Free in the City

Donna Every

Acknowledgements

I want to thank my editor Toni for her eagle eye, my daughter Kellie and my friends Gillian Morris and Maureen Earle for reading my manuscript and giving me their feedback. Thanks also to Kandace at the Barbados Museum for urging me to do the sequel every time she saw me and for promoting it to visitors before it was even written.

I could not have written this book with historical accuracy without the use of Richard Ligon's *True and Exact History of the Island of Barbadoes*, Matthew Parker's *Sugar Barons* and the research of Jerome Handler, Warren Alleyne, Pedro Welch and so many others. I hope I have done justice to their work while offering a somewhat different perspective of the slave/master relationships of the period.

Chapter 1

December 31, 1696
Bridge Town, Barbados

    *S*arah closed the door quietly behind her and strained her ears to hear any unusual noises before she locked it. It was the first time she had come back to the house since she and her daughter Deborah had moved out a few weeks before and she still felt a little uneasy after what had happened there. Richard, who had become her son-in-law that day, had insisted they stay with him until the wedding, for which she had been glad.

    The lock that had been broken to rescue Deborah from William, the master's son, had been fixed so she knew that she was safe. Although it was Deborah that William had sought, she would feel better when he was on his way to Jamaica where the master was sending him.

    She smiled wryly to herself as she realized that she still thought of Thomas as "the master". But then, it was hard to break a habit after nearly twenty years. She still couldn't believe all that had happened in the last nine months alone.

Who would have thought that when the mistress' nephew came from Carolina to stay at the plantation he would end up marrying Deborah?

That morning, when they became husband and wife, she had had mixed emotions. She was happy that Deborah would finally be with the man she loved and who loved her enough to turn his back on all he knew, but she was worried about what life would mean for them. After all, she and Deborah had been slaves as little as six months ago and the islanders would not easily embrace such a marriage. Would Richard come to regret that he had married a coloured woman? Would he end up leaving Deborah and going back to Carolina? She said a prayer that their marriage would be strong, knowing that they would face many challenges in the days ahead.

Instead of heading directly to change out of the dress she had worn to the wedding, she passed her room and stood outside the door of what used to be Deborah's room. The barrenness of the room, devoid of all Deborah's belongings, struck her hard. Even the bed had been stripped bare when they left. She was glad that Deborah had Richard, but she couldn't help the empty, lonely feeling that now became her companion.

Before she was seventeen, she had never known what it was like to be alone. She had lived with her mother at a small plantation in the country called Holdip Manor and, although their hut was just a small hovel made of wattle and daub, at least they had each other and they were constantly surrounded by the other slaves on the plantation. Until the day that everything changed. It was a day she would never forget.

August 3, 1677
Holdip Manor, Barbados

"Sarah! Sarah! Where you, girl?" Her mother's frantic voice carried through the undersized window of the back room where Sarah had just pulled off the handkerchief that covered her head during the day. She reached the doorway just as her mother was pulling open the door of their small hut. Her smooth black face was creased in distress.

"I'm here, Ma. What happen?"

"Girl, I don't know wha' to do," her mother agonized, grabbing her shoulders tightly. The fierceness in the grip of the work-roughened fingers told Sarah that something was very wrong. She vaguely wondered if her skin would show the bruises the next day.

"What happen?" she asked again, her voice rising in anxiety.

"The master sellin' you," her mother blurted out.

"Selling me?" Sarah repeated in disbelief. "Why?"

"Girl, he don't need a reason once the money right. When I come from the field just now Andrews tell me that a master from some plantation name The Acreage want to buy you and that he givin' the master nuff money for you."

"From The Acreage? That is Master Edwards. He was here today. I serve him and the master lunch because one of the other girls was sick. He was looking at me, but I didn't know he was sizing me up to buy me. Why he want to buy me?" she asked desperately. She remembered feeling his eyes on her as she served the meal and, even though she had kept her eyes lowered, she noticed that he was very good looking and well-built. After all, they did not often get such handsome visitors to the plantation.

"I don' know, girl. All I know is that Andrews say he sendin' for you Friday," her mother cried, dropping to one of their two rough stools as if her feet could no longer support her.

"Friday! That is the day after next!" Sarah said in a panic. "What to do?" She pressed her palm against her forehead as she paced the tiny hut as if it could somehow help to gather her frantic thoughts.

"The mistress like you. Go and see if she could change the master mind," her mother implored her.

"She didn' tell me anything when I left this evening, so maybe she don' know. She wasn't feeling good either, so she didn't take lunch with the master. Maybe she don' know. I goin' and talk to her."

Her mother was right. The mistress would not want her to be sold to another plantation. Yes, she could get the master to change his mind.

Sarah could see that the back door of the big house was open and she passed the kitchen quickly, hoping not to meet up with any of the other slaves. The heat that blasted her as she hurried past made her glad that she didn't have to work in the kitchen. From the time she was nine or ten, she had been companion to the Holdips' daughter who had always been sickly. When their daughter died a few years ago, Sarah and the mistress consoled each other and she began to keep the mistress' company instead.

The mistress had taught her many things, like how to speak better than she did and how to sew, which she now excelled at. They spent most of their time sewing in a small room off the main sitting room while the mistress gossiped about the goings-on at other plantations.

Raised voices from the direction of the master's office made her pause in the hallway and tiptoe towards the closed mahogany door. Her heart raced in fear of being discovered.

"…what do you mean you could not refuse his offer?" The mistress' voice demanded. "Other planters have offered you money for Sarah before, but you never entertained them. You know she keeps me company now that Marion has gone and she can sew even better than I can."

"He offered me £50! How could I say -?"

"£50?" The mistress interrupted in disbelief. Sarah knew that the newest of the mistress' dresses had cost six shillings so £50 sounded like a lot of money. "What on earth does he want her for? Nobody pays that kind of money for a house slave."

"He says…" Sarah strained to hear as the master's voice became muffled, as if he'd walked away, but she couldn't make out his words.

"Well, he can just find someone else," insisted the mistress.

"I've given my word and that is final." The master raised his voice again. "I'll take you for a shopping trip in Bridge Town and I'll find another girl to replace Sarah," he offered in consolation.

"I do not want another girl," insisted the mistress. "I want Sarah."

"So does Thomas Edwards, I'm afraid," said the master, putting an end to the conversation.

Sarah's head spun as she turned away from the door in a daze. She was going to be sold! The mistress could not save her. The man Thomas Edwards wanted her. What did he want her for? A terrible feeling of dread in the pit of her stomach made her feel sick. She held her stomach with one hand and covered her mouth with the other as she blindly stumbled down the hallway, no more able to control the bile that rose in her throat than she could control her fate.

Friday

Sarah curled herself into a foetal position on the sugar sacks that someone had thoughtfully spread on the rough floor of the cart to ease the discomfort of the journey. Tears streamed down her face and ran into the wild, curly hair that had come free of the handkerchief in the struggle as Andrews and one of the drivers parted her and her mother when the man from the

Edwards' plantation had come for her. She thought that after the tears she had shed in the last two days her eyes would be dry, but still more came.

The mistress had been crying herself when she told Sarah that she was to be sold. She had said that Thomas Edwards was a rich and powerful man and her husband had not wanted to vex him by turning down his offer. Although distraught, she tried to comfort Sarah with words of encouragement, saying that she had heard he was a good man and treated his slaves well.

The sound of her mother's wailing grew fainter as she was driven away from the plantation that had been home to her for seventeen years. The jostling of the cart caused her hip and shoulder to bounce roughly against the wood in spite of the sacks, but even that discomfort paled in comparison to the grief in her heart. She couldn't even rouse herself to wipe her tears and her running nose. Although she had not slept the night before, she was now too distressed and anxious to even fall into a blessed slumber so that she could escape her thoughts for a while.

A strong breeze blew her hair across her face and forced her to finally lift her hand limply to push it from against her nose. The automatic response to tame her hair brought to her mind a scene about ten years old and nearly forgotten.

She was sitting on the ground in front of her mother and looking longingly across the yard to where her friend, Annie, was playing with some other girls. Her mother was seated on a roughly made stool, tugging at her wild, curly hair with a broken comb that the mistress had thrown out.

"Ma, how come my hair is not like Annie's and yours?"

Her mother had paused from the task of combing her hair, giving her a brief ease from the torture.

"How come you askin' me that now?"

"Annie ask me today why my hair not like hers."

After a pause that was as long as two breaths (she had counted), her mother said: "Your hair is so because you' father hair was like the master's and the mistress'."

"That is why it softer than yours?"

"Yes."

"Andrews is my father?" The only other person Sarah knew with that kind of hair was Andrews, the overseer.

"No. It was another man that use' to work here."

"In the field with you?"

"No, child. He was the overseer, before Andrews."

"Oh. He was your husband?"

"No, child. Far from." She hadn't understood what her mother meant then.

A few years later, when the mistress asked for her to come to the house and keep her daughter company, her mother told her that it was because of the colour of her skin and her curly hair. It was then she explained how the overseer came to be her father.

Her mother had come from Africa which, she said, was far across the sea. She had been stolen from her tribe and sold to some white men who had shipped her to Barbados. The master had bought her in town and brought her to the plantation. Betsy, an old slave who had died a few years earlier, had taught her how to speak English and explained the way of life on the plantation to her.

She said that she had been put to work in the fields and that was when she first saw the man who had been the overseer. Her mother had said that he had wanted to lie with her the way a man lies with a wife. In her country it was wrong to lie with a man unless he was your husband, so she had refused and she had suffered for refusing.

Her mother had told her that when she was born Betsy had said to be glad for the colour of her skin and her curly hair because they would get her a place in the big house. When Betsy's words came to past and the mistress took her into the house to be with her daughter, safe from the whip and the lust of the men in the fields, her mother had rejoiced.

A particularly deep rut in the road jerked Sarah out of the past and painfully back into the present, causing thoughts of what might await her to torment her again. Where would she be put to work? The mistress had said that Master Edwards wanted her to mind his children. Was that the truth? She had also said that he was a good master, but how would she know? Did he beat his slaves? If she worked in the house would the new mistress be as kind as the mistress had been?

Some of the stories the mistress used to tell her about other plantations now frightened her as she drew nearer to The Acreage and farther away from all that was familiar. She had nothing to fear in the house at Holdip Manor, for Master Jonathan had never tried to lie with her and the mistress was good to her. She only hoped that her new master and mistress were like them.

The voice of the old driver, Abel he had said his name was, interrupted her thoughts, telling her that they had reached the beginning of The Acreage. She roused herself sufficiently to wipe her face on her sleeve and sit up, wincing as she did so, to look about her. They travelled for quite a long time under the shelter of trees that grew over the road until they emerged in a driveway lined with tall palm trees that almost looked as if they were waving a welcome to her. The sight of the plantation house painted a warm yellow with its green shutters and doors thrown open invitingly, somehow made her feel a little less afraid.

She was taken around to the back door and handed over to the housekeeper who said that her name was Ada. She looked to be a good ten years, or more, older than her mother.

"Girl, come and wash you' face. I can see you did cryin'. You ain' got nothing to cry for; you coulda gone somewhere worse. This here is a good plantation. Or if they was sendin' you to the fields you would got something to cry for because they does use the whip out there. But you is to help the mistress with the children," she informed Sarah to her relief. "The mistress lyin' down now because she ain' back to she full strength yet. The baby, Rachel, jest born four weeks now. The boy, William, is four and the little girl, Mary, is two. Sally tek the two of them out for a walk and she goin' feed them before they go to sleep."

10

Ada introduced her to the other house slaves and showed her the kitchen and the outhouse before taking her around the house and, finally, to the room off the nursery where she was to sleep. Although small, it had a window with a view of the back of the house. There was a little cot with a well-stuffed mattress and a small chest to hold her clothes. It was much better than the hut she had slept in at the Holdips. She had thought that the Holdips' house was nice, but next to the Edwards' house, it was like a house dress compared to a ball gown.

The baby had been sleeping when they peeped into the nursery and for this she was glad because she felt tired and drained after the parting from her mother and the long drive to the plantation. Ada made her sit down and drink some sweet water and eat a cassava cake which she said would make her feel better. Sarah had to force the cake past the rawness of her throat, but the sweet water revived her.

While she was eating, Sally came in with the children. She was a few years older than her and greeted her warmly, for which she was glad. The children were a little shy at first and clung to Sally's skirts, but she knew they would come around eventually, as children were usually drawn to her.

By the time the mistress woke up and rang her bell she was feeling better and followed Ada up to meet her new mistress.

Elizabeth Edwards was lying in a massive four-poster bed under a pristine white sheet pulled up to her waist. She wore a pretty blue nightgown that matched her eyes and blonde hair framed an attractive, if somewhat round, face and rested on her shoulders. She looked tired in spite of just having rested and she was cuddling the baby that the wet nurse had brought in after feeding her.

"This is Sarah, Mistress; the girl the master bring to help with de children."

Sarah stood awkwardly, not sure what to do or say. Her new mistress examined her, pausing at her hair which was still uncovered and a tangled mess and a strange look that Sarah did not understand passed over her face.

"Sarah," she repeated the name, offering no greeting. Her voice contained neither warmth nor hostility. "I can certainly use some help with the children. Come and take Rachel out for a little air. Did you meet the other children?"

"Yes, Mistress," she had answered quietly, taking the baby.

"Fine. You can take over from Sally tomorrow. Ada will show you where everything is."

"Yes, Mistress," she said again.

"Oh and Ada, get her a handkerchief for her hair." She dismissed them with a wave of her hand.

"Yes, Mistress," Ada agreed.

"The mistress ain' look too happy to see you," Ada whispered when she had closed the door.

"But I thought she would be glad to get help with the children," Sarah replied, puzzled.

"Yes, but I don't think it's the children she thinkin' 'bout. It's the master," she replied with a sly smile.

Chapter 2

*T*homas dismounted from his horse and handed the reins to one of the stable boys. He asked the boy if Abel had gotten back with the new girl and was pleased to hear that he had. A burst of anticipation caused some of his tiredness to dissipate as he remembered the beautiful slave girl that he had seen at Holdip Manor.

He had been looking for a girl to help Elizabeth with the children now that the baby had been born and when he saw her serving lunch at Jonathan Holdip's plantation he immediately wanted to own her. Not only was she beautiful, but there was also an innocence about her that attracted him.

He had broached the subject of buying her with Holdip.

"Who is the girl that served us?" he had asked.

"That's Sarah, my wife's girl."

"I need someone to help my wife with the children. I would like to buy her from you." Holdip had laughed quietly, shaking his head.

"I've had a few offers for her, but my wife is very close to her, especially since our daughter died, so I can't sell her. My wife would be distraught."

"You can assure your wife that she will be well looked after at The Acreage. My house girls are treated very well."

"I'm sure they are, but I cannot sell her, Thomas," he had insisted.

"I will give you £50 for her."

"£50! You can almost buy two house slaves for that. I'd be glad to sell you one of my other girls for £25."

"No. I want that one. She would be a good addition to my household. I will not take no for an answer, Jonathan."

Jonathan knew that it wasn't worth fighting him over the slave girl. Thomas Edwards had too much power on the island and, besides, he would need to grind his canes in the mill at The Acreage next year.

Holding out his hand he said: "That is an offer I'd be foolish to refuse, but my wife will not be happy," he had sighed.

"She will be fine. Buy her some jewellery," Thomas had advised, shaking his hand.

Now, as he reached the top of the stairs to head to his room to wash and change before dinner, he was pleased to see Sarah coming out of the room next to the nursery.

"Sarah," he greeted her. "I heard you had arrived."

Sarah visibly jumped at the sound of his voice and her heart started to race. She glanced at him, noticing that, unlike the day at Holdip Manor, he was in work clothes and his longish brown hair was almost free of the piece of leather that held it back. She quickly dropped her eyes to his dusty boots.

"Yes, Master Thomas," she replied shakily, shifting her eyes to the patterned carpet. She twisted her hands nervously behind her back.

His eyes lingered over the smooth tawny skin of her face before the nervous rise and fall of her bosom drew his attention.

"All settled in?"

"Yes, Master."

"Good. You met the mistress?"

"Yes, Master."

"And the children?"

"Yes, sir."

"Good. My wife will be glad for the help."

"Yes, Master."

"Alright, you can go." He dismissed her but stood watching as she hurried past him towards the stairs, eyes still downcast.

Sarah was relieved to escape. She felt uncomfortable in his presence. She hadn't realized he was so tall when she had served him at Holdip Manor. As she hastened down the stairs she imagined that she could feel his eyes burning into her as they had when she served him lunch. Was it only two days ago? However, when she chanced a glance back from the bottom of the staircase, he was at the door of the room at the end of the hall which Ada had said was his. Maybe he had not even been looking at her. It was Ada who had planted those thoughts in her head.

Thomas opened the door to his room with a satisfied smile. He had forced himself to tear his eyes from Sarah's retreating figure and walk to his room. Her walk had a natural grace and the sway of her hips was pleasant to watch. She was as beautiful as he remembered from his visit to Holdip Manor earlier that week and now she was here at The Acreage. He enjoyed the thrill of anticipation that stirred him.

The chirping of the crickets provided background noise as Thomas poured himself a glass of brandy and settled behind the large mahogany desk in his office. He was pleasantly full from dinner, which he'd eaten alone, and now the aged brandy warmed his stomach after sliding smoothly down his throat.

He pulled the folded and sealed parchment that had been left on his desk closer to him, broke the seal and perused it with satisfaction.

> *Know all men by these presents that I, Jonathan Holdip of Holdip Manor in the parish of St. Thomas, for and in consideration of the sum of fifty pounds, current money in the island of Barbados, paid before the ensealing and delivery of these presents, by Thomas Edwards, the receipt whereof I do hereby acknowledge and myself to be therewith fully satisfied, contented and paid having granted, bargained, sold and released, and by these presents do fully, clearly and absolutely grant, bargain, sell and release unto the said Thomas Edwards, a mulatto girl by the name of Sarah, born at Holdip Manor on the eighteenth day of September, 1659, to have and*

> to hold the said bargained mulatto girl unto the said
> Thomas Edwards and his heirs for their proper use
> and behoof for ever....

Breaking off his reading of who witnessed the document, he took a long ledger, in which he recorded all his slave transactions, from the bottom drawer of his desk. He opened it to a new page and recorded the following information:

> Date August 5, 1677.
> Purchased Mulatto slave girl, Sarah from Jonathan
> Holdip for £50
> Born at Holdip Manor on September 18, 1659.
> Age 17

So she was seventeen. He was a little more than twice her age and he certainly felt as if he had already lived two lifetimes. He'd moved to Barbados from England just over seven years ago after his father had died and he had discovered that the plantation he owned in Barbados, The Acreage, had been badly managed and was indebted. He had just married his wife Elizabeth, but he left her and came out to Barbados to see after the plantation. Her brother had come with him, but he soon moved on to Carolina to help establish a colony there.

After assessing the state of the plantation, he had been forced to take the hard decision to sell some of the slaves and make do with one overseer to pay off some of the debt. The first year had been the worst. It had taken him a while to become accustomed to the tropical climate and the water had made him ill. The deplorable state of the plantation and the slaves made him glad that he had left Elizabeth in England until he had assessed the situation.

He had been amazed at the extravagant lifestyles of the planters that he visited to introduce himself and to learn about the processing of sugar when he had first arrived. It had been equally appalling to see the way their slaves lived and were treated. Following the practice of Henry Drax who had given him a tour of his plantation, Drax Hall, he determined to provide better living conditions for his slaves as he could see the benefits that would result.

What had been most surprising for him was to discover that many of the planters had relations with their female slaves. He had heard talk of this in England. Masters taking advantage of servants was nothing new in some English households, but here the planters were quite brazen about it and often bragged that the slaves were much more receptive to sexual adventure than their wives. They did not see any wrongdoing in lying with their slaves; after all, the slaves were their property and for their use, the same as a horse or cart. They were certainly valued in the books of the plantations as such.

Thomas had been quietly disgusted and had resolved not to follow their example and held firmly to this while Elizabeth was in England. However, while visiting another plantation where he had been forced to spend the night after being caught in a storm, he had succumbed to the weakness of his flesh. The planter had sent him one of his slaves for the night, an exotic-looking, brown-skinned girl. At first he had resisted, certain he would be repulsed by bedding a slave. However, as soon as she divested herself of her clothing, he quickly realized that he found the dark sculptured body intriguing and rather than being repelled by their differences, the contrast of the smooth ebony skin against the white of his was surprisingly arousing and, more dangerous, addicting. An addiction he fought initially until the futility of it caused him to give up. It was just the way of the island and he had become an islander.

Two years later he sailed to England, which he no longer thought of as home, and escorted Elizabeth back to the island that had become a part of his soul. His timing, unfortunately, had been quite poor, for less than a year later the island suffered a violent hurricane which he would have spared Elizabeth had he known it was coming. Fortunately, the plantation survived, although with substantial damage which took from the earnings that he badly needed to put back into its running. Thankfully, the canes had already been harvested and the young ones and new plantings were mostly unaffected.

Two years after the hurricane a slave rebellion, led by one named Tony and one named Cuffee, had been exposed. It was discovered that they had been planning it for over two years and had intended to set the cane fields on fire and cut the throats of the planters. Thankfully, their plot was overheard by a house slave and reported to the judge so the plan was thwarted, sparing his throat and those of his fellow planters. The slaves, however, had not been so fortunate.

Of the seventeen that had been found guilty, six were burned alive and eleven beheaded. Another twenty-five were executed later and some committed suicide. The intended rebellion had shaken up the planters considerably and the following year new laws were passed that strengthened the militia and restricted the movement of slaves.

Those years confirmed to him that Barbados was not for the faint of heart. It was sheer hard work and determination that helped him to turn the plantation around. Thankfully, although the price of sugar had declined since the '50s, the increasing demand for it required larger volumes which more than compensated for the lower price. Persevering in spite of the challenges, he had managed to return the plantation to substantial profitability in the last three years and would soon be in a position to think about diversifying. He had plans to eventually invest in a ship once he could find the right partners. Then he would have his own means of transporting sugar to England and he would not have to pay merchants to do it, thus assuring him greater profits.

It was the wealth of his plantation that gave him power and influence on the island, which was why he was able to force Jonathan Holdip to part with Sarah. Over the years he had carefully chosen his slaves, as much for their physical ability as their looks, and his plantation had developed the reputation of having the best looking slave women, particularly the house slaves. Now he had Sarah, the most beautiful of them all. He wondered if she was untried. She certainly acted that way around him, or perhaps she was just nervous because she did not know what to expect from him.

A knock at the door interrupted his thoughts.

"Come in," he invited. He was surprised to see Elizabeth enter. She had had dinner in her room.

"May I disturb you?" she asked.

"You're not disturbing me, dear. I'm surprised you're still up."

"I slept quite a lot today so I'm not sleepy." She settled on a chair in front of his desk as Thomas leaned back in his leather chair.

"How are you feeling?" he asked solicitously. It had been a hard pregnancy for her, even though it was her third child.

"Better every day."

"Good. Now that you have the new girl to help, you can rest more."

"Yes. Thank you for getting her."

She wanted to insist that Sally was quite capable of dealing with the children. She wanted to ask if he had bought her because of her striking looks. Did Thomas really think that she didn't know that he lay with some of the female slaves? Nothing on a plantation was a secret — the slaves talked among themselves when they did not think she could hear. Granted, it was accepted on the island and she knew that a lot of the planters did it. It was the Barbadian way of life and the wives had learned to live with it, it seemed. After all, it was never openly discussed and they all looked the other way at the light-brown children that ran about the yards of the plantations and pretended that they did not know how they came to be. Thank God there were none at The Acreage. It hurt enough to imagine her husband lying with those women, far less getting any of them with child. That would kill her.

"Did you want something?"

"Not really." Only to spend some time with my husband. Only to have the man I married more interested in me than in his plantation.

Although theirs had been an arranged marriage, she had loved Thomas from the time she saw him. After all, he was one of the most handsome and sought after men among their peers. However, she had never deceived herself into believing that he felt the same way. He had, after all, married her and two months later left for Barbados. He was respectful and cordial to her, but words of love never passed his lips and there was no passion in their joining. Since coming to Barbados Thomas had changed. Barbados had changed him from the man she had married. He had become more distant and he seemed harsher somehow. She supposed that he had had to adapt in order to survive on the island and turn around the plantation, but at what price?

"I was thinking that I have not really seen you in ages."

"Elizabeth, you know that I have to put all my energy into the plantation to make sure it remains profitable. Besides, you have not been well during this pregnancy."

"I am recovered now," she intimated. Thomas felt a pang of something that felt like guilt. Although he would be hard pressed to say that he loved Elizabeth, he had respect for her. She had worked hard to make the house what it was now without complaint and she had given him a son and two daughters. He walked around his desk and pulled her up into his arms.

"I did not mean to neglect you, dear. I will arrange to rent a house at the seaside and we can take the children and spend a week there soon. Does that meet your approval?"

"Yes! Thank you, Thomas. That would be wonderful and the children will love it."

"We can take two of the slaves and Sarah to help you with the children."

Elizabeth was excited at the prospect of a week with Thomas and the children, although her excitement dimmed a bit at Thomas' words. Did he not consider Sarah to be one of the slaves as well?

Sarah tossed and turned in her small cot. Although it was far more comfortable than the pallet she had slept on the night before at Holdip Manor, it was not yet hers. It was not moulded to the shape of her body and she couldn't hear her mother breathing next to her. In fact, the room was very quiet. The only noise she could hear was the crickets in the grass outside the window. Loneliness cloaked her like the darkness now that she was not among the other slaves.

They had welcomed her and told her good things about The Acreage, but the mistress had not seemed too friendly and the master made her feel uncomfortable. It was not anything she could name, for he had not spoken many words to her, but still she felt uneasy.

Maybe it was because she had overheard Ada and Sally talking as she walked towards the kitchen after meeting him in the hallway that evening.

"How the mistress take to Sarah?" Sally had asked.

Ada laughed softly before replying. "She ain' no fool, girl. She look Sarah up and down and tell me to get a kerchief for she hair. That girl got some pretty long hair."

"And the master like he can' do without a brown girl, no matter how he try."

"Sarah look innocent enough. I don' know how long she goin' stay so. The master is a good man, but loss, you only got to look at Sarah to know that he ain' only buy she to help the mistress."

Sarah had made her presence known then, asking Ada what she meant by that.

"Girl, I don't know about the plantation that you come from and how you' master was with the girls, but Master Thomas like to lie with the slave girls sometimes. He like he can't help heself."

"Lie with them?" she had repeated, beginning to feel anxious. Her mother had told her that some men might want to lie with her as they would with a wife.

"Girl, you don't know that a lot of these masters does lie with their slave girls? How you think you come out that colour?"

"You think Master Thomas want to lie with me?" she had asked anxiously.

"Girl, if he don' want to, my name ain' Ada," Ada informed her.

She now shuddered at the thought and pulled the thin sheet closer around her as if to protect her from some unseen threat. She hoped Master Thomas was not thinking about her like that. Yet, she remembered the feeling that he was watching her as she hurried down the stairs.

Chapter 3

The sound of a cock crowing outside her window woke Sarah from a deep sleep. Cracking open one eye, her gaze encountered a wall, reminding her that yesterday had not been a dream; she was no longer at Holdip Manor in the hut with her mother. Sorrow squeezed her heart as she realized her life would never be the same again.

A little light was beginning to peer in the window of her room, so she forced herself to get up, knowing that the children might soon be waking. Thankfully, she heard no stirring in the nursery through the connecting door. The baby had woken several times during the night to be fed. The wet nurse slept on a pallet in the nursery and, although it was her business to feed the baby, Sarah had been awakened by the child's crying before the slave could satisfy her with her own milk. To her it was a strange sight to see the baby nursing at the breast of a slave. Thankfully, the children, who shared a room across the hallway, had slept through the baby's crying.

She dipped a small towel into the bucket of water that she had brought up the night before and washed herself automatically. After dressing in a simple cotton skirt and blouse, one of the three new sets of clothes that Ada had given her, she tamed her hair into a single plait and tied a handkerchief over it, forcing herself to get ready for the day. She would have preferred to curl herself into a ball and lie in bed all day, but that could not be.

Letting herself out of her room, she stopped abruptly as she almost collided with Master Thomas. He was dressed in clean work clothes and a quick glance showed that his hair was neatly combed and tied back with a piece of leather. Her eyes quickly dropped to his boots and she noticed that someone had cleaned the dust from them.

"Good morning, Master Thomas," she greeted quietly, waiting for him to pass.

"Good morning, Sarah. Did you sleep well?"

"Yes, Master," she lied. She waited for him to pass by her, but he seemed in no hurry to move on. She felt awkward, not sure if to ask his permission to leave or wait for him to move first. She chanced a quick glance at him and saw him looking down at her intently. Her breath caught in her throat as Ada's words came back to her. She dropped her eyes, afraid of what else she might see in his. She was startled when he reached out and tipped her chin up so that she was forced to meet his gaze.

"You're not afraid of me, are you, Sarah?" he asked softly, searching her eyes for she knew not what. His were so dark that she couldn't tell their colour.

"N-n-no, Master Thomas." She lied again, trying to still the shaking that had started in her knees.

"Good. You have nothing to be afraid of. I treat my girls well," he assured her before walking off, leaving her rooted to the spot.

She felt a slight, not unpleasant, tingling in her chin where the master's work-roughened fingers had held it gently. What did he mean that he treated his girls well? Somehow that did not make her feel any better.

A gentle breeze stirred the plants on the patio which was sheltered from the morning sun by nearby trees. Sarah sat at a small table feeding Mary small pieces of banana and pawpaw and porridge sweetened with sugar. William insisted that he could feed himself and managed the porridge quite well, but had a bit of a challenge picking up the slippery pieces of fruit with a spoon. In the end he allowed Sarah to help him.

She was told that she could eat the same as them, for which she was glad as she was treated well at Holdip Manor in that regard, often eating with the mistress in her small parlour. She now partook of the fresh fruit, forcing it past the lump in her throat that appeared as she thought about the mistress, her mother and her life at Holdip Manor.

"Can we go on a picnic today, Sarah?" asked William excitedly.

"Picnic, picnic," echoed Mary.

Sarah smiled slightly, her sadness being temporarily overshadowed by their excitement. They were already warming to her, as she had expected.

"Yes. You can show me 'round the plantation," she told them.

"Yaay!" William shouted, pulling at her hands to get going.

"I have to dress you first and then I will ask the cook to pack a basket so we can have the picnic somewhere nice."

"I am going to dress myself," shouted William, running inside. Sarah helped Mary from her high chair and took her upstairs to change. The feel of the small hand placed trustingly in hers touched a place in her hurting heart and the regret of being at The Acreage eased a little.

Half an hour later, armed with a basket holding their lunch, Sarah set out with her charges to explore the plantation. Sally had agreed to look after the baby until she returned.

"I know the best places," boasted William. "I can show you where they are."

"Me too," insisted Mary.

"Let's go see the windmill," insisted William.

"Alright. I never saw a windmill up close," Sarah admitted. She knew that the harvest had finished so there should be no one in the mill.

William was eager to rush ahead, so Sarah let him lead, picking up Mary whose little legs did not go as fast as her brother's.

"Slow down, William," Sarah called as he charged ahead. The last thing she wanted was for one of the children to get hurt on her first day with them. She was heartened when he obeyed her at once and slowed down so that she could catch up.

Up ahead she could see the circular windmill which was wide at the bottom and narrowed as it got to the top. The stone walls were thick with an arched doorway in one side. The wooden blades were stripped bare of their covering since the harvest was over and it was not needed to trap the wind. As they neared the mill, Sarah heard voices and slowed her steps, ready to leave, but William ploughed ahead.

"Father," she heard him say from inside, "I've come to show Sarah the mill."

"Have you? Well, where is she?"

Sarah hesitated, not wanting to see the master so soon after her encounter with him that morning.

"She and Mary are kind of slow," William explained, heading back to the doorway to wait for them.

Thomas followed him and saw Sarah hovering uncertainly a short distance from the doorway. He stood with his hands on his hips and watched as she adjusted her hold on Mary who shyly hid her face in Sarah's neck at the sight of him. She appeared to be already more comfortable with Sarah than she was with him, but that was not surprising since he hardly saw the children.

"Come, Sarah," urged William from next to his father.

Sarah timidly looked at Master Thomas for permission. He gestured with his hand for her to come in and turned to lead the way into the mill. When Sarah's eyes adjusted to the darkened room, she saw that two slaves were working with the machinery. They looked up at her as she greeted them, returned the greeting and just as quickly resumed their work.

"We are cleaning up and fixing the machinery now that the harvest is finished," the master said. Sarah wasn't sure if he was speaking to her or William, but she nodded just in case.

"The canes are crushed in here and then the juice is sent over to the boiler room where it is turned into sugar."

Sarah wanted to see the boiler room and was happy when William begged his father to show them. The boiler room was fairly large and had huge kettles of differing sizes. The master explained how they were used to make the sugar.

"It is unbearably hot when the cane juice is being boiled and no one likes to work in here during harvest, but this is the most important part of the process."

Sarah was thankful that she wouldn't have to work in the boiling house. She wasn't sure if the master expected her to answer him so she said nothing.

Having seen enough, William began to tug at her hand.

"Let us go and explore somewhere else," he urged. Sarah looked at the master for permission to leave, which he granted by a gesture.

As she walked away, she felt his eyes on her once again and hastened to get out of his sight.

The day was beautiful with clear skies and a strong breeze that kept the heat at bay. Sarah discovered that the grounds of the plantation were more beautiful than those of Holdip Manor, with all kinds of flowers and delightfully shady trees. In spite of herself, her spirits lifted a bit more as she enjoyed being outside and in the fresh air.

She suddenly realized that she had not spent much time outdoors as Mrs. Holdip had preferred to stay inside her parlour either reading or sewing, to avoid the sun. On the occasions that guests came to visit, they would sit on the patio in rocking chairs, so it was mainly on her trips to and from the hut that she shared with her mother, that she was outside.

William showed her the pond which most plantations had since there were few rivers in Barbados and they had to rely on rainwater which was caught in cisterns on the roof and in the manmade ponds. He had wanted to wade in the pond, but she forbade him since they had not brought any clothes to change into. Since he obeyed without protest she rewarded them by taking off their shoes and dangling their feet in the water in turn. Mary had squealed in delight, bringing a little more joy to her heart.

A lush gully was next on William's list of the best places to see on the plantation. It was quite dark and damp as it was covered by thick trees which did not permit much light to penetrate. Mary was not too keen on staying there for any length of time and Sarah had to threaten to leave William behind in order to get him to stop looking under the mossy rocks for slithery worms and other creatures.

Finally he led her to a grassy spot under some trees that overlooked what seemed to be a vast forest which stretched to the sea. Sarah was very excited to see the blue water of the sea with its white foamy waves, as it was a rare sight for her. She put Mary down on the grass, warning her and William not to go too close to the edge, while she stood staring at the beauty of the island before her.

Birds flew from tree to tree, filling the air with their songs. As Sarah's eyes followed them, she realized they were free to go wherever they wanted. Yet she was not. Tears caused the scene to blur as she remembered the day before. Was it only a day since she had come to The Acreage? Only a day since she had been torn from her mother's arms because Thomas Edwards wanted to own her? She dashed away the tears quickly before the children could see them.

It was because of him that she was here and, while the plantation was beautiful and the children were easy to deal with, at least so far, she did not know if she would ever see her mother again. She did not know if he would sell her when the children got older and no longer needed her. He owned her and controlled her life. Was he thinking about lying with her? She hoped not because she had lain with no man and she did not want to lie with one that was not her husband and certainly not Master Thomas.

A sharp cry from Mary snapped her head around in time to see her on the ground while the bird she must have been chasing was taking flight. Sarah hurried over to pick her up and was distressed to see blood oozing from a cut on her knee. Mary was equally distressed and made it known with intense screams. Sarah pulled off her kerchief and used it to press against the cut. She quickly instructed William to bring the basket while she hurried to get Mary back to the house.

She was relieved when Sally met her at the front door and took charge of the basket that William was struggling to carry while instructing her to bring Mary to the back room where her cut could be taken care of. Mary refused to release her hold on Sarah and sat on her lap the whole time that Sally tended to her cut while Sarah dried her tears. She fervently hoped that the mistress had not heard Mary crying. The last thing she had wanted was for either of the children to get hurt on her first day with them and not even that wish had been granted.

She took the children to their room for a wash before lunch since they had not started their picnic. As she was about to take them down for lunch on the patio, the mistress appeared in the doorway of her room. Mary broke away from Sarah and hobbled over to her mother to tell her about her cut which was now wrapped with clean strips of cloth.

Sarah braced herself for the mistress' displeasure and she did not have long to wait.

"What is this? On your first day Mary falls down and gets a cut on her knee? Your job is to watch the children. What were you doing? And where is your handkerchief? I told Ada to get one for you."

Sarah cringed in shame that she had failed at her job already. She couldn't tell the mistress that she had been lost in thought when Mary fell down. Instead, she answered her last question.

"I'm sorry, Mistress. I used the kerchief to stop Mary's cut from bleeding."

"What? You put your dirty handkerchief on her cut? You could cause it to become infected!" Her voice rose with each sentence, causing Mary to start crying again.

"What is going on?" The master appeared at the top of the stairs and hurried to the end of the hallway. His eyes quickly took in the scene and he couldn't help but notice that Sarah's handkerchief was missing and strands of her curly hair had escaped from her plait.

"This girl you brought hasn't even been here one day and already one of the children has been injured."

"What happened?" asked Thomas tersely, looking at Sarah. Sarah's belly quivered with anxiety, wondering if she would be whipped for this offence.

"I'm sorry, Master Thomas, but Mary was chasing a bird and she fall …fell and cut her knee. I used my kerchief to stop the blood." Thomas absently noted that that was the most she had ever said to him and that she was careful to speak slowly and as well as she knew how.

"Is that all? Elizabeth, dear, the children will get many cuts and scrapes as they play outside. They will be fine. There is no need to get so upset."

"But she used her dirty handkerchief to put on Mary's cut. It could get infected," she repeated.

"I hardly think so, dear. Besides, the cut looks like it's been cleaned and bandaged. I'm sure it will be fine." He patted Mary on the head as he headed for his room.

Elizabeth glared at Sarah before returning to her own room. The anger that Sarah had felt towards the master as she had watched the birds earlier diminished when she realized that he had not taken the mistress' side against her. But now her heart filled afresh with sorrow and fear. Holdip Manor and all that was familiar to her was not only far away, but now it seemed as if she had unknowingly made an enemy of the mistress of The Acreage.

Chapter 4

*S*arah was relieved to find that the mistress did not appear to hold a grudge for too long. After two days of treating her coldly, she began to thaw out and became civil again by the third day. Sarah knew, from the stories told to her by Mistress Holdip, that she was very fortunate since some slaves may have been whipped by their mistress for what had happened to Mary.

Elizabeth's return to civility, if not warmth, may have been inspired by the fact that a few days after the incident with Mary, Thomas announced that he had managed to secure a property to rent on the coast not too far from the plantation and that they would go there on Saturday morning which was three days away.

From that time the children and the mistress were almost beside themselves with excitement and Sarah found herself getting excited at the thought of seeing the sea and staying at the beach house for a week. She spent the next day choosing the clothes that the children would need on the trip and the night before they were to leave she packed them in a small trunk for the slave who would drive them to load onto the cart.

Saturday dawned clear and sunny, making it a perfect day for travel. Sally and the cook packed the cart with enough food and supplies to last them the week. A tall, good looking slave, who said his name was Jethro, came to collect the children's trunk. Ada told her that he used to work in the fields but the master had found him to be good with building things and had recently taken him out to be a carpenter and to help around the house and yard.

"I see he eyeing you, but I had to tell him don' even bother to look because the master done got he eye 'pon you," Ada had told her with a laugh.

"Ada, I wish you would stop saying those kinds of things," she had pleaded. "I been here a week and the master ain' trouble me. I don' even see him much now because he coming in late and leaving early."

"He only bidin' he time, girl. Mark my words."

Sarah was glad to get away from Ada and her talk, which only made her uncomfortable. Soon the mistress, the children and Sarah were settled into the carriage which was driven by Jethro while Abel drove the cart with Sally, the wet nurse and the food and trunks. The master rode his horse.

Sarah had never been in a carriage that fancy before. She had gone with Mistress Holdip to visit friends on occasion, but the Holdip's carriage was not as well-padded and comfortable as the Edwards' who could obviously afford better. She sat on one bench between the two children holding the baby while the mistress sat on the other one. The children looked eagerly out the windows at the passing scenery and could barely sit still at the thought that they were going to the beach.

Sarah was glad that the master had said that the trip would take no more than an hour because she didn't know how she would control the children and the last thing she needed was the mistress displeased with her again. She was accustomed to always being in favour with Mistress Holdip and she had been very uncomfortable with the mistress' coldness earlier in the week.

Thankfully, before the sun had reached its peak, they were pulling up to a two-storey bungalow next to the beach. The house was nowhere as fancy as The Acreage, but the mistress looked it over and said that it would do for the week. It had three bedrooms so the master and mistress would share one, she and the two older children would share another one and the wet nurse would sleep with the baby in the smallest room. Sally and Jethro would sleep on pallets downstairs.

The owner had cleared the bush leading down to the beach and from the patio they could see the waves gently rolling onto the clean, pale sand. The children could hardly wait until Sarah changed them into their play clothes to take them down to the beach. The mistress said she would sit on the patio in a rocking chair where she could watch them and the master took a book out of his bag and joined her.

"See that you keep a proper eye on the children this time, Sarah," admonished the mistress, reminding her that the incident with Mary was not forgotten. "The sea is quite calm, but you cannot be too careful around water."

"Yes, Mistress," agreed Sarah, taking the children by the hand. William pulled her urgently and she was practically forced to run to keep up with him. She scooped up Mary in her arms lest she fall and cause the mistress' wrath to be rekindled.

"Take off your shoes, William," she instructed as she bent down to take off Mary's. He needed no further prompting and threw himself down on the sand in delight before pulling off his shoes and digging his toes into the dry sand. Taking off Mary's shoes and then her own, Sarah took them down to the water's edge, cautioning William not to go into the water but to play where the waves rolled onto the sand.

Sarah was awestruck by the vast ocean spread out before her. It seemed to have no end, yet it met the sky somewhere far away. She would have loved to take off her kerchief and let the wind play in her hair. She would have loved to spread her arms out and twirl around at the delight of being in a world outside of the plantation where she was free to enjoy the sound of the waves rolling onto the sand, the warmth of the sun on her face and the crunchy feeling of the wet sand between her toes. It struck her that, here, she could enjoy the same things as her master and mistress because there were for everyone to enjoy, slave and free.

"Sarah, come and chase me," demanded William, taking off down the beach. Aware of the mistress' eyes on them, she grabbed up Mary and chased after him. She knew that if he fell he would not hurt himself on the soft sand so she let him enjoy her chasing him. The wind snatched her handkerchief from her head and she deposited Mary on the sand to chase after it, barely stopping it from blowing into the sea. She pushed it into her pocket rather than take the chance of it blowing away again.

"Dip me into water like you dipped me into the pond," begged Mary.

"Me too, me too," shouted William.

"I can only do one at a time."

"I'll go and get father to dip me," said William, taking off before Sarah could stop him. She kept her eyes on him until he reached the patio where she could see him explaining to his father what he wanted. Her pleasure dimmed as she saw the master get up and follow William down to the beach. She immediately tensed at his approach, losing the feeling of freedom that she had enjoyed moments ago.

The master sat on the sand and pulled off his boots. He had shed his jacket and had folded back the sleeves of his white cotton shirt to his elbows. It was tucked into a pair of brown breeches which he rolled up to his knees so they wouldn't get wet. As he stood up to follow William to the water's edge she noticed that dark hair covered his long legs which were very pale compared to his face and arms. They surely did not see the sun very often, if at all.

"Young Master William has pleaded with me to swirl him in the water," he told Sarah. Picking up William, he held him aloft and said: "How about if I give him a real dip in the ocean instead?" With that he pretended that he was going to toss William into the sea. William squealed in delight.

"Dip me in, Sarah," commanded Mary. Sarah complied, wading out a little to lower Mary's feet into the water.

The waves soaked the bottom of her skirt up to her calves. Thankfully, the water was quite warm and pleasant. She suddenly wished that she could sink into the waves and cool her whole body down.

"Swirl me around like William," Mary begged. Sarah did as she requested and was rewarded with childish laughs of delight. She felt the wind tugging at her hair and several strands teased her cheeks as they came loose from her plait. She chanced a glance towards the master and William and found that he was still swirling William in the waves a little way from them but his eyes were on her hair, making her feel very conscious of its mess. She quickly brought her attention back to Mary.

"My arms are tired, Mary. Let's go and play in the sand for a bit." She was glad when Mary happily agreed and soon William urged his father to let him run to the shore so that he could dig a big hole.

Thomas put down William so that he could wade through the gentle waves to the sand. Once he freed himself of the water swirling around his legs, he raced to where Mary was and dropped down near her to begin digging his hole. Sarah was kneeling next to Mary and started to dig into her pocket to find her kerchief. More of her hair had escaped from the plait and the soft-looking curls hung down one side of her face onto her shoulder. She self-consciously smoothed her hair behind her ears and made to put on the kerchief.

"Leave it off," Thomas commanded, joining them. Sarah tensed and stopped what she was doing. Her eyes instinctively flew to his as if to confirm what she thought he had said. He saw the wariness in them, even as she slowly lowered her hands in obedience and pushed the handkerchief back into her pocket.

He silently cursed himself for his impulsive words and the desire which she had no doubt seen in his eyes. He wanted her to begin to relax in his presence, but now he had frightened her and caused her to shy away like an unbroken filly. Patience, Thomas, he admonished himself silently. You have all the time in the world and anticipation is half the pleasure.

Sarah looked up to see the mistress making her way down to the beach to join them. She did not look very happy as she observed the scene before her; however, when the master turned to see what Sarah was looking at, she arranged a smile on her face and said, "You looked like you were having fun so I decided to come and join you."

"The children are certainly enjoying themselves," agreed Thomas.

"We're digging holes," William informed her. "Mine is the biggest," he boasted proudly.

"Good work both of you," his mother praised before turning to Sarah.

"Sarah, where is your handkerchief? You can't seem to keep one on your head," she accused.

"The wind blew it off, Mistress."

"Well, put it back on. You can go up to the house and start to get the children's lunch ready. The master and I will bring them up soon."

Sarah gladly scrambled up with a hastily mumbled, "Yes, Mistress," before she picked up her shoes and straightened to go to the house. From behind her she could hear the mistress say: "My goodness, she's almost like one of the children. Just how old is she?"

She didn't hear what the master replied, but she hoped that he knew she was young. Maybe that would stop him from looking at her as he did on the beach. She didn't know much about men, but what she saw in his eyes made her think that Ada was right. She shivered as the damp skirt brushed against her legs and she wasn't sure if it was because of the coldness of the cloth or if it was the thought of Thomas Edwards looking at her as if he was starving and she was a meal.

She walked around to the back of the house where she dipped some water out of a bucket to rinse the sand off her feet. Shaking out as much sand as she could from her skirt, she tied the two sides in knots so that the damp material did not rub against her legs and put on her shoes before hurrying upstairs to fix her hair and change her skirt before the mistress came in.

The excitement of being at the beach and the freedom she felt before the master joined them were now mere memories. She wondered how she would survive the week with the master around all the time and she fervently hoped that he would go to Jamestown on business or something so that she could have some peace.

Sally greeted her as she came into the kitchen. "You come to help with lunch?"

"Yes. The mistress send me up and say that she and the master would see 'bout the children."

Sally laughed quietly. "As Ada said, 'She ain' no fool'. The master sniffing 'round you like a dog looking for a bone."

"Sally, I don' know what to do. Just now my kerchief blow off and when I was going to put it back on he tell me to leave it off. I wish he would stop looking at me so." A thought suddenly occurred to Sarah and she looked at Sally. Sally was quite attractive and she was probably several years older than her.

"Sally, how long you been living at The Acreage?"

"About six years. Why?"

Sarah looked around cautiously before lowering her voice to ask: "The master ever...?" she trailed off, not knowing how to finish her question. "He ever lie with you?" she finally asked, grabbing the boldness before it left her.

Sally's usually open face became secretive and she said, "Girl, what you asking me my business for?" before turning back to the stove, leaving Sarah to come to her own conclusion. She dared not ask any more questions for she wasn't sure if she wanted to hear the answers, not that Sally was forthcoming with any.

She knew that she was safe at the beach house since the master and mistress were sharing a room and she was sleeping with the children, but what would happen when they got back to The Acreage? What would stop the master from coming to her room? She longed for the protection she had had at Holdip

Manor. At The Acreage, there was nothing that could protect her from Master Thomas if he wanted to lie with her and there was now no doubt in her mind that that was exactly what he wanted.

Chapter 5

The week went by quickly and Sarah was glad that the master did not join the children and her on the beach again. Instead, the mistress made it her business to spend time with them while the master read books on the patio and even went out on business two days as Sarah had hoped.

As their time drew to a close, apprehension began to mount in Sarah. Not only did she regret that she would lose the feeling of freedom that the beach gave her, but the thought of being more accessible to the master worried her.

She had just closed the trunk that contained the children's clothes when a knock on the opened door caused her to jump and turn around quickly. It was only Jethro who had come to take the trunk down to the cart that Abel had brought back.

"You alright, Sarah? Sorry I frighten you." His eyes searched her face as if it would reveal why she was so jumpy.

"Yes, I'm alright. I didn' hear you, so your knock jumped me."

"Sorry," he said again, not looking convinced. He looked as if he wanted to say more, but changed his mind and picked up the trunk effortlessly to go downstairs. Sarah followed him and went to find the children who were on the beach with Sally.

"Sarah," called Mary, "come and play with us." Sarah smiled a little at her. She was happy that the children had become accustomed to her and they had become quite close in the week that they had been at the beach. Even the mistress seemed more tolerant of her and trusted her on the beach with the children when she rested in the afternoons.

"There is no more time to play. It is time to leave now."

"No!" Both of them protested.

"I don't want to leave either, but it is time. Everything is in the cart and Jethro is waiting to take us back." That started tears. Sarah felt like crying too. She looked out over the ocean once more, not knowing when she would have the chance to see it again. The vastness of it somehow made her feel free. No, she didn't want to leave the beach house either but, like the children, she didn't have a say in what she wanted.

Sarah picked up the crying Mary while Sally pulled William along in spite of him dragging his feet and pouting all the way. They were greeted by the mistress on the patio.

"Now what has happened?" she demanded, taking Mary from Sarah and hugging her in comfort.

"Nothing, Mistress," Sally answered for Sarah. "The children don't want to leave."

"Oh, poor babies. I don't want to leave either, but this is not our house. We have to go back home."

Thomas chose that moment to join them on the patio. He was dressed for the trip and looked impatient.

"What is taking everyone so long? The cart has been packed and waiting for ages."

"The children don't want to leave and neither do I," Elizabeth said mournfully.

"It was a good holiday, but I need to get back to the plantation. I've been away for far too long and I for one am looking forward to going home. Let us go." His tone did not leave room for argument. As Elizabeth turned to go into the house with Mary, followed by Sally and William, Thomas was left with Sarah whose eyes briefly searched his before falling to the ground.

"And what about you, Sarah? Are you sorry to leave too?" he asked quietly.

"Yes, Master," said Sarah, meaning it with her whole heart. Thomas felt as if he could read her mind and knew that she was wary of returning to the plantation.

"You have nothing to be afraid of," he repeated the same promise he had made outside her bedroom the week before. Surprise made her look up at him quickly, wondering how he could know what she had not voiced.

He smiled slightly and turned to go into the house, leaving her to follow.

September 18, 1677

Something roused Sarah from a deep sleep. She had not slept well the night before as her thoughts had kept her awake long into the night. Life had settled down into a routine and she had relaxed since the master had not approached her or looked at her in that way that made her uncomfortable. She had told Ada that she was wrong about him, but Ada only shook her head and smiled knowingly. She had even begun to lose the grief of being parted from her mother and from the mistress at Holdip Manor.

She lay in bed for a minute. It was dark outside so surely it was not time to get up yet. A sudden peal of thunder shook the house and the fury of rain against the window spurred her from her warm bed to close it. It was then that she realized why there was no sun to urge her to get up. Another loud crash sounded as if the roof was falling in. She hurriedly pulled on her clothes so that she could go and check on the children. She was washing her face quickly when her door flew open and the mistress stood on the threshold with Mary, who was crying, and William, who was clinging to her nightgown.

"Sarah, did you not hear the children screaming in fright? I had to get out of my bed to see to them." She still looked sleepy and annoyed at the same time.

"Sorry, Mistress," she mumbled, wiping her face hurriedly before reaching out to take Mary.

"The thunder woke them up, poor dears!" She patted William's head as she turned to go back to her room, leaving the children with Sarah.

Sarah pulled them to her for a hug before settling them on her bed while she combed and tidied her hair and put on a kerchief.

"I wasn't scared," declared William. "It was Mary." The words were scarcely out of his mouth when a flash of lightning lit up the room, followed by another rumble of thunder. Both children jumped up and clung to her skirts.

"Thunder can't hurt you, but it can frighten you. When I was young I used to be frightened every time I heard thunder."

"You're not frightened anymore?" asked William in awe.

"No. Because I know it is nothing to be frightened of. When you see the lightning you can get ready because you know thunder is coming after that."

She had hardly finished speaking when lightning high-lighted their frightened faces.

"Get ready," she said and in a few seconds the thunder followed. "The longer the time is between the lightning and the thunder that means the thunder is going away," she explained. They looked happy to hear this.

"I'm hungry," complained William.

"Okay, let us go and get breakfast."

They ate breakfast in the dining room with the lamps lit because the day was so dark. There would be no going outside that day because of the rain, so the mistress got a book from the master's office and settled them down to read stories to them. She read to them about a man called Robin Hood who, she told them, lived in England where she and their father were from. He stole money from rich people and gave it to poor people. The children enjoyed the stories as did Sarah, although she gave no sign that she was listening as she mended a pile of the children's clothes.

"Do you know how to make clothes, Sarah?" the mistress asked her suddenly as she finished reading.

"Yes, Mistress."

"I will get some material so that you can make a few clothes for the children to play in because they are both growing at an alarming rate and they need some new things."

"Yes, ma'am," Sarah agreed.

"I'm hungry," William piped up.

"You're always hungry, William," said his mother, laughing. "That's why you're getting so big. Sarah will get your lunch for you now."

Sarah put down her sewing and made her way towards the kitchen. She was almost happy at The Acreage. The mistress had become a bit warmer in the last few weeks, the children were generally well behaved and the master had stayed away from her. She realized that her life could have been a lot worse.

Sarah washed with a basin of water and dressed in her shift for the night. She had settled the children in their bed about an hour earlier, but the baby had been a little fretful and it had taken a while to get her to settle down and go to sleep. Taking off her kerchief, she unplaited her hair and combed it through with a piece of comb that Ada had given her. She was about to braid it when her door opened quietly. Whipping around, she saw the master enter and close the door gently behind him and lock it. Immediately her heart began to race in her chest.

She slowly lowered her arms, folding them across her bosom with the piece of comb still in one hand. She wished she had not shed her dress already. Her frightened eyes sought his out. They were roving over her wild hair, making her want to hide it under the cloth again.

"Sarah. I could not let the day end without acknowledging that you are eighteen today."

Her eyes widened in surprise. It was her birthday? It was not something that she remembered; after all, slaves did not celebrate the day they were born, if they even knew it. What was there to celebrate?

"I have a present for you."

For the first time Sarah noticed that he was holding a small parcel in his hand. She could not help the tiny burst of pleasure, mingled with curiosity. Mistress Holdip had sometimes given her small gifts, but no one had ever given her a present wrapped up in paper.

"A p-p-present?" Her voice shook, betraying her nervousness.

"Yes. Here, open it." He extended it slightly. He had bought the gift when he was in town two weeks ago and he had kept it until now.

Sarah reluctantly put down the piece of comb and slowly took the few steps to reach him by the door. He took her hand and placed the parcel in it, holding it for seconds before releasing it. His was warm and rough from working in the fields. It was a strong hand. Sarah looked down at the parcel; one part of her curious to know what was in it and the other afraid of what it would cost her.

"Go ahead, open it," he urged.

She retreated a few steps and rested the parcel on her bed. Untying the string that held the paper, she unfolded the brown wrapping and discovered a beautifully carved wooden comb and a matching brush. Tears moistened her eyes. The master had given her a comb and a brush for herself; not someone's cast offs; they were new.

"Th-thank you, Master," she whispered, afraid of what he might demand as payment. The tears that threatened before rolled from her eyes and she quickly wiped them away.

"What is the matter?" The master quickly crossed the room to hold her shoulders. Sarah tensed.

Unable to articulate what she felt, she picked up the broken comb she had been using minutes earlier and showed him. "Ada gave this to me." He immediately understood all that she did not say.

"I can give you nice things," he said, drawing her closer. Sarah felt stiff against him and he could feel her shaking. "You don't have to be afraid of me, Sarah."

This was the third time he had told her that, but his closeness denied his words the power to assure her.

"Are you not going to thank me for my gift?" he coaxed her.

"Thank you, Master," she said again, although she had already thanked him.

"I meant a 'thank you' kiss." What was he saying? He didn't kiss his slave girls. Why would he even think of kissing Sarah?

"K-k-kiss?" Sarah stammered. She was sure that he could feel her heart beating frantically against his ribs; he held her that close.

"Have you never kissed before?"

"No, Master," she whispered.

"You can't turn eighteen without being kissed." Sarah felt dread uncurl in her belly. Ada had been right all along. The master had just been waiting for the right time. Her body shook violently.

Thomas felt Sarah shaking against him and he knew that all of his assurances were in vain. She was afraid of him and who could blame her? He owned her; he could do whatever he wanted with her and there was nothing she could do to stop him. So why was he not taking what he wanted? Why did he not have her on her back already? It was the fear coming from her in almost palpable waves that stopped him. He had no desire to force himself on a frightened girl, slave or not. The slave girls he lay with were willing, or at least they did not refuse him.

He looked down at her bent head and saw her pinkish brown lips and in spite of everything, he knew that he had to taste them. Tilting her chin up, he brushed his lips over hers. It felt no different to kissing a white woman, except that her tightly sealed lips were slightly fuller, appealingly so. Her eyes were screwed as tightly shut as her lips, as if by closing them she could somehow shut out what was happening. Her hands were clenched in tight fists at her side and she was shaking as if with a fever.

Abandoning her unresponsive lips, he dropped his head further to where her neck and shoulder joined and, pushing aside her hair, he nibbled the skin softly. Her hair was coarser than his but still soft to the touch. His caress caused goose bumps to roughen Sarah's normally smooth skin, making Thomas smile inwardly in triumph. He had found a weak spot; good. He pressed his advantage and was rewarded by Sarah's knees buckling slightly. He tightened his arms around her and began to draw her further into his embrace.

"Master Thomas..." she began, pushing back slightly, uncertain of what his reaction would be.

"Ssh, Sarah." He bent his head again and rubbed his lips against hers before delving in for a taste of her mouth. Her whimper, as he explored the virgin territory of her mouth, checked him. He was surprised at how badly he wanted to coax a response from her that was not born of fright. His body no doubt made it plain to her that he wanted her badly. His hands began to roam towards her hips to bring her closer.

"Master Thomas." Sarah finally unclenched her fists to stop his hands from venturing lower. Thomas reared back at her boldness. She flinched and whispered in a voice heavy with embarrassment, "It is my woman's time." Her face felt hot with the shame of admitting something so personal to the master.

"Your -?" Thomas swore under his breath and laughed mirthlessly. "This must be retribution for my sins," he said. Sarah did not know what he meant, but she was glad when he removed his hands and set her free.

"Happy birthday," he said and, turning the lock, left the room as quietly as he had come in.

Sarah sank down on the bed as her legs gave way. She pressed her hand to her mouth. She was shocked that Master Thomas had kissed her lips and her neck. She was even more shocked that the kisses on her neck had not been unpleasant, far from, although the other had felt strange. She was never so thankful that it was her woman's time; however, she knew that it wouldn't last forever. The master would be back.

Chapter 6

*T*homas finished his breakfast and pushed back his chair from his desk where he'd eaten today. It was later than his usual time to leave the house, but he had not slept well. After he had left Sarah's room, aroused and unfulfilled, he had cursed himself. Why had he not taken what was rightfully his as soon as she came to The Acreage? She was his property and he had every right to lie with her. And when he'd decided to wait until she turned eighteen, it was her womanly time! He scoffed at himself as he rubbed his tired eyes. Her untried lips had stirred a strong desire in him to taste all of her innocence and the remembrance of the feel of them as he coaxed them apart and explored her mouth had kept him awake long into the night.

He grabbed his hat and was on the way to the door when someone knocked. He opened it to find Ada on the other side looking rather anxious.

"Yes, Ada, what is it?" he asked somewhat impatiently.

"Sorry, Massa, but Bentley send one of the boys to tell you that the new slave George like he missing. He say that he wasn't there this morning when the gangs come out and he not sick in the hut so it look like he run 'way in the night."

Thomas swore. The last thing he needed was to have to chase down a slave when there was work to be done. It was always the new ones. He should stop buying them straight off the ships and get those who had been broken in to plantation life.

"The boy still out there?"

"Yes, Massa."

"Tell him to let Bentley know that I said to come up and bring one of the drivers to get the dogs. We will have to chase him down. I'm sure he's discovered by now that there're not a lot of places to hide in Barbados."

Within minutes, Bentley, the overseer, and one of the drivers rode into the yard to meet Thomas. They collected some cutlasses in case they had to cut through bush, put the dogs on leads and led them to the slave's hut to get the scent of the missing slave.

"He probably won't go towards the coast and Jamestown because there are too many people there. I figure he would have gone through the gully since there's already a rough path cut out," Thomas reasoned.

He and Bentley got on their horses and headed for the gully with the driver holding the dogs on foot in front of them. The dogs started sniffing and barking wildly as soon as they got to the entrance. The gully led deeper into the plantation where it was fairly heavily wooded. Most of the forests in the island had been burned and cleared to make room for sugar canes to be planted and it was only the gully areas and the hills that were still heavily wooded.

If he had left during the night, he would have gotten a good head start, but he had to stop and rest at some point. The dogs would sniff him out. He wasn't the first to try to escape and after he had been recaptured he probably wouldn't try it again.

Thomas didn't consider himself to be cruel, as some of the other planters were, but he had to teach runners a lesson and it was done in front of the other slaves so that they would understand the consequences of trying to escape. He never ordered more than thirty lashes. After all, he wanted them able to work again as soon as possible. The punishment for running was far more severe on other plantations.

Thomas and Bentley stayed on the track while the driver followed the straining dogs into the trees, coming back empty-handed. As one hour turned into two, Thomas grew increasingly annoyed at the time they were wasting chasing down the slave. He took off his hat and wiped the sweat from his brow with a handkerchief. Having not slept well the night before, he was tired and irritated, not to mention thirsty as they had not brought any water with them in their haste to leave.

When they came to the end of the track, a number of broken twigs revealed that someone had pushed through the bushes. The dogs strained to go in. Thomas and Bentley dismounted and found sturdy trees to tie their horses. Bentley took over the dogs and handed the cutlass to the driver who began to chop away at the bushes. Thomas brought up the rear. They followed the dogs for another hour into heavily forested areas until their frenzy increased and they lunged at a tree, barking frantically and trying to climb up the trunk. Looking up, they saw the escaped slave huddled against a 'V' in the bough, looking tired but somehow still defiant.

"Get him down and bring him to the yard," Thomas said as he turned and headed back the way they had come. He was glad the search had ended, but they had wasted all of the morning and it would be lunch time by the time they got back. He would deal with the runaway before the slaves went back out to the fields.

That was not part of plantation life that he liked, but he had to keep his slaves in order and this was the way that seemed most effective. He had never had a slave attempt to escape again after they had been punished the first time and those who witnessed the punishment thought twice about trying it. He had worked hard to build back up the plantation, many days working as hard as the slaves, and he was not about to let anything jeopardize it, especially not a rebellious slave.

The sound of dogs barking frantically and a commotion in the yard made Sarah tense. She had not too long put the children to bed for a rest after their lunch and had come out to the yard to join the rest of the slaves. She had been very anxious from the time Ada told them that a slave had escaped. In fact, all of them had been very quiet that day, keeping an ear strained to hear if the slave had been found.

"Lord have mercy!" Ada exclaimed. "They like they find the boy. It sound like they bringing he in now. You know what that mean."

Sarah was born on a plantation so she knew exactly what that meant. "Master Thomas going to whip him?" she asked anxiously.

"He ain' goin' do it himself. He will get Bentley to do it, but all of we have to watch."

"Why?"

"So that nobody else will think about escapin'," she explained.

"Why we would try to escape? We don't have it as bad as the field slaves."

"True, child. But we still slaves. All of we would still like to be free, no matter how much better it is in the house. Not you?"

Sarah remembered how free she felt at the beach and wished that she could feel like that all the time. Nobody to tell her what to do and where to go. No fear that the master would come and lie with her. Yes, she would like to be free too. She could understand how the slave George felt. If she were to escape where could she go? There weren't a lot of places to hide on the island. Freedom seemed like such an impossible thing. She could not imagine it.

Jethro appeared and announced that all the slaves were to come out by the whipping post. Sarah shivered in fright and looked at Ada and Sally as they moved to obey the order.

They clung together in a group to the side of the house, far enough away from the whipping post, but close enough to be seen by the master. Sarah's eyes immediately swung to the slave stripped to the waist and tied to the whipping post. She had seen the post before, but never gave it much thought until now. She shivered as she contemplated what was to come. Her eyes sought out the master. Gone was the man who had kissed her the night before and told her on other occasions that she had nothing to be afraid of. In his place was a man whose face was hard and expressionless as he declared that the slave, George, had escaped from The Acreage and would be given thirty lashes with the whip as punishment. He warned anyone who thought of doing the same to think carefully before they did it, lest they wanted to suffer the same fate.

Thomas gave Bentley the order to start and watched impassively as he delivered the punishing blows. Sarah stood biting her lip with her hands clasped around her waist. She cringed with each fall of the whip. The slave set his face like flint, barely flinching with the first ten lashes. However, by the time she had counted ten more he was grimacing. Sarah closed her eyes to avoid seeing the pain on his face. She was relieved when the rope holding him was cut and he slumped against the post, unable to move.

"Anyone else thinking of escaping can expect the same," Master Thomas promised. "Now back to work," he added before heading to the house.

Sarah and the other house slaves quietly moved back to the house. No one spoke and they avoided each other's eyes. Sarah had a sick feeling in the pit of her stomach and could not even face lunch. The others seemed to feel the same way.

"You best put the master lunch on the table, Sally," advised the cook. "He goin' be hungry."

"I goin' to peel some aloes to put on the boy back," Ada said at last, heading to the small patch of herbs and plants in the yard.

Sarah didn't know what to do with herself. She felt like hiding in her room as she certainly didn't want to encounter Master Thomas. It was a good thing that the children were resting because, after what she had just witnessed, she didn't know how she could entertain them as if nothing had happened. It only reminded her that they were slaves and that Master Thomas could do whatever he liked to them. And that meant her too. How she longed for the safety of Holdip Manor. But even there wasn't safe, for she had been sold to Master Thomas, exchanging one master for another and this one seemed cold and cruel. In spite of what he had told her, she now felt more afraid of him than ever.

Ekow gritted his teeth as Ada smeared the slimy paste over his bleeding back, but no sound escaped his lips. Anger burned in him, both at himself for getting caught and for the master who ordered his whipping. He was not even man enough to do it himself, getting the overseer to do the deed for him.

"Sorry that I hurtin' ya back, George, but the aloe goin' help it."

Ekow thanked her, though he silently rejected the name that had been given to him when he came to the plantation. George? His name was Ekow. It meant "eager for battle". He was a warrior from the Ashanti tribe, even though the English traders called all of the people of that region in Africa Coromantees. He would never bow to these people and accept what they threw at him like a dog. He came from a tribe rich with gold and full of powerful men. They owned slaves; they were not owned. How he hated this white man who hunted him down like an animal and then had him stripped and beaten in front of the slaves. He would avenge himself for this disgrace. He would make the white master suffer as he had suffered.

Thomas looked down at the food on his plate with little interest. He had no appetite after witnessing the flogging, but he forced himself to eat. He certainly could not send his plate back to the kitchen with his food uneaten as if he was affected by the punishment. He took no pleasure in it, but it had to be done, otherwise the slaves would rebel. As there were far more of them than there were whites on the island, they had to be kept in control at all costs and he could not appear to be soft to his slaves, especially after the failed rebellion a few years earlier.

He had already lost valuable time that day searching for the runaway and he was sure that the productivity would be down that afternoon as the slaves rebelled with a slowdown in work. He was surprised that his food wasn't more salty, or perhaps it had been prepared before the cook and the other slaves were forced to watch the flogging. They had their ways of making their displeasure known, but they also knew that they had it better than on most of the plantations on the island. It was because of that that he had very few runners and the only other cause for flogging was stealing sugar. Thankfully, apart from the usual whips to hasten the work along, they rarely had floggings on the plantation.

Sarah had been at The Acreage just over a month and she had witnessed one of those rare floggings. He had caught a brief glance of her across the yard with the other house slaves and she had looked distraught. She would no doubt look at him with a new fear in her eyes now, and with good cause. Not that he would ever have her whipped. He would never sanction causing her smooth skin to be scarred. Thinking about her smooth, brown skin and remembering how it had felt under his lips last night whet his appetite for more. He didn't intend to wait much longer.

Elizabeth came in as he was finishing his meal. He looked her over and noted that she was looking a lot better.

"Thomas, I'm glad I caught you. What was that flogging about? I couldn't help but hear the commotion in the yard. Thank God the children were sleeping."

"One of the new slaves ran off during the night. We spent the whole morning looking for him and he had to be taught a lesson."

She nodded understandingly, seeing the strain on his face.

"You've been pushing yourself too hard, Thomas. You're out in the fields as early as the slaves and you're back late. Now that you have Bentley you don't need to work so hard."

"I'll slow down once the planting has finished," he assured her.

"I enjoyed our time at the beach house," she hinted. "I've hardly been alone with you since then."

Thomas looked at her and realized that he had only been to her room on two occasions since they returned from the beach house.

"I'm sorry I've been neglecting you, dear. I know I've been working too hard, so when I come in at night all I want to do is sleep. I will come in early today since most of the day has been fruitless anyway."

"I'll look forward to having dinner with you then."

"Yes, I'll see you for dinner." He pushed back his chair and kissed her briefly on the forehead before heading out.

She was an attractive woman, but he found that her blonde hair and sun-sheltered skin paled in comparison to Sarah's, whose dark, curly hair and light brown skin he found fascinating. He was already thinking about Sarah more than he should and he had not even lain with her yet. He would have to change that soon. He would give her a few days to get over the whipping and her womanly time.

Chapter 7

arah washed quickly and dressed for the day. It looked as if it was going to be a beautiful day, so she decided to take the children outside to explore the gardens. She had encouraged them to plant a few seeds in a small part of the yard and they had been checking every day to see if they were starting to grow so they would want to do that first, no doubt.

She combed through her hair with the beautiful comb that the master had given her. When she had returned the broken one to Ada and told her that the master had given her a new one, Ada had simply shook her head and said that it was only a matter of time now.

Sarah could no longer deny what the master wanted, but he had kept his distance in the last week, for which she was very glad. She knew that he was only waiting until her time had finished.

She left her room and checked on the baby and the children to make sure they were still sleeping before going down to the kitchen to get their breakfast ready.

"Jethro and the master gone town this morning," Ada announced to her.

"They gone for a few days?" Sarah asked hopefully.

Ada laughed. "It don't look so. The master didn' have no bag with him. He gone to buy goods and he must be buying another present for you," Ada teased her.

"I don't want any more presents," Sarah insisted. The master's presents would no doubt come with a price and she knew she would be called on to pay soon. "I going to take the children outside to play today," she said, changing the subject.

"I think I see their seeds beginnin' to come up," Ada told her. Sarah smiled slightly as she thought how excited they would be. They could always bring a smile to her face.

She enjoyed looking after the children and now that the baby was sleeping less she sometimes took her out for walks in the morning before the sun got too hot or in the evening when it was cool. She was happy that she and the mistress had had no more incidents and life had settled down into a pleasant routine. She still thought about her mother and Holdip Manor, but the pain had lessened. Her life here was harder than before as she was constantly at the beck and call of the children, but at least she had every other Sunday off when Sally or Ada looked after the children.

By the time she got back upstairs, the children were waking up and she helped them to wash and dress before going down to eat their breakfast. She waited until they were almost finished to tell them that Ada had said that their seeds had started to spring up. She knew that the breakfast would be abandoned once they heard that, which was why she had waited.

William scrambled out of his chair and was waiting impatiently for Sarah to take Mary from her high chair when the mistress came in.

"Mother, the seeds we planted are growing!" William announced. "Come and see them." He tugged at her hand. Elizabeth allowed herself to be pulled along while Sarah carried Mary.

"I'm coming," she laughed.

"We're going exploring today," William informed her. "I am going to look for treasure and I will show it to father when he comes in."

Sarah tensed at the mention of the master. She could tell that William craved his attention but hardly saw him. She felt sorry for him, but at the same time she was glad that his father was not around them more. His presence disturbed her in ways that she could not explain.

"He has gone into town today," his mother told him. "Maybe he will bring a present for you," she added, to make up for her husband's lack of attention. She had already hinted to Thomas to bring a surprise for the children. It would be nice if he brought something for her too, although that was not as important to her as receiving his attentions. She could empathize with William. Thomas had come to her room late last night. She smiled to herself as she remembered their time together. He was always gentle with her and very controlled. She sometimes wished that he would be more passionate and lose some of that restraint, for then she would feel as if he really desired her and was not just performing his husbandly duties.

The talk about presents reminded Sarah that the master had said that he could give her nice things. Would he bring her something from town as Ada had teased her? Not that she wanted anything else from him, for she was well aware that she had not paid for the first gift as yet. She kept her brush and comb hidden in her trunk in case the mistress came in and saw them.

The day passed pleasantly. She helped the children to water the tiny seedlings without drowning them and then all of them walked in the garden so that the children could look for treasure. The mistress was very pleasant to her and, as Sarah looked around at the beautiful surroundings, she was thankful that she had been brought to The Acreage and not sold to another plantation.

Thomas climbed down from the cart and headed for the front door while Jethro continued around the back to unload the goods they had bought. He had hurried to get back to the plantation before the sun slipped behind the horizon. He was tired but satisfied with his day's purchases. Several ships had come in from England and France with good wine and brandy and beautiful merchandise to buy. He had bought toys for the children, a new perfume for Elizabeth and a small gift for Sarah which he would also appreciate.

As he entered the house, he was greeted by a very excited William and a more subdued Mary who must have been looking out the window for him.

"Father, I found a lot of treasure today. Come to my room and see it."

"Treasure? That sounds exciting! Then you probably don't want what I bought for you in town today."

"You bought me a present?" William danced excitedly around his father.

"I bought everyone presents." He gestured with the parcels he held in his hands. "Let me go to my room for a moment and wash up and then I will bring your presents and see your treasure."

Minutes later, Thomas entered the children's room with two parcels in his hand. His eyes immediately travelled to where Sarah was standing folding a pile of clothes that took up most of one bed.

"Hello, Sarah," he greeted her quietly.

"Good evening, Master Thomas," she answered, looking at him briefly before turning back to her task. She silently acknowledged that he looked particularly handsome in the clothes he had worn to town.

"Look at this, Father," William diverted his attention. "I found something that looks like a little spade. Mother said that it could have belonged to the Indians who lived here before."

"That is interesting," praised his father, taking it in his hand and inspecting it. William lapped up the praise like a thirsty puppy.

"And what treasure did you find?" Thomas asked Mary.

"I found some pretty flowers," Mary shared shyly, pointing to a vase on the chest of drawers.

"Very pretty," agreed Thomas. "Here are the presents that I bought for you in town." He helped Mary to open her present. It contained a small doll that looked surprisingly like her. She squealed in delight, forgetting her shyness around her father, and hugged the doll.

William looked expectantly for his gift and was rewarded with a set of wooden toy soldiers. He whooped with pleasure. Both ran off to their mother's room to show her their gifts.

Being alone with the master made the room seem smaller as his presence seemed to fill it, making her aware of him in a disturbing way. She tried to appear as if she did not feel his eyes on her, but her heart raced in a way she did not understand. However, she knew it was not truly fear that she felt.

"I brought you a present as well, Sarah," he said quietly. Her eyes flew to his. She did not want any gifts from him, but she couldn't help but be curious about what he could have bought her.

"I'll leave it in your room later. Use it tomorrow night."

Sarah stared after him in dismay as he left the room. She pulled the dress that she was folding to her bosom and held it there as if for comfort.

Thomas retreated to his room briefly, after which he joined the children in his wife's room.

"I bought you a present from town, my dear," Sarah heard him say before closing the door.

She dropped to the bed as her legs suddenly felt weak. The master was ready for her to pay for the presents he had given her.

Sarah hardly slept. When she had returned to her room after feeding the children and settling them down for the night, she had found a small parcel on her bed. She had stared at it for some time, reluctant to open it and yet wondering what it was that he would want her to use the next night. Finally opening it, she had found a bar of soap wrapped in soft paper. When she held it to her nose, she was rewarded with a burst of a wonderful floral scent. She had never bathed with anything smelling so fine and she would have been delighted to do so, except that the master wanted to smell it on her.

Forcing herself to get out of bed, Sarah went through the motions of getting dressed for the day, but her mind was far away. It was on the night. Reaching the kitchen, she found Jethro, Ada and Sally talking about the trip to town the day before.

Sally asked her, "Sarah, you ever been to Bridge Town?"

"Yes. My last mistress used to take me with her when she went, but I ain' been for a long time. Why?"

"I was just telling Ada and Sally about the amount of ships that was in Carlisle Bay and all the things they was unloading at

73

the wharf," Jethro explained. "Town was real busy. The master buy a lot of drinks and fancy food."

"Don' think that they don' spend nuff money 'pon the'selves, though," Sally commented.

"He buy presents for the children too. They were real happy," Sarah added.

"He buy anything for you?" Ada asked pointedly. Sarah felt uncomfortable and did not answer.

"You ain' hear me?" Both Jethro and Sally now looked at her with interest, waiting to hear her answer.

"I hear you, Ada," Sarah admitted quietly.

"Oh, that mean he buy something. You getting a lot of presents and he ain' ask for no payment yet? You like you bewitch the master." She laughed while Sarah burned with embarrassment. She threw a quick glance at Jethro and saw him looking as uncomfortable as she felt.

She liked Jethro and he seemed to like her too, so the last thing she wanted was for Ada to be discussing the master and what he wanted in front of him. She sometimes caught him looking at her, but he did not make her uncomfortable like the master did. Maybe it was because he didn't look at her the same way.

"Girl, get the most you can out of he, hear? And if you get money keep it an' see if you could buy your freedom one of these days," Sally advised. Sarah's interest pricked at that. She had never considered that she could buy her freedom. Would the master ever let her?

"You know anybody who buy their freedom?" she asked.

"No, but it goin' soon start happening, you wait and see."
Sarah began to imagine saving up enough money to buy her
freedom when the truth hit her, making her heart heavy.

"I don't know how I could ever buy my freedom because
the master pay £50 for me."

"£50!" Ada exclaimed. "The master did want to own you
real bad."

Sarah could not deny it, as she had heard what Master
Holdip had told the mistress. She couldn't understand it.

"So what present you get?" Ada persisted.

"I have to get the children's breakfast." She avoided
answering.

"Oh, it must be something real special. That mean the
master goin' want something special from you soon."

"Leave the girl, Ada," Sally chided. "Don't mind her,
Sarah."

Sarah briefly smiled her thanks before escaping with the
children's breakfast on a tray.

Jethro's eyes trailed after her and Ada told him, "Boy, I
tell you already, don' even bother to look. She belong to the
master and I surprise that he ain' had she yet, but you mark my
words, it ain' going to be long now."

Jethro's heart pained him at her words. He knew that Ada
was not being cruel, she was only telling the truth, but that
did not make it any easier. From the time Sarah had come to
The Acreage he had been drawn to her. Not only because she
was a beautiful woman, but she was kind too. He liked how
she was with children and not only the Edwards' children, but

when she came across the other ones in the yard. He would have liked to marry her, but he knew that she was the master's. According to Ada, nothing had happened between them yet, but it was only a matter of time. He wished that he could protect her and take care of her, but he was powerless to do so. Slavery made a man powerless.

Chapter 8

The lengthening shadows became Sarah's enemies. She wished that she could stop the sun from going down, but its descent was as inevitable as the master coming to her room that night. After she had put the children to bed, she washed with the soap he had given her and dressed in one of her thin chemises.

Sitting on the bed, she brushed her hair, more to occupy her hands than anything else. Her stomach churned with nervousness and growled in hunger as she had been unable to eat anything that night. Uncontrollable shivers erupted in her from time to time, betraying her anxiety. She had nothing to be afraid of, she told herself; the master had said so more than once. The same master who had ordered George to be whipped for running away.

She jumped when the door finally opened and the master entered. The sound of a key turning in the lock froze Sarah's heart before it restarted with a rapid beat. Her wide eyes sought him out in the dim light of the room as her hands slowly dropped from her hair. He was dressed as she had never seen him, in a pair of loose breeches with a white shirt that hung outside. The open neckline revealed dark hair sprinkled across his chest. His longish hair of the same colour was unrestrained from the usual leather thong that he bound it with. He looked handsome and not as frightening now that he was dressed casually.

Thomas leaned back against the locked door. His eyes were immediately drawn to Sarah's curly hair which she had tamed somewhat with the brush that he had given her. The brushing seemed to have lengthened it and straightened the curls which now rested below her shoulders. He simply enjoyed feasting his eyes on the picture she offered with her smooth, brown skin contrasting with her white chemise and her hair framing her face. He pushed away from the door.

Stopping in front of Sarah, Thomas drew her up against him, feeling her firm arms through the soft chemise. The soap that he'd bought her teased his nostrils and he bent his head to nibble the sensitive spot he'd discovered last time. Sarah shivered and her knees buckled slightly. Thomas raised his head and, lifting her chin, brought her mouth up to meet his. Her lips were as soft as he remembered from the last time.

Thomas teased her lips before coaxing them apart with his. Her mouth was like nectar to him, feeding the desire that he had held in check since last week. There would be nothing to stop him tonight. His hands roamed her back through the thin garment and he could feel her body shaking as he pulled her closer, crushing her softness against him.

Reluctantly releasing her mouth, he once again sought the sensitive skin of her neck and was rewarded by a small sound of pleasure from Sarah that encouraged him to seek her mouth again. His heart began to race as he anticipated possessing her body in a similar manner.

Stepping away briefly, he drew the thin shift over her head, leaving her vulnerable before him. Before she had time to cover herself, he quickly stripped off his shirt and drew her against his hair-roughened chest. The sight of her brown skin against his and the feel of her softness against his chest, aroused him beyond measure. What was it about that sight that so fascinated him? Why was it that Sarah, this innocent slave girl, made him want to lose all control and take her now?

He took a breath to steady himself and put a little space between them, bringing Sarah's hands up to his chest. Sarah's eyes sought his and widened slightly, shocked by the intensity of the desire in his. How was it that the master wanted her so? His eyes sought her lips and she involuntarily licked them, causing him to plunder her mouth with barely restrained passion. Her fingers curled in his chest hair in protest, but that only seemed to arouse him further.

Divesting himself of his remaining clothes, he pulled Sarah over to the bed. Sarah felt the mattress under her back and panicked, pushing at the master's shoulders as she felt his weight on her. The softness of her body under his almost overcame him, but the panic on her face sobered him and he forced himself to restrain the urge to take what he wanted immediately, knowing that she was untouched.

'She's just a slave. What is stopping you?' a voice taunted him. His flesh urged him to obey, but something deep within stayed him. A twinge of conscience stirred as he knew that he was taking her innocence rather than she giving it to him. However, he was too far gone. He had to have her and, after all, she was already his legally. He joined their lips again, before fitting his body to hers, to capture the soft cry and the stiffening of her body that marked her as his in all ways. He tried to hold back, but found himself unable to delay his gratification long enough that she could find hers.

Sarah turned to face the wall, silently wiping the tears that rolled from her eyes as the master moved away to sit on the side of her bed. He was still breathing heavily as if he'd just come from chasing a runaway slave. She could not believe it. The master had lain with her! Other than when he had kissed her neck and her mouth, she had known no pleasure, but thankfully less pain than she had imagined. She wanted him to leave so that she could get up and wash, but he sat holding his head in his hands.

Thomas' body was satiated, but he knew that because he had lost control of himself he had given Sarah no pleasure and for that he felt somehow less of a man, which was ridiculous. He didn't have to give the slaves pleasure; they were for his pleasure, but something in him, some strange vanity perhaps, wanted to satisfy Sarah. He normally had enough control to ensure that he did not impregnate any of his girls, for he did not want his weakness to be known or to bring shame to Elizabeth with unwanted children.

Sarah was different. He had lost control with her and only fortuitous timing prevented a babe from now forming in her womb. He didn't know what to say to her. One did not apologize to a slave, but for some reason he felt to say sorry and to tell her that next time it would be better. Already he was eager for the next time. He wanted to ask Sarah if she was all right, but he could not. A master did not ask a slave such things. It did not matter if a slave was all right or not. So why did her quiet tears make him feel like the lowest of men?

He turned slightly and laid a comforting hand on her shoulder, unable to voice his thoughts. She instinctively flinched away from him, making him disgusted at himself all over again. Picking up his clothes, he dressed quickly and let himself out of her room, but the guilt went with him.

Sarah was relieved to hear the door close so that she could get up and wash away the evidence that the master had lain with her. He had taken her innocence. Angry tears made her eyes fill again and she impatiently wiped them away. She would not cry anymore. What sense did it make? The master had taken what he wanted, so maybe he would be satisfied and not come again.

Thomas was up even before the sun. He was sorry that it was not a work day because he would have liked to get out into the fields and let the heat of the day and the hard work purge his thoughts of Sarah. He knew that she would probably be even more wary of him now, while he was even more desirous of having her again. He could not rid himself of the memory of her soft body and the feeling of the resistance that evidenced her innocence giving way to him. Next time she would shed no tears; he would see to that.

Today was church, after which his friend and neighbour, John Bowyer, and his family would be coming for dinner. The Bowyers ran a smaller plantation a few miles away and had a son a year older than William and a daughter around Mary's age. They would be good company for the children and it had been quite some time since they'd had visitors over, so Elizabeth would be pleased.

He washed and dressed in his Sunday suit and went downstairs to wait for Elizabeth and the children. About a half an hour later, Elizabeth came down, followed by the children, with Sarah carrying the baby and bringing up the rear. They had not been to church since Sarah had come to the Acreage as Elizabeth was still recovering from the birth, so he had not thought about her accompanying them. Something stirred in his belly as he looked at her drawn face with dark circles under her eyes as if she had not slept well. He was becoming quite acquainted with the feeling which he recognized as shame.

"Sorry to keep you waiting, Thomas, but Sarah couldn't seem to get out of bed and the children had to wake her up. Imagine!" Elizabeth puffed. Sarah said nothing, keeping her head down.

"We should still be in time. Never fear," Thomas assured her. "Jethro has the carriage waiting."

Sarah dreaded being in the carriage with the master. How could he act as if nothing had happened? As if he had not taken her innocence last night? Now they were going to church to hear about their God. She had gone to church with Mistress Holdip on a few occasions and heard about him, but she knew that he was not her God. Her mother had told her about Olódùmarè, whom she worshipped in her country before she was brought to Barbados. Maybe Olódùmarè was more interested in what happened to people like her, because their God did not seem to be.

Thomas helped Elizabeth into the carriage and then the children. He seemed to hesitate as if he was about to help Sarah up when he caught himself and climbed in, seating himself on the other end of the seat that Elizabeth had taken. Sarah climbed in last and sat next to the children, drawing as far as possible away from her master's knees which protruded into the space. Her gaze focused on the passing scenery as they moved off.

"I'm looking forward to the Bowyers coming to lunch today," announced Elizabeth. "I haven't seen Margaret in ages. In fact, we have not had company in a long time."

"Yes. I must admit that I'm looking forward to John's visit. We haven't spoken in quite a while. I was very glad to run into him in town this week."

In a short time they arrived at the parish church in Jamestown. The wooden building had been severely damaged by the hurricane that devastated the island a few years earlier, but repairs had been done to it so that services could be held there. Many people greeted the family warmly as they walked to their pew at the front of the church, befitting their position as owners of one of the largest plantations in the parish. Sarah and the children sat at one end, followed by Elizabeth and finally Thomas.

Looking around curiously, Sarah saw that the church was filled mainly with people like the master and mistress as well as several slaves, like herself, who were brought along to keep the children quiet and see to their needs. She couldn't help but wonder if any of them had to suffer their master's attentions as she did. Did their God not see the evil that they did? Did he not care? For here the master sat in the church as if he had done no wrong. Maybe in his eyes he had not.

Thomas struggled to get comfortable on the wooden pew. He tried not to look in the direction of Sarah who was holding Mary on her lap while trying to keep William from wiggling around. The last thing he needed was to be having lustful thoughts in the house of God. His conscience pricked as he remembered one of the commandments that said, "Thou shall not commit adultery". Surely adultery involved the emotions, so that did not apply to what he did with the slaves or to what he had done with Sarah. That satisfied his conscience. Anyway, the slaves were his property, his assets and he could use them as he willed. He didn't mistreat them as some of the other planters did; he fed them and clothed them well, so he was being a good steward.

They stood as the service started and, after singing a few hymns to the accompaniment of a piano, the congregation was invited to sit and the priest stood behind the wooden pulpit and opened a large Bible.

"Today I'm going to read from the book of Joshua. In the first chapter and verse 5, God says to Joshua: 'There shall not any man be able to stand before thee all the days of thy life: as I was with Moses, so I will be with thee: I will not fail thee, nor forsake thee.' God made a promise to Joshua that in the same way he was with Moses he would be with him. He said that he would always be with him and not fail him. We too can have the assurance that God will always be with us and that he will not fail us."

Sarah did not know who Moses and Joshua were, but the words that this God promised to be with them caught her attention. Did he mean her as well? If he did, why had he not been with her when the master had made her lie with him last night? He had not stopped the master, so maybe the words did not apply to her. Sorrow filled her heart at the thought that there was no one to care what happened to her, no one to protect her, no one who would always be with her. She was at the mercy of the master and there was nothing she could do about it.

Chapter 9

"John and I will be in the mill house to see some of the new machinery I bought," Thomas told the women as he and John Bowyer headed off in that direction, talking about the last harvest and the price they had gotten for their sugar as they went.

"Elizabeth, it's been too long since we've visited," declared Margaret Bowyer as she walked with Elizabeth to the house followed by the children and their nannies.

"Yes, indeed!" Elizabeth answered her friend. "To tell the truth, this last pregnancy has taken a lot out of me and I was very tired most of the time. I'm only now coming back to myself."

"It is fortunate that you got the girl to help you then. I don't know what I would do without my girl. Henry never seems to stop moving and I do not have the energy to run after him in this heat."

Elizabeth laughed as she led her friend to the patio. They had eaten the refreshments which they had taken to church with them, so they were content for a few hours until dinner was ready. They made themselves comfortable in the rocking chairs.

Sarah took the Bowyers' slave girl and the children up to the children's room while she put down Rachel, who was sleeping.

Elizabeth looked out across the yard towards the men as they made their way towards the mill house. She absently wondered what they were talking about. Margaret followed her eyes and drily made the comment, "I imagine that John is asking Thomas about your new girl. I am not blind to the looks that he was giving her in the churchyard, of all places. I don't understand what it is about those women that capture the attention of our men."

Elizabeth said nothing, not caring to share her concerns with Margaret, although she wondered the same thing. Thomas, at least, was not quite so distasteful as to openly admire such women in her presence, although she knew that he had lain with some of the slave women. Had he lain with Sarah? Such a thought made her stomach revolt. Surely he would not be so bold to lie with her under the same roof.

Once the men were a good distance away, John gave Thomas a knowing look and remarked, "I see you have a new addition to your household, Thomas. And a very attractive one as well, I must say. The reputation of The Acreage continues to be upheld."

"Oh, you mean Sarah?" he replied dismissively, hoping that John would not dwell on the subject of Sarah.

"Yes, if that is the name of your delectable-looking child minder. I wouldn't mind her minding me," he joked.

Thomas was surprised at the surge of possessiveness that he felt for Sarah which John's words elicited. 'I'll be damned if I share Sarah with any man,' he thought to himself. He forced a smile and answered noncommittally, "I'm sure you wouldn't. So, have you heard about the goings-on in Jamaica?" He changed the subject.

"You mean the latest slave rebellion?" Thomas nodded. "My God, it seems that every year they have one. At least ours are not as frequent! That last one that was attempted here was apparently led by some from a tribe called the Coromantees or some such name. They are the same ones that stir up trouble in Jamaica. They seem to have a penchant for trouble."

"You're right. I had a new slave run on me just a few weeks ago and I do believe that was the name of the tribe that he came from. Found him in the south gully. The new ones learn the hard way that there are few places to hide in Barbados. Not like Jamaica. Those maroons that the Spanish set free have been living in the hills there for years and no one can capture them."

"You know, it's surprising that ours don't overthrow us and cut all our throats in our sleep. They have the numbers to do it, but they just can't seem to work together to carry out a plan successfully, thank God."

"I find it quite remarkable that a lot of the slaves on Drax's plantation were from that same Coromantee tribe but, from what I heard, they did not join the rebellion. I tell you, there is something in treating your slaves well, the way he treats his; you gain their loyalty. That's what I try to practice here."

"I don't hold to that. You have to let them know who is boss, or else they will steal you blind and only do half the work they are capable of. I hear he gives his slaves all kinds of food like cassava, plantain, corn, molasses and fish, but I'm not going to end up in the poor house to fatten up my slaves. And if they won't work, they will feel my whip, field slave or house slave. They are all the same to me."

Thomas realized that they were not all the same to him. His house slaves were like family. He had come and found Ada who had been at the plantation almost from the time his father bought it. She was like the matriarch and ran the house with great efficiency. All the girls worked well and he had nothing to complain about. Sarah looked after the children admirably and they seemed to be thriving under her care. No, she was not the same as the field slaves and he would never see her whipped. He didn't know what it was, but there was something different about Sarah, even from the other house slaves.

Sarah and the Bowyers' nanny settled on two chairs as the children sat on the floor to play with their toys in the nursery. The boys set up battles with the soldiers that William's father had given him a few weeks before while the girls played with their dolls. Sarah was happy that they had other children to play with for a change. A smile softened her face and she looked up to see the Bowyers' nanny, Betsy, looking at her.

"How long you been here?" she asked.

"Nearly two months," Sarah told her, realizing that it seemed a lot longer.

"They does treat you good here?"

"Yes. Why? They don't treat you good at the Bowyers?"

"Girl, you wouldn't want to live there! You see the mistress who look so holy and good at church? Well, she nearly as fast to throw a whip as the master."

"What? My mistress ain' like that and since I was here I only see one man get whipped. That was for running away and the master didn't even do it himself."

"You lucky that you live here, girl." Sarah bent her head as she remembered the night before and silently disagreed with Betsy. "And don't talk about when the master had some drinks!"

Sarah wondered if Betsy had to suffer her master's attentions as well, but she would never be so bold as to ask.

"To tell the truth, I don't know how they could be so evil and then dress down in their finery and go up in the church like nothing ain' happen. It like if they does forget God every day of the week and then remember him on a Sunday."

Sarah looked at the children quickly to see if they were listening, but they seemed to be engrossed with their toys. She wondered what they would be like when they grew up. And what would become of her? Would she perhaps be sold to cruel masters like the Bowyers? Would she be sent to work in the fields? She shivered at the thought and prayed that she would never suffer such a fate. All her life she had been in the house; first at the Holdips and now here.

The only reason she had lived such a life was because of the colour of her skin and the texture of her hair. To her it didn't make any sense. Why should the colour of your skin or your hair make a difference to how you were treated? Not that she was sorry for hers because working in the house was, by far, better than working in the fields. But what did her mother have to suffer to end up with a child who looked like she did? She now knew what her mother meant and she understood why she had refused to lie with the overseer who was her father. It was shameful.

She was obviously not as brave as her mother, for she had not refused Master Thomas; she had let him do to her what he wanted. Not that he had been cruel, but he still took what she did not wish to give and now she could never go to a husband untouched. She would probably never have a husband at all. The unfairness of it brought tears to her eyes which she hurriedly wiped away lest Betsy and the children saw them. She looked towards her future without joy or hope, for what joy or hope was there to be found in a slave's life?

"Would you believe that some of those Quakers came to the plantation last week asking if our slaves could come to one of their meetings?" Margaret asked in disbelief.

"Yes," confirmed her husband. "Ever since that Edmunsen fellow actually had the audacity to come out and condemn us for keeping slaves a few years ago, they have been doing everything to preach the gospel to the Negroes. If you ask me, all they are doing is planting the thought of rebellion in their heads with all that talk about being set free."

"We've seen none here, thank God," Elizabeth answered. "Why on earth would Negroes need to hear the gospel anyway? Aren't they under a curse? I've always heard so."

Sarah put down the dishes she had brought in near to the end of the long dining room table where the Edwards and Bowyers sat. She could feel John Bowyer's eyes on her and she hastily followed Sally who had added her dishes to the table and turned to go back to the kitchen for more. Her ears had immediately picked up the mistress' words and she wondered if that was why her life was so miserable. Was she, and all black people, under a curse? She followed Sally out of the room, sorry that she had been asked to help serve. She did not want to be around the master or his friend who looked at her like he wanted to lie with her.

Thomas saw John's gaze following Sarah from the room and was surprised to find himself annoyed by his friend's interest in her.

"I'm surprised they were so bold," Thomas said, forcing himself to contribute to the discussion and ignore John's reaction, "because it's been over a year since the act to prevent Quakers from bringing Negroes into their meetings was passed."

"They are nothing if not bold and rebellious to boot. Not only do they condemn us for owning slaves, but they flaunt their rebellion by not contributing to the support of the militia. Who do they think keeps the island from being taken over by the French, the Spanish or even the slaves, if not the militia?"

"How dare they try to tell us how to treat our slaves?" Margaret was obviously quite put out by the boldness of the Quakers.

"Well, we treat ours very well here so they cannot accuse us of misusing our slaves," defended Elizabeth.

Thomas was disquieted by Elizabeth's words, especially as Sarah chose that moment to come back into the room to put down the last of her dishes. He caught her eye briefly to see if there was any indication that she had heard his wife. Did she feel that he had misused her? Hadn't he? He had not abused her really, he justified himself. He had tried to be as gentle as he could and he really couldn't be faulted for losing his control; she was just too desirable. He would buy her a gift next time he went into town, he thought, to appease his conscience. What could he give her that would not attract the attention of Elizabeth? It would have to be something that she wouldn't see; maybe like a new chemise. The thought of seeing Sarah in a fine lawn chemise and feeling the softness of it against her skin was enough to make him adjust himself on his chair. He would give her until Saturday before he approached her again. That would give her a whole week to recover. That could hardly be considered misusing her, could it?

Chapter 10

Ekow quietly pushed open the door of the hut that he shared with another slave. It was long past the time when the slaves would have settled down for the night and the only noises he heard were the crickets in the grass. He was glad for the moonless night as he crept through the slave village towards the cane fields. Bypassing the ones they had planted mere weeks ago, he made his way to the fields with canes that were not yet as tall as him but would be by harvest time.

In his hand he carried a rusty bucket in which he nursed glowing embers that he had earlier removed from the cooking fire, adding small bits of dry wood and leaves to it once he passed the last slave hut. He now stoked the fire until it caught into a healthy flame. He smiled as he pushed his way into the thick of the canes and set down the bucket. When the flames began to lick greedily at the green leaves nearby, he hurriedly made his way through the canes and ran back to the village.

A dog barked in the yard as he silently slipped between the huts until he reached his and let himself in. He stood just inside the door and took deep breaths to quiet his rapid breathing before he crossed the dirt floor to the back room where he lowered himself to the thin pallet that was his bed, satisfied that the one he shared with lay as he left him.

He smiled to himself even as he turned to lie on his side to ease the pressure on his back that was not fully healed. Hopefully the master would lose a lot of canes tonight before anybody smelled the smoke or heard the crackle of the flames. This time his payment would be in the loss of his property, but that was only the beginning. He would learn that no man shamed Ekow without paying the price.

By the time shouts were heard all over the village, he did not have to feign sleep for he had fallen into a deep sleep for only an hour. He had been tired from the work of the day, his weakened body and the hours since he had left his bed the day before. Through the commotion and confusion that burst through the village, he heard the crackling of fire in the distance and took satisfaction in knowing that his effort had not been in vain.

Thomas was woken by a quiet but insistent knocking on his door. Instantly awake, he threw off the sheet and stumbled to open it. Ada stood on the threshold wearing a dress that appeared to have been hastily donned.

"Massa Thomas, Bentley say that the canes on fire and to come quick."

"On fire?" he repeated in disbelief before rushing to look out of the window that provided a view of the front of the house and across to the fields. Orange flames lit the night sky and the dreaded sound of crackling flames could be heard.

His heart leapt in fear at the sight as he picked up the clothes he had shed earlier.

"Tell him I'm coming," he instructed tersely as he closed the door and rapidly pulled on his clothes and boots.

He absently noted Sarah peering out of her door in confused sleepiness as he ran past her and down the stairs. Thoughts of how to handle the fire raced through his mind. Fighting it with water in the dark would probably be pointless. They would have to fight it with fire.

He found the stable boy pacing anxiously as he threw open the front door. He had a horse saddled and ready.

"Where's Bentley?" he asked, pulling on his hat.

"He gone to the fire. He say to tell you it look like the fields to the north."

Dread curled in the pit of Thomas' belly as he knew that was where the canes for next year's harvest grew. He mounted his horse and took off towards the fire, sending up prayers along the way. The orange of the flames lighted the night sky and guided him to the blaze where Bentley was already issuing instructions to the slaves who had been roused from their sleep. At this proximity, the heat and the crackling of the hungry flames gave urgency to their actions.

Further downwind, a track was being cut to create a firebreak while a back fire had been lit to burn up the canes in the path of the advancing fire so that it would have no fuel to sustain it and would burn itself out. Thomas joined the slaves who were cutting the track while Bentley saw to the back fire.

An hour later, hands raw, covered in ash and coughing from the smoke, Thomas saw the last of the flames go out and relief poured through him, dispersing the adrenaline that had kept him going. With the fire out, they could not see the full extent of the damage so he mounted up and tiredly led the way from the burnt fields, spying a few glowing embers as he went.

Anger fuelled him now that the adrenaline had gone as he considered the loss that he had suffered that night. He had taken years to build the plantation back up and now this. He didn't know the full extent of the damage and he dreaded what the morning light would reveal.

The sun stinging his eyes made Thomas turn his head instinctively away from the source and try to settle down for some more sleep. As he turned, the smell of smoke from the clothes he had dropped on the floor before falling into his bed assailed his nose. His eyes flew open, only to close again in hope that he was still in a dream and that he had not really spent several hours fighting to save the canes that were to be harvested the following year.

However, the soreness of his hands and the stiffness in his back confirmed that it had been no dream. Throwing his feet off the side of the bed, he took a moment to catch himself before standing to painfully stretch his aching muscles. A quick wash and a change into clean clothes and he was hurrying out of his room eager and reluctant, in equal parts, to discover what damage the fire had wrought.

He already found Bentley and a number of slaves surveying the damage. His heart plummeted as he saw the acres of charred canes; his Muscovado gold, the promise of a good harvest, turned to worthless black stalks. He felt to weep at the loss.

"How the hell did this start?" he asked in a voice still hoarse from the smoke and from shouting.

"I can't say, Mr. Edwards. It looks like it started in the middle of a field. See there where the east side is not fully burnt? I'll look through the trash and see if I see anything."

"Do you think any of the men could have started it?"

"We've had no trouble here before. The slaves know that they are treated well and have no reason to do something like this."

Thomas did not answer; instead, he turned his horse around to head back to the house. Who really knew what the slaves were thinking? He and Bentley might not think they had reason to rebel, but did *they* think so? Bentley was right; they had never had trouble before. Before the new slave George came. Could it be him? Then again Sarah had not been here for long either. Not that she could have done it, but could she have gotten one of the men to do it to get back at him? Jethro maybe? He didn't know what to think. All he knew was that he had lost a good part of his harvest for the next year and that would significantly impact his profits. The pain of the loss hit him hard because he had poured so much of himself into making the plantation profitable. If one of the slaves had done this, they would pay for it.

The atmosphere in the kitchen was subdued as the slaves discussed what had happened in whispers, as if to talk about the fire in their normal voices would draw suspicion to them. Jethro, who had been to see the burnt canes, reported that a good few acres had been destroyed and that he was there when Bentley went through the trash and found a burnt, nearly melted bucket near the place that the fire may have started. Bentley had taken the bucket to show the master and they had discussed how it could have been used to start the fire.

"So you mean that somebody like they set it?" Ada asked.

"Look so," confirmed Jethro.

"But who would do that?" Sally asked.

"It could be any of the men, but all of we was in we huts when Bentley hear the crackling and wake we up," Jethro said.

"It could be slaves from another plantation," Ada suggested.

"Yes, but why they would set the master canes on fire and not their own master's?" Sally asked.

"I think the master and Bentley planning to question everybody to see where they was when the fire start," Jethro added.

"I feel real sorry for the master," Sarah said. She was surprised that after what had happened last week she could still feel sorry for him. When he had passed her that morning heading downstairs he had hardly noticed her. He had looked distracted and troubled as he hurried to see what damage had been done. Although the fire had shifted his focus from her for now, she couldn't be glad about what had happened.

Next time she saw him she would gather her courage and tell him that she was sorry. She knew how hard he worked on the plantation and that losing all those canes would be hard for him. She couldn't understand it, but she found herself wanting to offer some comfort to him.

"How bad is it, Thomas?" Elizabeth asked him at lunch.

"Bad. I lost a quarter of next year's harvest." He barely picked at his food, having no appetite due to the pain of his loss and the soreness of his throat from breathing in so much smoke.

"I'm sorry, Thomas. I know that you work hard on the plantation, but what does it all mean? All it takes is a fire or some other catastrophe to make it all seem almost pointless. It is times like this that I feel as if we should move back to England."

Thomas felt anger rising in him at her words. He would never move back to England. Did she not understand that the work he did was about more than just making the plantation profitable again? It was about proving to himself that he could run The Acreage successfully and that he could survive the hardships of Barbados.

Years before his father had died he had asked him to let him come to Barbados and run the plantation, but he had refused, telling him that he knew nothing about running a sugar cane plantation and he probably could not survive in Barbados. Instead he had left the plantation in the hands of his unscrupulous manager. Although his father was dead, he somehow needed to succeed just to disprove his father's words and the sting he had felt when he said them.

"It is the hard work that I do which allows you to dress in the finest apparel, eat the best foods and have a house full of slaves to do your bidding," he countered coldly. "And I will never leave Barbados," he added, before taking himself from her presence lest he said more than he ought.

Sarah met him in the hallway as she was coming from the children's room. He idly thought how often he met her in this hallway and always she was eager to escape his presence. Today was different. Her voice stopped him in his tracks.

"Master Thomas?"

"Yes, Sarah?" He looked at her curiously, even more so when she did not lower her eyes as she usually did.

"I am real sorry to hear about the canes you lost."

Those few words simply spoken, but with a wealth of sympathy giving weight to them, flooded him with warmth and caused him to feel a tenderness towards her that surprised him.

"Thank you, Sarah."

He marvelled that after what he had done to her; taken her from her home and made her his in all ways against her will, she could still find it in her heart to be compassionate to him. Some hitherto untouched place in his heart warmed at her words and the lust he had felt for her began to transform into something else. What it was, he could not give a name to.

Chapter 11

Thomas could think about nothing but the coming night. The whole week had seen him dealing with the matter of the fire. They were no closer to finding out who had started it, but he was sure that it had been done deliberately. The days had been spent clearing the burnt thrash from the fields and preparing it for replanting. He had come home every day bone tired and filthy from the trash. Once he had washed away the stench of the day he fell into bed, many times without even the desire to eat. His desire for Sarah had not dwindled; he just did not have the energy to do anything about it.

Although he worked hard, work did not purge Sarah and her words from his mind. When they had finally succeeded in clearing and replanting the canes, he was once again able to turn his attention to her. He considered lying with her again a reward for his hard work. That morning he had told Ada to send her to his office when she came downstairs.

She had timidly knocked at the door and looked poised for flight even as he had beckoned her to come in. The plain garb she wore did little to disguise her womanly form and the curve of her neck, left bare by the simple white blouse, reminded him of the sensitive spot he had discovered. He couldn't wait to rediscover it and feel her response. He did not keep her long; he could not without giving in to the temptation to test the sturdiness of his desk. Reigning in his wayward thoughts, he tersely told her to ready herself for him tonight, ruthlessly pushing away the twinge of guilt he felt at the look of dread that crossed her face before she fled the office.

Now his conscience pricked him again as he thought that he had not been in to Elizabeth for two weeks and had no desire to. Had this young, brown-skinned slave girl somehow bewitched him? He knew that some of the slaves dabbled in the practices they had brought from their own lands which were said to have strong magical powers. Not that he really believed they had any power and, in any case, he was sure that the only spell Sarah would put on him, if she knew the black arts, would be one to keep him away. It was obvious that she had no desire for him, nor had she thought to use her charms to get whatever she could from him. Maybe it had not dawned on her yet. As for her lack of desire for him, which his poor performance the last time had not helped, he planned to change that tonight.

He forced his mind to the job at hand – going over the books of the plantation – which was especially important in light of the loss that week. This was something that he did not enjoy, but he had committed to do it himself because of his father's lack of good stewardship. He had recently received payment for his last shipment of sugar and, after recording the revenue he had earned and the expenses for the last two months, he was pleased to see that the plantation was continuing to show a good profit. He had been looking at buying two hundred acres on the north side of the plantation before the cost of land became even more expensive than it was, but now that would have to be put off. The forced delay to expand the plantation was almost like a physical pain. Maybe lying with Sarah would help to ease it.

Returning to the books in front of him, he turned to record assets he had purchased in the period. The receipt for the £50 he had paid to Jonathan Holdip was between the pages of the book, together with the receipt for the machinery he had shown Bowyer and some other small tools he had acquired. Apart from the machinery, the payment to Holdip was one of the largest for the period and it drew his mind back to Sarah yet again. He smiled ruefully, as he realized that even the drudgery of doing the books did not succeed in taking his mind away from her. Reminders of her were everywhere.

He was honest enough with himself to admit that paying the amount he had for Sarah was a poor business decision. No one paid more for an asset than was necessary, especially when they could obtain one to perform the same function for less money. Sarah was listed as an asset in his books, along with the very desk that he was writing on. That made him pause. An asset had no feelings, but he had felt her fear, seen her tears. So what did that make her?

He could not fathom this possessive feeling he had with regard to her. When John Bowyer had expressed his interest in her, he had immediately rejected the idea of sharing Sarah with him or anyone else. The thought actually repulsed him. She was his and his alone. So why was he having these thoughts about whether she was an asset or not? An asset was something that could be bought or sold, so she was an asset and she was his. And tonight she would be his again in every sense of the word. The night could not come fast enough for him.

Sarah hoped that the night would never come. After speaking to the master in the hallway, she had done her best to avoid him for the rest of the week. Not that it had been hard, with him working all hours of the day and coming in late. However, when Ada greeted her that morning with the message that the master wanted to see her in his office, she knew she could no longer avoid him. He had told her to ready herself for him tonight. Why had she thought that he would not want her again? It may not have been enjoyable for her, but perhaps it had been for him. She remembered the groans he had smothered against her neck and the shaking of his body on hers and she shuddered in revulsion. Afterwards she had felt dirty and used. But that was what she was to the master, something that he had paid a lot of money for that he could use at his will, like his horse or cart. Her mind recoiled at that thought.

"Sarah! What are you daydreaming about? I asked you where my blue silk dress is."

The mistress' strident voice interrupted her thoughts and her hands stilled in the act of pulling the needle through a pair of pants that she was repairing for William.

"I gave it to you to sew back on the lace yesterday and I would like to wear it to dinner tonight."

Her mind returned to the present abruptly and for a few moments she struggled to the answer the mistress' question.

"I gave it to Sally to press, Mistress. I will ask her where she put it."

Even as she spoke, an unexpected thought sprung to her mind of what the mistress would say if she knew what she was daydreaming about. What would she think if she knew that her husband wanted to lie with her? Was she hoping that the blue silk dress would make the master go to her room tonight? Sarah fervently hoped so. She did not understand it; she wore no silk dresses, her skin was not pale and her hair was not soft and golden. Why would the master want to lie with her instead of the mistress?

"Bring it to my room when you find it," she instructed.

"Yes, Mistress," Sarah agreed, securing the needle in the folds of the pants before putting it down.

Sarah found Sally who was getting ready to bring up the clothes she had pressed.

"Sally, give me the mistress' blue dress. She just asked me for it because she want to wear it tonight."

Sally smiled. "She does look good in that dress. She like she hoping to catch the master eyes tonight."

"I hope so," Sarah murmured. She would have liked to talk to Sally about the master, but she was too ashamed. She was only glad that Ada had not questioned her too closely last week when she took her sheets out to wash away the traces of the loss of her innocence.

"Girl, don't get too much hope," Sally advised knowingly.

"I don't understand it," Sarah burst out. She couldn't seem to help herself.

"Girl, these men must be don't understand it neither. On the one hand they think that black people ain' no better than animals and the same time they can't stay away from the black women. The master ain' no different, although he got a little more decency than some. As far as I know, he never force heself on any of the women and he don' treat them bad. He force you?"

Sarah hid her face behind the blue silk dress in shame. She didn't know how to answer. He didn't exactly force her, but he didn't give her a chance to refuse him either.

"You can say no to the master?" she asked Sally instead.

"Girl, you can always say no. But if he want you so bad, you may as well use what you have to get what you want."

"What I have? What you mean?"

Sally shook her head. "You real sweet and innocent for true. No wonder the master can't keep he hands from you. You best prepare yourself because no matter how good the mistress look in that dress tonight, I could tell you she can' keep the master from you' room. You got something that she ain' got and it is that that got the master."

Sarah did not know what it was she had; she only wished that whatever it was would leave her.

Thomas thought that Elizabeth would never go to bed. She dragged out dinner for an inordinate amount of time until he begged her indulgence to retire to his office for a brandy on the pretext of finishing off some work. It wasn't a lie, since earlier he had thrown down his quill in disgust after only a few hours of updating the books and gone for a ride around the plantation to clear his head, avoiding the burnt cane fields. He had found it hard to concentrate when thoughts of Sarah had lodged in his mind after he recorded the receipt for her purchase.

He had bought Sarah, not just to help Elizabeth, but because she attracted him from the very first time she served him at Holdip Manor. So he had lain with her, but far from quenching his desire, he now could think of nothing else. That had never happened to him before, certainly not with Elizabeth, and it disturbed him.

She was the slave and he was the master, so why did he feel as if he was the slave, as if she had a hold over him that he did not have over her? Curse his weak flesh! He wanted her to want him as he wanted her. He would show her who the master was tonight in the most pleasurable way.

He closed the ledger he had been staring blindly at and pushed back his chair. His body leapt in anticipation as he left his office to go to his room to wash and change. As he passed Elizabeth's room, he could hear no sound and there was no light coming from under the door. He sighed with relief as he entered his room, hastily stripping off his clothes.

Within minutes he was letting himself into Sarah's room. She was sitting on the bed, almost in the same position that he'd found her last week. The sound of the lock turning in the door caused her eyes to fly in his direction before she lowered them to look at her hands that twisted in agitation.

Distress filled her as she briefly caught the blaze of desire in the master's eyes. She had known that the fire would only keep him away for so long and today when he had called her to his office she knew, even before she got there, what he wanted and she had dreaded what the night would bring.

Although she could not say that he had really hurt her very much the last time, she had not liked how she felt afterwards, as if she wanted to scrub her whole body with a harsh soap. And now he wanted to lie with her again. Sally had said that she could say no, but fear trapped the word in her mouth. What would he do if she said no? Would he have her whipped? Somehow she knew that he would not.

She tensed as he walked quietly towards her and took her hands in his, pulling her to her feet.

"Sarah..." he began.

She opened her mouth to say no, but her tongue felt too heavy to form the word, so instead she shook her head silently in refusal, looking down at her feet.

Thomas gently slid his hands into her hair to stop her from shaking her head and tilted it back so that she would be forced to meet his eyes. "Don't be afraid, Sarah. It won't be like the last time. I promise you."

With that he bent his head and reacquainted himself with the sensitive skin of her neck, knowing that she enjoyed that caress. He was rewarded with a slight shudder of her body and this time he knew it was not fear. His lips tormented her with their pleasurable caress, shocking Sarah that her body could respond to his touch even while her mind was saying 'no'.

Pushing aside the pleasure she felt, she stirred up her courage and opened her mouth.

"No." Even as the word spilled from her mouth, she was not sure if she was speaking to the master or to herself. Thomas stopped, surprised. He saw the torment in her eyes and his heart softened towards her.

"I know that the last time you had no pleasure, but it will be different this time," he coaxed.

Sarah knew that he could take what he wanted whether she said yes or not, but he did not press her. It was as if he was waiting for her to give her consent and he would not force her if she said 'no' again. For the first time she felt in control. Maybe if she let him do what he wanted he would be satisfied and not want her again. Maybe it wouldn't be like the last time. She gave a barely perceptible nod, which Thomas did not miss, as he was watching her intently. She heard him release a breath that he must have been holding and pulled her closer, murmuring something that sounded like "Thank you", but she could not be sure.

Giving her no further opportunity to change her mind, he gently sipped at her full lips until she relaxed enough for him to coax them apart and explore the secret places of her mouth, tilting her head so that he could deepen the kiss. He was pleased that she did not resist, but neither did she participate. He lifted her hands to his hair which was unbound from its usual leather thong and she tentatively felt its texture and then more boldly explored its softness with her fingers as she relaxed. He shuddered in response.

Sarah felt the master shudder and marvelled that she could draw such a response from him by just running her fingers in his hair. His hair was soft and silky to her touch. She found that she enjoyed the feel of it. He lifted his head and laid his forehead against hers, pulling her close to him. He was breathing rapidly and their closeness did nothing to disguise his desire. Yet he did not pull her to the bed as he had before, he simply held her in his arms.

Sarah was surprised at how comforting it felt to be held. She could not remember being held by anyone for a long time, except when she and her mother had clung to each other the day she had been taken from Holdip Manor. But that was not the same as this. The master's embrace made her feel cared for and somehow protected. Her hands fell from his hair and settled on his shoulders, neither holding him nor pushing him away.

Taking a deep breath, he gently kissed her forehead. She thought she heard him murmur something about being sorry, but she must have been mistaken. Masters did not tell slaves sorry for anything. Gently raising her chin, the master kissed her with such gentleness that Sarah could not help but be wooed by his kiss. For the first time she responded, tentatively tasting him in turn which made him shudder and bury his hands in her wild hair, kissing her passionately. Sarah didn't resist when he quickly shed their clothes and drew her to the bed. Rather than falling on her, he turned her to face him so that he could explore the contours of her smooth, tawny body, causing Sarah's breath to catch as she experienced her first taste of desire. Thomas couldn't help the triumphant smile that crossed his lips before they trailed where his hands had explored. He was gratified to feel Sarah's response to his caresses and the secrets her body unknowingly yielded, telling him that she was ready for him.

Minutes later he caught Sarah's muffled cries in his mouth as her body trembled in his arms. Only then did he allow himself the release that he craved. A feeling of intense satisfaction filled him that was in part due to the physical release he had experienced, but much more to do with the fact the he had given Sarah her first taste of pleasure.

He was surprised at how much he wanted to just sleep with her in his arms, but he reluctantly roused himself from her, kissing her one more time before he rose from the bed. Tonight there were no tears on her cheeks. The dim light of the room was not enough to hide the languorous look of a woman who had been well satisfied. Thomas dressed quickly before he was tempted to return to the bed.

"Thank you, Sarah," he said quietly.

She said nothing, lowering her eyes in embarrassment as she pulled the sheet up to cover herself.

As he unlocked the door and left quietly, Sarah wondered at his words. The master had thanked her. Since when did a master thank a slave for anything? But Master Thomas had thanked her. For what, she was not sure. Maybe for not refusing him. At least this time she did not feel the shame she had felt before.

However, her shame was that her body had responded to his touch in ways that she had not expected and could not control. Ways that made her face hot when she thought about them.

Thomas closed the door behind him and headed for his room. How he wished he could have stayed in Sarah's bed all night. Far from diminishing the desire he had for her, lying with her had only increased it. He smiled as he recalled her response to him and felt his body begin to stir again.

As he passed Elizabeth's room, a thought put an abrupt end to his budding desire. He realized that he had so lost himself again that he had not protected her from possible pregnancy.

Chapter 12

*A*lthough it was Sarah's day off, she found herself waking up early and getting out of bed. She could have lain down for longer, but her disturbing thoughts and the smell of the master's scent on the sheets made her leave the bed. She was confused. How could she have responded to the master's touch like that last night? Her face went hot with shame as she remembered how her body had shuddered with pleasure and how her hands had grabbed him as feelings she had never experienced rippled through her.

As she stood, her head felt a little giddy and her stomach queasy, reminding her that she had been too anxious to eat anything the night before. She would make sure she had a good breakfast later when the family had left for church. Washing and dressing quickly, she let herself out of her room quietly and headed downstairs and out the back door before any of the other women saw her.

She made her way to the spot that William had taken her to the first day she was at The Acreage. As she settled down against a tree, she remembered how she had been lost in her thoughts when Mary had fallen and cut her knee. She had thought that the master would have had her whipped when the mistress had complained about her carelessness in watching the children, but he had brushed aside the mistress' concerns and had not punished her.

She tossed her head restlessly as scenes from the night before plagued her mind. What was happening to her? She hated the master, didn't she? He had bought her and taken her from the only home she had ever known. He had forced her to lie with him and stolen her innocence. So how could her body betray her so? Even now her thoughts caused a twinge of anticipation in her body. She closed her eyes as if that would block out the shame and confusion she felt.

A sound behind her caused her eyes to fly open and she whipped her head around. Her heart jumped and began to race before slowing when she saw that it was Jethro.

"Jethro, you frightened me," she scolded.

"Sorry, Sarah. I didn't do it for purpose. I thought you hear me coming."

"I was thinking too hard to hear you."

"What you thinking so hard 'bout?" he asked, coming to sit down next to her.

"Nothing to do with you. So what you doing out here so early?"

"I watch you coming out here and come to see if you alright."

"Why wouldn't I be alright?" she challenged.

"I don' know." He was uncomfortable with the conversation. He could hardly ask her if the master had hurt her in any way. In any case, what could he do about it if he had? He was just a slave like her.

"I am alright. I just wanted to come out here and get some air."

The air was cool and fresh as the sun was just beginning to come up.

"I like this time of the day," Sarah continued. "It is fresh and sweet."

"Like you," Jethro murmured under his breath.

"What is that you said?"

"Nothing," he denied and fell silent. It was not an uncomfortable silence. Both of them looked into the distance at the forest that spilled down to the sand where the waves tumbled to the shore.

"When we were at that beach house, I used to look out at the sea and I would feel free," she confided. "You ever think about being free, Jethro?"

"All the time," he admitted.

"What you would do if you was free?"

"The same thing I doing now, but for myself. I would build things and repair things for other people, but I would be earning money. And I would find a good woman and marry and have nuff children."

"You could marry now. Some of the slaves at the plantation that I come from were married to one another and here too. So why you can't marry now?" Sarah turned to look at him.

"The woman I want to marry belong to somebody else." He looked pointedly at her. Sarah turned her head back to the view. She didn't want to see what was in his eyes. She would not encourage him and, in any case, she did not want him thinking about her in that way. What would be the point? She liked him alright, but would she want to marry him? Would she want to lie with him the way she lay with the master? She wasn't sure about that, especially after last night.

"You know I mean you, Sarah, so don' play that you don' know," he challenged her boldly.

Sarah was silent. Jethro had never been so bold before. Why was he being so now? Now that she was already confused about her feelings for the master.

"You mean me? So what you want me to say?"

"I wish we was free so that I could marry you, Sarah. I wish you didn' belong to the master to do with as he like," he said angrily.

"Jethro…" she began weakly, not knowing what to say to his words. They were fruitless anyway because there could never be anything between them. This was the first time they had been alone to even talk to one another. She didn't know how he could know that he wanted to marry her and they never even been together without Ada or one of the other slaves there.

"It ain' fair that the master could have you just because he own you," he went on. "He treatin' you good? Or he just taking what he want and he don' care 'bout how you feel?" Jethro asked angrily.

"Jethro…" Sarah protested, uncomfortable with the conversation.

"He does kiss you or he don' kiss slaves? He does kiss you like this?" He turned her head and kissed her. Sarah did not stop him. She wanted to see if his kiss would make her feel the same way that the master's made her feel last night.

"Jethro! What the hell are you doing?" The master's angry voice made them spring apart guiltily and stand up. "I asked what the hell you are doing kissing Sarah?" The master's voice was cold and menacing. Jethro had never seen him like that and he felt dread creep into his belly.

"Sorry, Massa. Sorry! I couldn't help myself." His admission took some of the steam out of Thomas because he knew exactly what he meant. Nevertheless he was still furious to find Jethro and Sarah kissing, especially after last night.

"How dare you touch Sarah! Get the hell out of here and I will meet you at the whipping post when I get back!" Jethro backed away a few steps before turning to run back to the yard.

"Master Thomas, Jethro didn't mean anything by that. Nothing happened." Sarah appealed to the master.

"Nothing happened because I came upon you." He pulled Sarah to him. "Did you arrange to meet him out here?" he demanded.

"No, Master Thomas. I come...I came out here to think and he saw me and came to see if I was alright."

"You came out here to think and Jethro just happened to follow you? You expect me to believe that?" he challenged, still enraged at the memory of Jethro's lips on hers.

"It is the truth."

Sarah hung her head, not wanting to tell him why she was out there and what was confusing her. He lifted her chin and looked into her eyes as if trying to read the truth. He could see no guilt in them, but jealousy spurred him to bend his head and roughly possess her mouth as if to erase Jethro's kiss. Sarah was taken aback at the roughness of his kiss and stiffened.

Thomas' mouth immediately gentled on hers and he began to explore her mouth with a sensuality that caused her to melt with budding desire. Thomas felt the change in her and moved his hands from holding her head in place to caress her back and pull her against him. He would have loved nothing more than to pull Sarah down on the grass and possess her as he had last night. He reluctantly broke away, resting his forehead on hers.

What was ailing him? He felt out of control. He wanted to take her in broad daylight where they could be discovered! He was jealous of his own slave! What a ridiculous notion. This woman had truly bewitched him.

"What were you thinking about?" he asked more gently, remembering what she had said.

"About last night," she confessed quietly. "I was confused."

"Confused about what?" he prompted.

"About how I felt when you came to my bed."

"Did I give you pleasure?" he asked, already knowing the answer. She nodded, hiding her face.

"You do not have to feel ashamed. There is no shame in giving each other pleasure."

"I gave you pleasure?" she asked shyly. He laughed out loud.

"More than you can imagine." Sarah smiled shyly at that before she sobered again, remembering Jethro.

"Master Thomas, you really going to whip Jethro?" she asked plaintively. He stiffened against her.

"I have every reason to strip the skin off his hide," he said angrily. "How dare he touch you!"

"He didn't do any harm. Please don't whip him."

"Are you begging for mercy for your lover?" He asked jealously

"Master Thomas, you are the only man I ever laid with. I never had any dealings like that with Jethro." She laid a hand on his arm in appeal and the anger melted away from Thomas. He knew he was being suspicious without reason.

"Alright, I will give him a chance. But let him know that if I catch him sniffing around you again, there will be hell to pay!"

"Thank you, Master Thomas." Sarah smiled at him and he gently stroked her cheek. She was surprised, but happy, that he had listened to her.

"Today is your day off," he stated, leaning back against the tree that she and Jethro had rested on minutes ago and pulled Sarah against him, clasping his hands low down on her back.

"Yes, Master."

"What do you do on your day off?" Sarah couldn't believe the master was asking her these questions.

"Uh, wash my hair, wash my clothes…"

Thomas released his hold on her to take one of her hands in his. It had a few callouses. All she did was work, even on her day off. "That's still work." He gently kissed the palm of her hand, making Sarah shiver slightly. Sarah didn't know what he wanted her to say. He had bought her to work, so why was he saying these things now? She was a slave and slaves worked. He did not remember that she was a slave?

"I wish I could stay here all day, but I have to go and get ready for church," he remarked. "I want you to come to my room tonight," he added, straightening and releasing his hold on her.

"Your room?" she repeated. Thomas nodded. "Yes, Master Thomas."

She thought that he would kiss her again, but he stroked her cheek and walked off, leaving Sarah staring after him, in confusion once again, wondering why she felt disappointed that he had not kissed her.

Jethro was in the kitchen with Ada and Sally when Sarah came back. He jumped up and looked around worriedly.

"The master come back?" he asked.

"Yes. He gone to dress for church. Don't worry, he ain' going whip you no more," Sarah assured him.

"How you know?" Jethro was not convinced.

"It would serve you right if he was to beat you, Jethro," Ada interrupted unsympathetically. "I tell you to keep 'way from Sarah, so I don' know what you doing kissing the girl."

Sarah looked accusingly at Jethro. He told the other women that he had kissed her? She was glad to see that he looked shamefaced.

"You sure he ain' plannin' to do it when he come back from church?" he asked, still looking fearful.

"Yes, I sure. I asked him not to whip you and he said he would give you a chance, but to tell you that if he catch you sniffing around me there will be hell to pay."

"Thank you, Sarah," he said, looking relieved. Sarah nodded.

"Wuhloss, you got real power 'bout here, Mistress Sarah," Ada cackled. "Hell to pay? I hope you hear that loud and clear, Jethro. The master ain' mekkin' no sport."

"Why you call me Mistress Sarah, Ada?" Sarah asked, ignoring the rest of her comment.

"Well, if you got the power to stop Jethro from getting a beating, you must be the mistress of the house. You got the master bewitch for true."

"Stop that kind of talk, Ada, before the mistress hear you. I goin' and lie down for a little bit. I get up too early and I still feel tired."

"You didn' get no sleep last night?" Sally teased. Sarah felt her face go hot with embarrassment and she quickly escaped from the kitchen.

There were no secrets on a plantation. Everybody was always in everyone else's business. She was surprised that the mistress did not know that the master had started to come to her room. At least she didn't act as if she knew. And the master wanted her to come to his room tonight? She couldn't help a little tingle of anticipation as she thought about what that would mean. Why did he want her to come to his room? Not that she minded going; not after last night. She wondered if that was why he listened to her today. Had he been pleased with her?

She smiled a little to herself as she remembered how she, who was so afraid of him before, had had the courage to ask him not to beat Jethro. She was surprised that he had done what she asked. Was Ada right? Although she was the slave, did she really have some kind of power over the master?

Chapter 13

Thomas could barely concentrate on what the minister was saying. His thoughts jumped from the night before to that morning when he had come upon Jethro kissing Sarah. He had seen Sarah heading out to the eastern side of the plantation when he had been eating his breakfast at the dining room table. He had hurriedly finished the meal and made haste to follow her, but was delayed by Elizabeth who came down to breakfast as he was leaving and stopped him to ask if they were still to visit the Terrills at Cabbage Tree Hall after church.

Barely stopping to answer her, he had left the house, intent on seeing Sarah before the family left for church. He had slept soundly but had woken with memories of the night before fresh in his mind. He had wanted to see how Sarah looked at him. He was sure that she would no longer be regarding him with fear. Would there be desire in her gaze now? Thoughts of her response stirred him afresh and had hastened his steps.

The hot anger that had surged through him when he saw Jethro kissing her frightened him. He had felt quite capable of whipping him to within an inch of his life. Never had he felt such fury and it was beyond disturbing. What was this manner of madness that had come over him? He had seriously begun to wonder if Sarah's fear of him and her shyness had been a pretence while she had been really carrying out the black arts to madden him while she was dallying with Jethro.

All of those thoughts disappeared when she had shyly confessed that she was confused because of the night before. He believed her because he, too, was confused. He had wanted to stay with her the whole night and not only to join their bodies again; he had wanted to hold her. A feeling of discomfort stirred in his stomach. He was beginning to have feelings for his slave. What master had soft feelings for a slave girl? He knew of none, or at least none had ever confessed such feelings to him. Something must be wrong with him.

"And Sarah said to Abraham 'The Lord has kept me from having children. Go, sleep with my slave, perhaps I can build a family through her.' Genesis 16:2. So we see that from the beginning of the Bible, men have been lying with their slaves."

The minister's voice, heavy with cynicism, penetrated Thomas' thoughts and brought him back to the present with a jerk. He felt as if the minister had read his thoughts and exposed them to the whole church. Glancing around, he saw John Bowyer and the planter who had offered him the first slave girl he had lain with and smiled inwardly, thinking that most of the men in the church were probably doing the same as Abraham and if he was called the father of faith, then it was obviously not an unpardonable sin.

"But don't be fooled that God allowed it. He has given man free will, but there are consequences to using our free will. The Bible says later that when the slave, Hagar, became pregnant she began to despise her mistress and her mistress mistreated her. That sin caused much trouble in Abraham's household. When we do things out of God's will, trouble will follow."

Thomas forced himself not to squirm in his seat. Maybe he should talk to the governor about moving this minister and replacing him with one who preached messages that comforted the soul and not that stirred the conscience. That was a little too close to the truth for him, especially since he had once again not taken any measures to prevent getting Sarah with child. He began to offer up a prayer for divine intervention before the irony of it stopped him from being a hypocrite. He would have to be more careful in the future lest his household became filled with turmoil, as Abraham's did.

The journey to Cabbage Tree Hall in the north of the island took a little under an hour in the carriage. Sally did her best to entertain the children and keep them from fidgeting, but Thomas couldn't help but notice that Sarah generally seemed to have better success with the children than she did. When the baby woke up and began wailing, Thomas fervently wished he had ridden his horse so that he would be free of the confines of the carriage.

"That was certainly an interesting sermon today," remarked Elizabeth once the baby had quieted again. "I'm sure that most of the men were squirming in their seats," she added with a cynical laugh. "That is, if their consciences are not dead."

Thomas said nothing, wondering if she was referring to him. Did she somehow know that he had been to Sarah's room on two occasions? He did not see how she could because he had waited until he was certain that she had been sleeping before he left his room. He had asked Sarah to come to him tonight. Somehow it would give him the feeling that he was not forcing her but that she wanted him as much as he wanted her. He was being ridiculous! She didn't have to want him; she was his to command. But it gave him immense satisfaction to know that fear was no longer her master, but desire was. Maybe this was the same reason that God gave man free will – so that he would have the pleasure of knowing that they chose to serve him out of desire rather than out of fear.

"I am looking forward to this visit," Elizabeth continued. "I have not seen the Terrills for some time. In fact, since I was so ill during my confinement with Rachel, I have hardly been sociable. We should arrange her baptism soon and have a party to celebrate it."

"Yes, by all means," Thomas agreed absently.

"You seem rather distracted today, Thomas. Is everything all right? Have you managed to deal with the burnt canes?"

"Yes dear, everything is fine." Unless the fact that I can't stop thinking about our child minder is a problem, he thought. Glancing over at Sally, he would have sworn that he had seen a smirk on her lips before she schooled her expression. Did she know what was distracting him?

Thankfully Elizabeth fell silent and turned to look out of the window at the passing scenery. In a short time they turned in the entranceway of Cabbage Tree Hall, lined by the magnificent cabbage palms that gave the Hall its name. It was not as big as The Acreage, but it had a solid appearance and boasted many windows.

Unlike the Acreage, the patio was at the back of the property rather than the front. As they disembarked from the carriage, the front door opened and their host and hostess came out to greet them.

"Thomas, Elizabeth, wonderful to see you." Michael Terrill greeted them, shaking Thomas' hand before leaning down to kiss Elizabeth on her cheek. His wife, Jane, held her cheek for Thomas' kiss before giving Elizabeth a hug and ruffling the children's hair affectionately.

"Oh and this is the latest addition to the family," she cooed, stroking the baby's head softly. "How precious she is."

The women turned to follow the men into the house, leaving Sally to bring up the rear with the children.

"I'll get one of my girls to show your girl and the children to the nursery where they can play. Our William has been eagerly looking forward to your William coming over. I will have some beverages sent up as they must be parched and they can eat their lunch there too."

Elizabeth eyed her surroundings with appreciation. The plantation house was well appointed and comfortable. Persian rugs covered the floors of the rooms that led from the hallway while beautiful furniture made of mahogany and other dark woods graced the rooms.

"It's such a beautiful day, I thought we could have our lunch outside," Jane said as they by-passed the dining room with its long table. At a glance, Elizabeth could see that it was polished to perfection with a beautiful flower arrangement in the centre.

"I totally agree with you. It's a wonderful day, considering that we're still in the rainy season," Elizabeth agreed. "I'm so glad that we've been spared a hurricane again this year, although we did have a very bad storm a few weeks ago."

"Yes, indeed. That was rather violent. Lightning struck one of the palms in the entranceway and snapped the top right off!"

"My word!" Elizabeth exclaimed.

They reached the back veranda which overlooked a beautiful garden. A slave girl was waiting with a tray of beverages which Thomas and Elizabeth accepted gladly before taking their place at the table.

"Have you heard that John Yeamans' widow has recently come back to the island?" asked Jane.

"No, I hadn't heard that. To tell the truth I do not know her, although I have heard of the Yeamans," admitted Elizabeth. "But then, I feel as if I've been cut off from civilization for a long time," she joked.

"Yes, my dear and she's on her third husband. We all know what happened with Colonel Berringer, her first husband."

"That would have been before I came to the island."

"My dear, the poor man was poisoned by Yeamans and he was barely cold in his grave before Yeamans married Margaret and merged the two plantations, naming it after himself."

"What! How shocking!" Elizabeth exclaimed.

"Yes, rather. They were having a relationship while she was married to the Colonel, so it seems that Yeamans killed the Colonel so that he could marry her and take over the plantation," Jane said with authority.

"Jane, dear, you should not repeat rumours and gossip," chided her husband.

"But, my dear, it is widely known. Anyway," she went on, "she has recently returned from Carolina and has a third husband. Some are lucky to get even one, but she has had more than her fair share."

"Yeamans did very well for himself in Carolina. Not only was he governor, but he also amassed considerable wealth and left her well taken care of, so she obviously did not marry for money," Thomas remarked.

"I did not know all of that, but now you mention it, I remember my brother's wife, who lives in Charles Town, writing to tell me when he died three years ago, thinking that I may have known him. Apparently, he was not very well liked in several circles," Elizabeth confided. "Maybe people suspected that he did away with the Colonel, as you say, in order to marry his paramour. The rumours must have followed him all the way to Carolina."

"Ladies, perhaps we should not perpetuate the rumours and instead speak of other things," suggested Michael.

"I heartily agree," said Thomas. "I met the new husband only recently and he seems quite a decent chap. Name of William Whaley."

"Yes, indeed. Have you heard that an Act was passed to empower Benjamin Middleton to sell his estate to settle debts?" Michael asked Thomas, changing the subject.

"You don't mean Middleton from Middleton's Mount, do you?"

"I believe it is the same one. Maybe he just means to sell off a piece of his estate."

"If that is the case I can commiserate with him because that is exactly what I had to do when I first came here. While I managed not to sell off any land, I certainly had to part with a lot of my slaves and let go one of my overseers, but thankfully I have managed to restore my work force and turn the plantation around. I had wanted to buy a couple of hundred acres, but I just suffered a bad fire. Lost a quarter of the canes that would have been ready to harvest next year."

"My God! That's tragic. What caused it?"

"I don't know for sure. It looks as if it may have been set deliberately, but we don't know who did it. We questioned the slaves, but no one knows anything, of course. Up until then I was having a good year, particularly the last couple of months," Thomas confirmed. Yes, especially the last two months, he thought silently, since Sarah came to The Acreage.

Elizabeth looked at him thoughtfully, wondering what had made the last few months so good. Maybe Thomas meant that they'd had a new addition to their family because the only other major change that had happened at the plantation was him buying Sarah to help with the children. Could he mean that? Was Sarah his latest interest? It would devastate her to discover that Thomas was lying with one of his slaves under her roof. Knowing that he sometimes visited them in their hut was bad enough. She would have to keep a closer eye on him and Sarah.

Chapter 14

Sarah quietly closed her door and waited for her eyes to adjust to the darkness of the hallway. She crept past the nursery, running her hand along the wall to feel her way. When her hand encountered the doorjamb of the mistress's door she quickly removed it lest she make any noise. Her heart thumped with fear as she imagined the mistress throwing open her door as she passed by and demanding to know where she was going in her thin chemise, with bare feet and her hair "wild", as she referred to it. Thankfully, it remained closed and no light escaped from beneath it, telling her that the mistress was asleep. At least she hoped so. She knocked as loudly as she dared at the master's door and waited anxiously for him to open it.

Thankfully, the master opened the door quickly and stepped back to allow her to come in, closing the door quietly behind her. Sarah's eyes landed on the huge four poster bed which dominated the room and which looked high enough to need a step to get into. There was a slight indentation on it and the sheet was wrinkled where the master had been lying down.

A closer inspection of the room revealed night stands on both sides of the bed, a large, solid-looking wardrobe, a chest of drawers, a desk and a wash stand. Two rugs, with a striking blue and brown pattern that matched the highly polished wooden floor, lay on both sides of the bed. Dark blue curtains were drawn back on either side of the windows, allowing a small sliver of moonlight to add to the light provided by the lamp on the night stand. The room, which was bigger than the hut that she had shared with her mother, suited the master. She wondered why he and the mistress had separate rooms; this was certainly big enough for both of them.

Her perusal of the room was interrupted by the master who stood watching her as her eyes darted around the room.

"Does everything meet your approval?" he teased quietly.

"It is a very nice room."

"I'm glad you like it. I would like you to visit it often," he invited, moving closer to her. He was dressed in a loose pair of breeches and a robe that was untied. A part of his broad chest, with its dark hair, was visible through the opening. She remembered the coarse texture of that hair from last night and was tempted to feel it again, but she was not so bold. It was funny how the hair on his body was not as soft as the hair on his head.

"How was your day off?" She started at the unexpected question.

"It was alright. I went back to sleep after I came in," she answered. She had managed to rest for several hours so now she was wide awake.

"Good, you're well rested then. Did you deliver my message to Jethro?" he asked, reminding her of what he had told her earlier that day.

"Yes, Master."

"Good. I won't be so generous if I catch him so much as looking at you again. You are mine," he declared, tilting her chin up so that she was forced to look at him. The intensity of his gaze burned through her and she nodded.

Sarah's hair beckoned to his hands and he could not resist burying his fingers in the thickness of it, tilting her head back so that he could possess her mouth passionately. He felt he could never tire of kissing Sarah. Her responses were still innocent, but were now becoming bolder under his tutelage. When she lifted her hands to his hair of her own volition, an involuntary shudder went through his body and he pulled her closer until their bodies were melded together.

Sarah delighted in the master's response to her simply playing with his hair. She could feel every contour of his body pressed against hers and she could tell that he already wanted her. When he parted his mouth from hers and trailed his lips down her neck to that place that made her shiver and made her knees weak, she clung to his strong shoulders and boldly felt them through his cotton shirt.

"Undress me, Sarah," he invited huskily. She shyly obeyed, taking delight in the fact that she was in control and took time to discover all the treasures she unveiled, driving Thomas quietly to the brink of his control. Before he could lose it completely, he stilled her hands and swept her up in his arms to deposit her on the high four poster bed before joining her eagerly. He was gratified to see an equally eager smile on Sarah's face before he captured her lips once more.

Thomas held Sarah to him spoon fashion, amazed at how content he felt with her in his arms. He wondered if she felt the same way. He really should get her to go back to her room before they fell asleep and were discovered, although Elizabeth hardly entered his room. He would let her go in a little while.

"Are you awake?" he whispered.

"Yes," she answered quietly. She didn't add the word 'Master'. Somehow it did not seem necessary. He did not feel like her master right now and she did not feel like his slave. She felt like his woman. He had made her feel that way. She mentally squirmed now as she recalled all they had done and the way she had responded to his passionate touch.

"Are you happier here now? At The Acreage?" he clarified.

"Yes. I am happier now. I like to look after the children and everyone is good to me."

"I'm glad to hear that. You must let me know if anyone does not treat you well." They were silent for a while, but it was a comfortable silence. Sarah felt herself growing drowsy in the warm comfort of Master Thomas' arms.

"Should I go back to my room now?"

"Yes. I should let you go, but I like having you here. I will have to get up and go to work in a few hours."

"Master Thomas, how come you work in the fields with the overseers? Master Holdip didn't use to do that." It took quite a lot of courage for Sarah to ask that, but she felt that she could.

"It's a habit now, I think. When I first came to Barbados seven years ago the plantation was in a bad way because the manager didn't run it properly. In fact, he was stealing from my father. I had to sell some of the slaves and make do with one overseer, so I started to work in the fields myself. Now I find that I prefer it to sitting around the plantation all day long like some of the other planters. Of course, my hands have become rough with callouses."

"I don't mind them," Sarah admitted, feeling one of them and appreciating the callouses because they told her that he was not afraid of hard work. She was amazed at how comfortable she felt with him. In fact, she had almost forgotten that he was her master.

"What did you use to do for Mrs. Holdip?"

"Mostly keep her company and sew. She taught me a lot of things, like how to speak properly and she showed me how to sew and then she used to say that I could sew better than her." He could hear the smile in her voice.

"I noticed that you speak better than most slaves. I find it easy to understand you. You like to sew?" She nodded. "Well, I will buy you some material when I go to town the next time," he promised. "You can make something nice for yourself."

"The mistress might wonder where I got it from," she reminded him regretfully.

Mention of the mistress brought Thomas back to reality. "Oh, yes, the mistress. I had almost forgotten about her," he admitted. "How remiss of me," he chided himself, even as he shifted to disentangle himself from her reluctantly. Sarah didn't know what 'remiss' meant, but she had forgotten about the mistress too. That reminded her that it was time to go back to her room and her small bed. She was glad that the master had told her to come to his room. The large bed was much more comfortable than hers and fit the master and her better. She wouldn't mind coming to his room again.

Climbing out of the bed, she pulled her chemise over her head and headed for the door, feeling the master's eyes on her. She slipped out, closing the door behind her as quietly as she could. The darkness of the hallway made her feel her way along the wall until she reached the mistress' door. She held her breath as she passed by and touched the frame of the nursery door. She was just about to open hers when the mistress' door flew open. She froze, her head flying around.

"Sarah? What are you doing creeping around the hallway in your nightclothes?" She demanded suspiciously.

Words temporarily deserted Sarah, leaving her hostage to the mistress' suspicion.

"I- I thought I heard the children cry out, so I was checking on them," she lied. Her racing heart betrayed her and she was glad that the mistress could not see it beating frantically beneath her thin chemise and that the shadows were the friends of her guilty face.

"Oh. Mayhap that is what disturbed me as well," the mistress concurred, the suspicion leaving her face. She turned and went back into her room without another word.

Sarah quickly entered her room where she sagged against the door in relief. Had the mistress believed her story?

Thomas closed the door to his room and immediately caught sight of Elizabeth leaving hers. He had hoped to avoid her, but he had woken up late so he knew it was a distinct possibility. He had fallen asleep as soon as Sarah had left his room, but by then it was the early hours of the morning so that he had slept well past his usual time.

"Good morning, Thomas," Elizabeth greeted him. "Surely you're not only now getting up? That's not at all like you. Were you up late last night?"

"Uh, yes. Rather late."

"It seems that we were all up late last night."

"Oh?" Thomas paused and waited expectantly. Had Elizabeth heard him and Sarah in his room?

"Yes, I found Sarah going into her room in the early hours of the morning." She searched his face, which remained impassive. "She said that she was checking on the children." He nodded unconcernedly.

"Maybe we can have breakfast together for a change. You're always off to the fields long before I get up."

"I don't really have time for a leisurely breakfast, but you can certainly join me while I eat," he offered.

"Thank you. I will." They walked down to the dining room side by side and waited a few minutes while one of the slaves brought in their breakfast.

"I don't know why you go off to the fields every day," complained Elizabeth. "It's not as if you don't have two overseers."

"I prefer to be directly involved in the running of the plantation, Elizabeth. I won't make the same mistakes my father did. If he had not been so absent, his manager would not have had the opportunity to almost ruin the plantation."

"I can't imagine that one day off will lead to ruin, Thomas. I was hoping we could do something together. Perhaps visit town. It's been ages since I went into town. I wanted to buy some material so that I could get Sarah to make a few articles of clothing for the children; they are growing like weeds."

"Well, be that as it may, I can't just drop everything and go off to town today. We can plan it for Friday."

"Alright, dear. I will look forward to going on Friday. Do you think we should bring the children?"

"No!" Thomas said vehemently. The last thing he needed was to be closed up in a coach with Sarah who would no doubt be going to keep an eye on the children. He was sure that Elizabeth would somehow get wind of his interest in Sarah if they were in close proximity. He was having a hard enough time being around her as it was.

"Alright, dear. It will be just the two of us. That will be nice. We haven't spent very much time together recently."

"We were together at the Trellis' only yesterday," he corrected.

"That's not quite the same, but it was rather fun. I had never even heard about the goings-on between Margaret Berringer and John Yeamans. Do you really think he poisoned the Colonel?"

"I certainly don't know, Elizabeth. It does not behoove us to speculate and, anyway, that was several years ago."

"Yes, I know. But if it is true, then he got away with murder, which is totally unjust. I am a firm believer in justice. Therefore, if we sin we should pay for our sins."

Thomas laughed a little mockingly. "You are sounding very religious, Elizabeth. What has possessed you?"

She made a face at him. "I do not mean to sound religious. I'm just a believer that what is done in the darkness should come to light."

Thomas said nothing. That hit a little too close to home for him.

Chapter 15

Three weeks later

Sarah dressed herself automatically for the day and headed downstairs for breakfast, but anxiety caused her stomach to revolt at the thought of food. Her womanly time was late. It had never been late in her life and she shied away from what that meant.

She rested her hand upon her flat stomach as if it would give up its secret, but nothing was forthcoming. In fact, she felt no different. The only thing she had noticed was the day after Master Thomas' visit, the one where she had felt pleasure for the first time, she had woken up and her head had felt a little giddy and something had not felt right. She had dismissed it, thinking it was because she had not eaten the night before and she had gone to sleep late.

Now she wondered if that was her body letting her know that something was happening; letting her know that a babe was forming in her womb. She started to shake with fear. What would the master say? Worse yet, what would the mistress do? Would she be sold to another plantation? Would her baby be taken away from her? She prayed to her mother's God and to the master's God, in case he was listening, that she was not with child.

"Morning, Ada," she said quietly as she entered the kitchen.

"Morning, Sarah. You want some porridge or you going to eat with the children?"

"I don't think I could eat anything, Ada," Sarah confessed. Ada inspected her face and saw the distress all over it.

"What happen with you, Sarah? You don' look so good."

Sarah hung her head to hide the tears that sprang to her eyes. "I think I might be with child," she whispered.

"Oh loss," Ada lamented. "How late your monthlies is?"

"A week."

"A week ain' nothing. Don' worry your head, girl."

"I never been late in my life."

"The master never get any of the slave girls 'round here with child. He know what to do. You mean to tell me that you had his head so turn that he didn' do nothing to stop you from breeding?"

"Nothing like what?"

Ada shook her head at Sarah's innocence. "Girl, I hope that you ain' really with child because I don't know how the mistress would take to that. A lot of masters does get the slaves with children, from what I hear, but it never happen 'bout here yet."

Sarah decided to go for a short walk to clear her head. Ada wasn't helping and she didn't know what to do. She didn't want a child if she had no husband, especially a child from the master. Everybody would know that she had lain with him. Shame and fear accompanied her and, far from calming her, the walk only provided the opportunity for thoughts to torment her. Her feet took her towards the east side of the plantation where the master had seen Jethro kissing her a few weeks ago.

"Sarah!" Master Thomas' voice arrested her. She tensed as she turned to face him. How had he found her?

"What are you doing walking out here so early?" He searched her face and found misery inscribed on it. "What's the matter?" he asked concernedly.

"Nothing, Master Thomas," she denied.

"'Nothing' has got you very upset. Has someone bothered you? Has the mistress ill-treated you?"

"No, Master Thomas." Tears filled her eyes at his concern, but she was afraid of what would happen if she told him what she suspected.

"What is it, Sarah? Tell me," he demanded, taking hold of her shoulders.

"I-I may be with child," she confessed in a whisper.

"With child? Are you sure?" Thomas searched his mind to recount the times he had been with Sarah. And his mind reluctantly recalled the fact that he had been unable to control himself on each occasion and knew that any of those times could have resulted in putting a babe in her womb.

"My monthlies are late," she confirmed.

"Don't fret, Sarah. It may not be so." He knew he was offering vain hope and he silently cursed himself for his weakness.

Elizabeth would be furious if he had gotten Sarah with child. He had been into her once since Sarah became his and that was only because she had made him feel guilty for not giving her any attention. He had performed his husbandly duty, trying not to compare Elizabeth's pale body, which had borne three children, with Sarah's lithe, young body with its smooth tawny skin that contrasted with his in such an appealing way.

At the same time, a part of him was pleased that he may have made Sarah pregnant and was intrigued to see what a child made by he and Sarah would look like. The thought of her belly swelling with his child stirred something in him that he had not felt before. Not only did he feel possessive about Sarah, but now it was coupled with a new feeling of protection for her.

"Don't worry," he assured her. "Everything will be fine."

Three months later

Sarah struggled to remember the words of assurance that the master had given her that morning months ago as she faced the mistress.

"Sarah, what is wrong with you? You look ill and have done for weeks, yet I swear you have put on, rather than lost, weight. In fact, your skirt seems to be fitting you tighter…" Her voice trailed off as a new light dawned in her eyes. "My God! Tell me you're not with child!"

Sarah began to tremble. Words failed her as she grappled for a response to the mistress.

"Who was it? Jethro? I will have the master flay the skin off him! How are you supposed to look after the children if you will be waddling around here in a few months? This is most inconvenient!"

"Sorry, Mistress. I will still be able to mind the children." Sarah almost fainted with relief that the mistress did not realize the truth. She did not know how the mistress could miss what was happening under the same roof, but she was glad.

The master now only asked her to come to his room once a week, rather than two or three times like before and he treated her with such gentleness that her heart was beginning to soften towards him. He had taken to buying her gifts when he went into town, saying that he enjoyed doing so. His last present was material and ribbon. She had made a bonnet with it, hoping the mistress would think she had brought it with her from Holdip Manor.

"Stop daydreaming and get the children ready. We're going over to the Bowyers' to spend the day." That abruptly pulled Sarah out of her daze. Not the Bowyers! Not only was she not looking forward to the bumpy carriage ride, but she hoped that Mr. Bowyer was not at home. The one time she had seen him months ago, she had felt him looking at her in the way that the master did when she first came and she had been uncomfortable.

"Yes, Mistress."

"Oh, and go and tell Ada that we won't be home today and that we will need Jethro to take us in the carriage."

Sarah escaped from the mistress' presence with relief. If the mistress was so vexed at the thought that Jethro had put the babe in her belly, what would she do when she found out that it was the master?

Minutes later she found Ada in the parlour instructing Sally about cleaning the silverware. She looked up as Sarah walked in and said, "Mistress Sarah, you lookin' for me?"

"I wish you all would stop calling me that," Sarah complained, annoyed.

"Why do they call you Mistress Sarah?" a curious voice asked from behind her.

Looking around, startled, Sarah saw that William had followed her.

"I thought you were just Sarah," he added.

Ada and Sally both laughed and shook their heads.

"She ain' just Sarah anymore," Ada told him, still smiling.

"Hurry up, Sarah," William urged, losing interest in the conversation, "I want to get to Henry's house."

"You all going out today?" Ada asked.

"Yes, that is why I was looking for you. The mistress said to tell you and for you to let Jethro know she will want him to take us in the carriage soon."

"Yes, Mistress," Ada teased her again. Sarah sucked her teeth and took William's hand to lead him back upstairs. She hoped that the mistress never heard them with that foolishness. They had taken to calling her that from the time she had saved Jethro from the beating. Ada also told her several months ago that the master no longer went to the slave huts, which was another reason they called her Mistress Sarah. It seemed as if she was now the only one that he lay with. She had felt pleased with that information, as it made her feel that she was special to the master.

Elizabeth eyed Sarah's bonnet with interest. It was finely sown and had a brightly coloured ribbon that tied under her chin. And it matched the new dress that Mary had proudly shown her on her doll only that week, which she said Sarah had made. Where had she gotten the cloth and ribbons? Did she bring them from the Holdips? Or did Thomas buy them when he last went into town? And why would Thomas buy her gifts? A dawning horror began to fill her as she looked closely at Sarah and the noticeable increase of her belly. No, No. It couldn't be. Thomas would never be so bold as to be bedding a slave under her very roof! He would not be so foolish as to get her with child! It had to be Jethro's. She knew that Thomas sometimes gave Jethro a little money for jobs he'd done well so he probably got the material for Sarah. But slaves were not allowed to buy and sell. She eyed Sarah afresh as if she would find the truth in her face.

Sarah tried not to squirm as she felt the mistress' eyes on her. She knew that it had been foolish to wear the new bonnet that she had made from the cloth the master had given her, but something in her wanted to show it off. Did she somehow want the mistress to know that the master favoured her? That would be foolish indeed, but a little pleasure stirred in her heart at the thought that he did. She remembered what he had said to her only a few nights ago when he had come to her room long after everyone had gone to bed.

"Mary showed me the dress that you made for her doll today," he had said quietly, holding her against his side. He had taken to spending time lying with her before he left her room. She liked those times.

"Her doll needed a new dress," Sarah said. "The one it came in was getting to look real old and washed out."

"You are remarkable, Sarah." The master had said. She had waited for him to explain what he meant, but he had said no more, only pulled her to him and kissed her gently before rising from the bed as if he didn't want to leave. She found that she didn't want him to leave either.

"I will show Helen my doll's new dress that Sarah made for her," Mary announced, interrupting Sarah's thoughts. She turned her attention to the doll that Mary was hugging to her chest. Her heart skipped a beat when the mistress answered.

"It's very pretty. Sarah, where on earth did you get that mat-?"

"I brought my soldiers to play with Henry and Jethro built me a fort for them to hide behind," interrupted William. Sarah could have hugged him as he and Mary competed to tell what they planned to do when they got to their friends' house.

She gratefully looked out of the window of the carriage, thankful that the mistress did not have the chance to ask any more questions, but she knew that she would probably not escape so easily the next time. She would have to be more careful. Suppose the mistress searched her things and found the comb and brush that the master had given her, or the two beautiful handkerchiefs edged with lace, not to mention the beautiful soft chemise that he had bought her the week after she had told him she was with child? She would surely demand that she be thrown out of the house or even sold. Sarah shuddered at the thought. The Acreage had become her home and she couldn't imagine living anywhere else.

"Thomas, did you know that Sarah is with child?" Elizabeth demanded. They had come back from the Bowyers' more than an hour ago and she had had to wait until Thomas came in from the fields to talk to him.

Thomas felt as if he had been hit by a cart and was momentarily unable to respond. He didn't want Elizabeth taking out her wrath on Sarah and he had not as yet decided how to deal with the situation. As he searched for a response, she continued.

"It must be Jethro. I said as much to her and she did not deny it! This is most inconvenient. How is she to adequately look after the children when she becomes big with child?"

Jethro? Thomas had a moment of doubt before he caught himself, knowing that the child was his. Sarah was not one to lie with different men. In fact, he acknowledged that she had not chosen to lie with him at all; at least not at first. Now she welcomed him willingly.

"What would you have me do, Elizabeth? The damage has already been done, if she is indeed with child."

"Yes, so it has."

Now was not the time to deny that the child was Jethro's. Elizabeth would make Sarah's life a misery, not to mention his, if she knew the truth. In six months or so the truth would be known. He would deal with that when the time came. Not that he would openly admit that the child was his; that was not done. Elizabeth would not dare question him about it; it would be an unspoken truth. He was lord of his house and he was answerable to no one. If she didn't want to be put on a ship to England, she would watch her words and keep her mouth shut when the child was born. Many other wives dealt with the evidence of their husband's coupling with their slaves and it was not mentioned. It would be no different here. Not that he considered lying with Sarah as mere coupling; she had become very dear to him and the time with her was special.

"Just get one of the other women to take on some of her responsibilities when it gets hard for her to move around," Thomas suggested. Elizabeth snorted in an unladylike manner at the thought of making Sarah's life easier when she had brought the situation upon herself.

"That's just the beginning. Then she'll have to be looking after her child and ours at the same time. That is beyond inconvenient! We can only hope that the child does not survive. That would certainly make things a lot easier for everyone."

Thomas stared at her as if seeing her for the first time. How had he not noticed how self-absorbed she had become, even to the point of hoping that the babe would not live so that she would not be inconvenienced. Right then, any remaining feelings that he had for her dried up and the guilt he had felt about how the child in Sarah's belly would affect Elizabeth left him. She would just have to live with it.

Chapter 16

*E*kow sat outside his hut idly carving a mask from a piece of wood that he had gotten from Jethro. To anyone looking at him he seemed focused on his task, but he was subtly watching Sarah who was telling a story to some of the children in the slave village. It must have been her day off from minding the children in the big house.

He had seen the family leaving to go to their church earlier. He scoffed to himself. Their religion was a joke. They went to their church and came home and bedded their slaves and beat them to get them to work harder. What did their God say to that? They seemed to be prospering, so maybe he turned a blind eye. So it was up to him, Ekow, to see that justice was done; to punish them as they punished his brothers and sisters.

He looked again at the woman across the yard. He knew who she was. She was no sister to him. She was the white man's whore, Sarah. Jethro had seen him watching her one day and had warned him that she was the master's woman. He had told him that he had barely escaped a beating when Massa Thomas, as he called him, had caught him kissing her. Ekow smiled cynically. The master must have been afraid that if she lay with

Jethro she would know what a real man was, instead of a pale-skinned man who didn't even have the stomach to beat his own slaves. Maybe he would show her.

Not that she aroused any desire in him, with her skin the colour of a river full of mud after many rains. No, she could never compare to the women of his tribe with their pure, undiluted black skins. She had probably used her colour to get into the white man's bed. In this country it seemed that the paler your skin, the more favoured you were. It was not so in his country. That must be why the white man favoured her. Ekow smiled slightly. Good. He was glad that she was her master's favourite because when he struck, it would cut him as deeply as the whip had cut into his back. The way the burned canes had hurt him.

He could see that her belly was swelling with child, the white man's child. It would be another slave to add to the wealth of the plantation and another whose even paler skin would give it the privilege of working in the house, away from the heat of the sun and the sting of the whip. How he hated this country and longed for his own.

He had waited for three full moons after the fire so that when he struck no one would think that the two were done by the same hand. Now the time had come. From watching her he knew that she sometimes went to that part of the plantation that looked out over the sea. Out there was lonely. If she went there today, he would follow her. He would not even have to do much more than push her over the edge of the cliff. People would think that she had slipped.

He smiled again as he heard her telling the children that she would tell them stories another time. Hopefully, she would head for her favourite spot and he would be close behind her. He put down the mask he had been carving, keeping the knife he had been using concealed in his hand. Casually looking around to make sure that no one was watching him, he walked in the opposite direction to which she had gone. Once he cleared the last hut in the village, he doubled back and followed her silently, like the warrior he was.

Jethro saw Ekow leave the village and followed him. He knew that he wouldn't be trying to escape during the day, but he was curious to find out where he was going. When he realized that he changed his direction to follow Sarah, he kept him in his sight. Why would he follow Sarah? He had warned him that she belonged to the master. Surely he did not want another whipping when his back had only now healed from the last one. Maybe he had not understood what he had told him. He had, after all, only come to the island a few months ago and was still learning the language.

Although the slave, who insisted his name was Ekow and not George, spoke little and preferred to spend his time whittling and carving wood, Jethro liked him. He appreciated the strength in him and he secretly admired the fierceness he saw in his eyes. Fierceness that must have been in his own eyes many years ago, but which had now burnt out with years of

155

being slave to another and not his own man. If he was his own man, he would have been able to marry Sarah, rather than having to admire her from a distance. He would not have to envy the master for putting a babe in her belly, as it was now plain to see.

When she had told him that the mistress thought the babe was his, he had been surprised at the pain that had squeezed his heart to know that it was not, nor could ever be. The mistress had never asked him anything about it, but if she had, he had been prepared to protect Sarah as best he could.

He had to admit, though, that the master seemed to treat her well, for which he was glad. He often bought gifts for her when they went into town and, according to Ada who seemed to know everything, he no longer lay with any of the slaves in the village. Still, he felt protective of her, which was why he hid behind a tree and watched as Ekow approached her.

Ekow moved so silently that he was almost upon Sarah when she finally heard him. She jumped and put a hand on her tummy as if to calm the babe.

"George, you frightened me! What are you doing out here?"

"My name is Ekow."

"What are you doing here?" Sarah asked again.

"I walked behind you." He followed her? Why would he do that? Sarah began to feel uneasy.

"What do you want?" She looked around but saw no one.

"You de master's woman?" he asked, ignoring her question.

"What is that to do with you?" Sarah asked, surprised he would ask her that.

"You lie with the white man and have his child in your belly? You would be the shame of you' mother if you were in my country." Sarah knew she would be the shame of her mother here too.

"You do not know anything about me." Her uneasy feeling intensified. Something was not right with him. Maybe the beating had affected his mind. "I will tell the master what you said." She would not, but she wanted to frighten him as he was frightening her. She turned to leave but he blocked her path. He was tall, dark and powerful. Anger came from him so strongly that she could almost feel it touching her.

"I not frighten for you' master. He not a man. He lie with you when he got a wife and he could only beat me by tying me to a post and gettin' Bentley to do it. He would never fight me like a man, 'cause he is a coward. I goin' kill he when I get the chance." Sarah was now terrified. She knew that if he told her this, he would not allow her the chance to tell the master. She began to fear for her life.

"He is a good man," Sarah protested, trying to ease her way around him.

"You are his whore so you say that." Sarah recoiled at the venom in his voice and turned to run. Ekow caught her before she had run four steps and swung her around, bringing her close to his chest. Sarah put out her hands to push him off. His chest felt like rock beneath her hands; an immovable rock.

Jethro was too far to hear what they were saying, but when he saw George grab Sarah, he started to run towards them.

"I should show you what it is to lie with a real man, but I don' want what the white man had already. So I goin' do you like I do the canes."

Sarah began to panic as she realized that it was he who set fire to the canes and he intended to do her some harm. She began to struggle, but her struggles were in vain. He easily turned her around with her back to him and, pinning her arms to her sides, he lifted her slightly off the ground and began to walk towards the cliff.

Sarah screamed as she understood his intention. She frantically tried to turn her head to see if anyone was nearby and screamed again before Ekow took one hand away to cover her mouth. She wanted to kick and thrash her body, but she feared for the babe in her belly.

"George! George! What you doing? Put down Sarah!"

The sound of Jethro's voice almost made Sarah weep with relief.

"You gone mad? Let go Sarah!"

Ekow swung Sarah around and Jethro saw that he held a knife to her neck. He inched towards the cliff, glancing over his shoulder to see how close they were to the edge.

"George, what you doing?" Jethro asked again. The tremor in his voice betrayed the fear in his heart.

"I gettin' my revenge for what you' master do me."

"Usin' Sarah? She never do you nothin'. He own she the same way he own me and you. Let she go."

"She got he chile in she belly. You tell me that she is he favourite so I goin' tek she from him."

"He buy she from another plantation and force she to lie with he. She ain' do nuttin' wrong. Let she go." Jethro appealed again.

Ekow seemed to waver. He could not see Sarah's face, but he could feel her shaking against him. A picture of her telling stories to the children and hugging them to her flashed in his head and it was as if the hatred that blinded him fell away and he was able to see that she was a good woman and maybe as much a victim as he was. By seeking to take her life for something she had no control over, he was being as unjust as the white man. He let go of Sarah and stepped back so suddenly that she stumbled and would have fallen if Jethro did not rush forward to catch her.

"I sorry," he apologized to Sarah. "Since I get carry away from my land, my head not de same. I am a warrior from de Ashanti tribe," he told them proudly. "My tribe is powerful and rich in gold. We own slaves; we not slaves."

"Wunna does own slaves?" Jethro asked in disbelief. "You ain' no better than the master then."

"We treat our slaves good," Ekow insisted. "If a master treat a slave bad in my country the slave can ask for a new master. Sometimes a master will marry a slave and make she his wife and our slaves can marry and have children."

"Here, too," Jethro pointed out.

"Yes, but in my country the children born free. Not here. Here, you is a slave forever and your children too." Sarah instinctively put a hand on her belly as if she wanted to protect her child from the truth of his words.

"Our law say that a man is not to lie with the wife of a slave. For that he can be put to death. Here the master could lie with any slave even if she got a husband and the slaves does get treat worse than the animals. I never see the white man beat he horse thirty times with a whip."

Jethro silently agreed with Ekow.

Ekow suddenly stood up straighter and declared passionately, "I am a warrior. I can't live as a slave no more. If I can't go back to my land it better for me to be dead and go to my ancestors. They will welcome me." With that he turned and leapt off the cliff with a loud war cry.

Sarah and Jethro stood stunned as they heard the snap of branches breaking under the weight of Ekow's body until everything went deathly still. Sarah put her hand over her mouth in horror and turned trembling into the comfort of Jethro's chest. In spite of the horror of what they had just seen, Jethro could not help but to be glad to have Sarah in his arms as she turned to him for comfort.

The sight of Ekow jumping off the cliff replayed in his mind and convicted him of weakness. How had he become so weak that living as a slave seemed better than death? Shame consumed him. Slavery made a man less than a man.

By the time the Edwards came back from church Sarah had calmed down. Ada had made her drink chamomile tea to calm her nerves and afterwards she went to lie down in her room.

Jethro made sure that the mistress and children had gone inside before telling the master all that had happened.

Thomas was shaken to learn how close he had come to losing Sarah. If he had any doubt of his feelings for her, the thought of her being thrown from the cliff convinced him of the love that had birthed in his heart. He was glad that the slave had thrown himself off instead. The fact that he was the same one who burned the canes angered him, but the fury that consumed him at the thought of the harm he had planned to do to Sarah frightened him. It was a good thing he was already dead.

He would have liked to have gone to Sarah right away and to hold her in his arms to assure himself that she and the babe were alright, but he could not as Elizabeth was about. As it was, he had asked Jethro to tell the other slaves not to discuss what had happened lest Elizabeth discovered why the slave had taken Sarah. He cursed the circumstances that prevented him from going to her and comforting her.

He thanked God that Jethro had followed the slave to see what he intended. He shuddered to think what may have happened to Sarah if he had not. He owed Jethro a debt of gratitude.

Chapter 17

Six Months Later

"Ada, I think the baby is coming," Sarah exclaimed, clutching her tummy as it tightened.

"The water break?" she asked calmly.

"Early this morning."

"So why you didn' say nothin', girl?"

"You told me that when the water break it is still a few hours before labour start and I had the children's clothes to fold up and some to sew."

"Alright, you better go and lie down. I goin' boil some water and bring up some cloths and things. Don't worry, girl. I help deliver nuff of the children 'bout this plantation."

Sarah felt comforted by Ada's calm words. As she turned to go, another contraction tightened her tummy, causing her to gasp. Walking up to her room, her throat ached with suppressed tears as loneliness and sorrow engulfed her. She had no one to go through this with her. For the first time in many months, she longed for her mother. She would be there for her if she was still at Holdip Manor. Then again, if she was still at Holdip Manor, she would not be carrying the master's child.

She could not help but wonder what the child would look like and whether it would be a boy or a girl. She didn't know which she preferred. If it was a boy would he eventually be sent to the fields? If it was a girl, would she suffer at the hands of some master when she blossomed into womanhood? Whether it was a boy or girl, her child would be a slave. Her heart hurt at the thought of that. Would the master, one day, sell them? She could not imagine that he would sell his own flesh and blood.

The master had gone into town early that morning. He would not even be there as she went through the pain that she knew was to come. Not that he would be able to be with her, although she knew that he would want to in his heart. She thought back about how he had been in the last six months and smiled. Her smile quickly turned to a grimace as another pain tightened her belly.

The night of the day that George had jumped over the cliff, he had barely waited until the mistress had gone to sleep before coming to her room. He had held her to him and told her how glad he was that Jethro had saved her. That night he loved her tenderly as he never had before.

He did not speak of his feelings for her. She did not expect him to, but he was good to her. He always brought her gifts from town and he had brought her soft cloth to make things for the baby. And he shielded her from the mistress. In the last month he no longer lay with her in that way, but many nights he would come to her room and lie on her bed. He would hold her and put his hand on her swollen belly and feel the babe leap in her womb as if in response to his touch.

A particularly strong contraction caused her to gasp and stumble to the bed to sit down. She was glad when Ada came in with a basket full of necessities, issuing instructions about taking off her clothes and putting on an old chemise, and showing her how to squat on the bed with her back braced against the wall.

"I goin' get somebody to bring up a basin of hot water for me when you ready. The pains coming closer now?"

Sarah could only nod as her belly tightened again and she squeezed the hand that Ada offered.

"You want me to get a stick for you to bite on?"

"No. I think I can bear the pain. But tell Sally to take the children out for a picnic."

"I already tell her that and I tell the mistress that you in labour."

"Oh." Sarah fell silent. In a few hours everyone would know the truth and her life would never be the same again.

Three hours later

"Alright, Sarah. The next time you feel like you got to push, push hard. I can see the head. Look like he or she got reddish hair," Ada encouraged her while Sarah panted and braced herself to push when she felt the next wave. She strained with the effort, grabbing Ada's broad shoulders as she bore down with all her might.

"Good, good. One more push and it goin' be out. Good. It all over now." Ada caught the slippery baby in her hands and rested it on a clean sheet while she cut the cord.

"You got a little girl," Ada announced, putting the babe to Sarah's breast once she lay back on the bed. I gine clean her off as soon as I deal with the rest. When you feel to push again, go ahead and push."

Several minutes later both Sarah and the baby had been cleaned up and the baby was nursing at Sarah's breast.

Tears pricked Sarah's eyes. She had birthed a beautiful baby girl with soft reddish brown hair and when she opened her eyes and looked at her, her eyes had been green. The exact shade of green as the master's. Her heart turned over with a love that she had never felt before. It was a fierce protective love that burned within her. She would do anything for this child.

"What you goin' name her?" Ada asked.

"I don't know. I will ask the master what he want to name her."

The master came in from town not long after and Ada told him that Sarah had had the child.

"How is she?" he asked anxiously.

"Both of them good. It is a girl. She real pretty and got green eyes," Ada added, looking at him.

"Thank you, Ada. I will go up and see them now."

Thomas eagerly mounted the stairs and let himself into Sarah's room. She was still holding the now sleeping baby to her breast and was dozing a little herself.

"Sarah? How are you feeling?"

She raised tired, but happy, eyes to his.

"Good."

"Ada said that the baby is a girl."

"Yes," she said, shifting slightly so that Thomas could see her.

"She is beautiful," Thomas praised. Sarah smiled.

"Ada asked me what her name is to be, but I didn't know what you wanted to name her." Thomas thought for a moment and then he said, "Deborah."

"Deborah?"

"Yes. Deborah was one of the judges in the Bible. She was a strong woman and she was a leader. She led her people into war."

"A woman?" Sarah asked in disbelief. She had never heard that story and the idea of a woman leading men into war seemed a little unbelievable.

"Yes."

"Deborah," Sarah repeated, letting the name settle on her. She looked at the baby and nodded.

"Has the mistress been in?"

"No."

"OK. I will see that she doesn't come in today, but she will soon see the baby."

Sarah nodded, not needing further explanation.

"You don't have to worry. I will keep both of you safe."

The master left a few minutes later and Ada came back to put the baby in an old basket.

"The master name the baby?"

"Yes. He named her Deborah, after a woman in their Bible."

"She real pretty," Ada acknowledged. "And don't think she don't look like the master already."

"I don't know what the mistress goin' do when she see the baby." Sarah fretted. "You know she think that Jethro is the father."

"Don' worry your head, girl. The master gine deal with that. That baby there, she goin' be a strong woman. She goin' to cause nuff trouble 'bout here because she going do she own thing and she goin' do things that we never do," Ada prophesied. "You mark my words."

Sarah did not say anything, but she pondered Ada's words in her heart.

Elizabeth heard of the successful birth of Sarah's child with both regret and trepidation. It would have been so much better for the child to have died. Now she would have to deal with it. She would go in and see the child, a girl, Ada told her. She hoped that its skin would be brown like Jethro's and put to rest the suspicion that had birthed in her that day in the carriage. However, she already knew it was a vain hope. Her woman's instinct told her that Thomas was bedding the slave and, worse yet, he appeared to have a softness for her that he did not have for her, his own wife. He would listen to no complaints about her and he had made sure that Sally helped her with the children as she had grown large with the child.

If she had any other doubts, the fact that he rarely came to her room anymore convinced her, as well as the haste with which he did his husbandly duty when he deemed it necessary to visit her. It was as if he could barely stand to touch her. She wondered why he bothered. Maybe he wanted to get her with another child in case the diseases of the island should take any of their children. Or maybe, as his mistress grew great with child, he used her to relieve his physical needs. She should turn him away, but if that was all she could have of her husband, she would take it. How had she become so lacking in shame?

She roused herself from where she sat at her dresser, smoothed her hair back and steeled herself to go into Sarah's room. As she opened her door she remembered the night that she had surprised Sarah in the hallway. Had she been coming from Thomas' room rather than seeing to the children as she claimed? She walked the few steps to Sarah's door, took a deep breath and pushed open the door. Her eyes immediately sought out the child. She was nursing at her mother's breast. Sarah's eyes flew to hers before lowering to the babe. She pulled the child a little closer to her, as if to protect her.

Elizabeth schooled her face into an emotionless mask as her eyes confirmed what her heart had already told her. The pale skin of the babe contrasted with the light brown of Sarah's smooth breast. Soft reddish brown curls capped her small head and, although her eyes were closed, she somehow knew they would confirm that Thomas had fathered her, if there was any doubt. The pain and shame of Thomas's betrayal, now evidenced for all to see, almost caused her to retch. Turning quickly lest she shamed herself in front of the slave who was her husband's mistress, she groped for the door knob and blindly stumbled into the hallway. The closing of the door covered the sob that rose to her throat from the depths of her soul.

December 31, 1696

Sarah came back to the present with a start. She was still sitting on her bed, alone in the house. So much had happened in the last eighteen years since Ada had spoken the words about Deborah. All of them had come to pass. Deborah was certainly a strong woman and had never been one to act like a slave. She always did what she wanted and, to tell the truth, Thomas had allowed it. He had always protected her, until that day when the mistress had waited until he went into town and ordered Jethro to whip her. Thank the Lord that Richard had been there.

Deborah had certainly caused trouble at The Acreage, from the time the mistress had set eyes on her and knew the truth. She had done things that none of them had ever done, like learn to read and write with the children. And today she had also done something that none of them had ever done. She had gotten married. Not only that, but she married as a free woman and to the mistress' nephew from Carolina. Now that was a story worth telling. Sarah was sorry that Ada had not lived to see all of her words bear fruit, but she had seen enough to know that the rest would be fulfilled.

Rousing herself, she found sheets to put on the bed. Even after six months she sometimes couldn't believe that she was not only free, but that she had her own house, which Thomas had bought for her, and that she had a business which was doing well. Of course, it did not start out that way and she and Deborah had learned some hard lessons. She was still learning something new all the time and each time she used it to make the business better. She had come a long way since the day that they left The Acreage and Jethro had brought them to their new house with Mamie and Jacko, slaves that the master had given her in spite of her protests.

She changed into a house dress and went into the front to throw open the doors to the balcony to let some wind in. The sound of a cart rumbling past in the street below triggered her memory of the day they had moved in. Was it only six months ago?

Chapter 18

Six months earlier

*A*s the cart carrying her, Deborah and Mamie rumbled through the streets of town, Sarah's eyes devoured the sight of the shops and taverns lining the roads. She had not been into town for a very long time.

Most of buildings were two storeys and made of stone with wooden balconies spanning the width of the upper floor. One would never know that the city had been almost totally destroyed by fire several years ago, as it was now rebuilt and was one of the busiest and most prosperous cities in the colonies.

The streets teemed with people of all descriptions. Ladies escorted by slave girls carrying umbrellas to protect them from the sun, men dressed in uniforms, slaves loading and unloading merchandise and men patronizing the many taverns. She felt somewhat overwhelmed by the noise, the smells and the heat that was trapped by the buildings.

Looking at Deborah squeezed in beside her, she only saw excitement on her face, although this dimmed from time to time as if reflecting the ebb and flow of her sobering thoughts.

After all, it was only a few days since Richard had sailed back to Carolina to marry the girl he was engaged to. Her heart ached for Deborah, for she knew that in spite of how she had hated Richard when he first came to the island, he had captured her heart even before he had set her free.

"We nearly there yet, Jethro?" she called.

Jethro had seen to the setting up of the house that the master had bought for her. She had asked him endless questions about it on the way and he had patiently answered as many as he could until he had finally told her, "You goin' soon see it for yourself."

"We turning up High Street now," he informed her. "That is where the house is."

Both she and Deborah sat up expectantly and peered about. They looked at each other and laughed at their almost identical reactions. Joy burst in Sarah's heart. They were free! The master had given her a house, some money to help start businesses and two slaves. She didn't really want slaves and she would free them as soon as possible, but the master had insisted she would need them.

"This is it," Jethro announced, slowing down. He turned the cart into a small dirt-packed area next to a house. Sarah eagerly looked at the building he had parked beside, noting that the walls of the bottom floor were painted a warm yellow and its two sets of double doors were painted in green. It reminded her of The Acreage. The narrow wooden balcony which ran the width of the upstairs part of the building cast no shadow on the road below as the sun scorched down from right above them. A staircase at the side of the house led to the living quarters upstairs and a wooden fence blocked the yard from the view of passers-by.

Jethro jumped down, with Jacko following more slowly, and headed around the cart to start unloading the trunks. Jacko, who had lost his right hand in the sugar mill a few months before, was not able to lift the trunks, but helped to carry the lighter things which he held between his left hand and the stump of the right.

Sarah and Deborah wiggled from the bed of the cart and led the way up the stairs, leaving Mamie to help with the unpacking. Sarah took the iron key from her pocket and paused as if savouring the moment when she would open the door to her own house for the first time. Deborah smiled understandingly at her.

The key turned in the lock easily and she stepped over the threshold into the small hallway. The house smelled slightly musty as it had been shut up for a little while, but she didn't care. It was hers! She owned a house. Tears flooded her eyes and she hastily wiped them away with the back of her hand.

"I can't believe we're actually here, Ma. In our own house." Deborah sounded as much in awe as she was.

"Me neither, child."

"Let's look around," Deborah encouraged, heading for the bedrooms.

The bedrooms were identical and bigger than any either of them had slept in before, except when Deborah had shared Richard's room at The Acreage. Each room had a window which was quickly thrown open to let in the breeze. A bed with a plump mattress dominated each room and a chest of drawers with a mirror on the wall above it completed the furniture.

"We even have our own mirrors," Sarah said in awe, looking at herself in the mirror.

Jethro came in to put down Sarah's trunk in her room before heading back downstairs to get Deborah's.

Deborah dropped onto Sarah's bed, delighting in the soft mattress under her.

"After sleeping in Richard's bed, I've been spoiled," she admitted shamelessly. The fact that she could even talk about that bed where her innocence had been ripped from her was a testament that she was healed by Richard's tenderness and caring, even if he had never said he loved her.

"Let's go and see the rest of the house," Sarah suggested.

The kitchen, with a small table and four chairs, was next to Sarah's room. Across the hallway was a little parlour and a larger living room with several doors which opened onto the balcony. The house was completely furnished. It wasn't furnished like The Acreage, of course, but Master Thomas had ensured they had everything they needed and more. Sarah was moved that he had taken such care of them.

She and Deborah eagerly unbolted the doors so that they could step out onto the balcony. When they leaned over they could see down the road both ways. Smiles wreathed their faces as they observed the activity in the road below them.

Across the street in the balcony of a house that was a stone's throw down the road from theirs, a well-dressed woman was sitting in a straight-backed chair. A young slave girl waved a small palm frond over her to cool her down. She glared at them and her voice carried clearly across the narrow street.

"You would think they would go and get the house ready for their mistress instead of looking out as if they own the place."

The smiles immediately vanished from their faces as they realized that, although they were free from slavery, they were not free from the colour of their skins and the hatred of people who could not see past it.

Somewhat hampered by the comments of their neighbour, Sarah and Deborah withdrew to the sanctuary of their living room.

"We do own the place," Deborah corrected defiantly, even though she knew the spiteful woman could not hear her. Sarah smiled as her joy returned.

"The master even bought furniture," she said in satisfaction, looking around.

"He's not the master anymore," Deborah reminded her.

"It's hard to break a habit after nearly twenty years, child. I remember when I first went to The Acreage, I was so frightened. I didn't know what kind of man the master was and how I would get treated. One of the first things Ada told me was that the master liked brown girls. That only made me more frightened. The first morning I opened my door I met him coming from his room. My knees started to shake and he asked me if I was frightened of him."

"What did you say to that?" Deborah butted in. She had never heard this story before.

"I said, 'No, Master Thomas', but I was trembling." Sarah smiled reminiscently. "Then he took my chin and made me look up at him and said, 'You have nothing to be afraid of'. And he was true to his word. He was a good master."

"But still a master. At least we're free now. Come let's go and see downstairs where we will have our shop," Deborah said eagerly.

"After what that woman said just now, you think anybody will buy from us?" Sarah asked worriedly.

"Of course," insisted Deborah, "because we will give them things that they need. Don't worry, everything will work out."

Sarah hoped so.

Downstairs was divided into two parts. The front, which was to be the shop, was an open space and was separated from the back by a partition. The back had two small rooms where Jacko and Mamie were to sleep and a storeroom.

"We will need a countertop with a little door at the side," said Deborah, remembering a store she had seen when she came into town with Richard a few months ago.

"You goin' have to ask the master if I could build it for you," Jethro told them, coming into the room.

"I wonder how much that would cost," said Deborah. The master had already spent a lot of money on the house. Would he be willing to spend any more or would that have to come out of their money? And would they have customers to sell to anyway? In spite of her assurance to her mother, she was a little worried. When she had visited town with Richard she had seen no coloured shopkeepers and not that many slaves working in the shops. She hoped that the people in town were different from the ones in the country, but if they were anything like the woman across the street, they would have more than their fair share of challenges.

The two women spent the rest of the day unpacking and settling in. They had brought a little food from the plantation with them, but they would need to venture into town the next day to buy food and supplies for the store. That would also give them the opportunity to see what the shops were selling and how their goods were laid out.

"Ma, we need to think about what we're going to sell in our shop," Deborah said as they sat in their small kitchen drinking herbal tea.

"We should do what we know best," Sarah advised. "I know how to sew so I will make and sell clothes."

"But there are a lot of stores that are selling clothes already so what will make people come to you, especially since you are coloured."

"I did not think about that, Deborah. What is going to make my clothes different?" She thought about it for a while, then her face brightened and she said, "I'm going to make clothes that look as good as the ones that come from away, but do not keep the women so hot. I know that the mistress and the girls like the clothes from away, but they make them sweat because the material is too heavy for here."

"That is good, Ma. But how are they going to find out that you're making those kinds of clothes?"

Sarah smiled and said, "That is where Master Thomas could help. He know a lot of people. He could start to tell people about the shop and the kind of clothes I will be making. They will come because he tell them about it. Then when they see how good the clothes look and that they don' keep them as hot as the ones from away, they goin' to buy them. Then when their friends sweating in theirs and they see that the women wearing my clothes not sweating like them, they goin' to ask where they get those clothes from." She smiled again confidently.

"How you know that, Ma?" Deborah teased her.

"Something in my spirit just know. I could see it happening in my head already."

"I believe you, Ma. And I know that you can make clothes even better than some of the ones that come from away. Like that green dress you made for me when I was sixteen."

Sarah smiled. "According to Cassie, when Richard see you serving at the party in that dress he couldn't keep his eyes off of you."

"Yes, but that same dress got me into trouble," Deborah reminded her.

"It wasn't the dress that get you in trouble, it was you," Sarah corrected. "Anyway, all of that behind us now. So what you plan to do in your business?"

178

"Well, I know about herbs so I can grow some in the yard and dry them and sell them, but I can also bring in different kinds of herbs and other things like soaps and perfumes. I can make soaps too, with flowers to make them smell different, like the one I make with lemon grass. And before you ask me what will make people come to me, I will tell you. When I came to town with Richard, we went to a lot of places and they were selling all kinds of fancy things, but I did not see any selling herbs to make tea or to help with sickness."

"So you will be the first person to sell herbs."

"Yes, and in small amounts. And I can tell people which herbs to use for different sicknesses."

"Like the chamomile you gave Richard to help his stomach when he had the runnings?"

Deborah laughed, remembering how she had thought she had poisoned Richard when he had first come to the island. Her laugh faded as a picture of him flashed into her mind, bringing with it a pang of sorrow.

"Sorry to make you think 'bout him," Sarah apologized, squeezing her hand.

Tears sprang to Deborah's eyes and she hastily wiped them away.

"Don't be sorry, Ma. I knew he had to go back to Carolina. If he had not come we may not be free now, so I am not sorry. Time will heal my heart and this store is going to keep me too busy to think about him all the time."

"That is true."

They fell silent for a few minutes. The noise from the street below intruded the quiet in the kitchen; the clip clop of horses' hooves on the road as carts passed, the voices of men shouting to each other in the taverns and the sound of drunken men singing as they stumbled down the road.

"I wonder if I will ever get accustomed to this noise," remarked Deborah.

"I was just thinking the same thing," Sarah smiled. "I prefer how quiet the country is, but I would rather be free in the city than a slave in the country."

"Me too."

A fierce joy burst in their hearts as they realized again that they were free.

Chapter 19

The light that filled the room told Sarah that it was past the time that she would normally wake up, but she deliberately ignored it. For the first time in her life she did not have to get up with the sun. She could lie in her bed all day if she wanted to. She was free!

She snuggled under the sheet and enjoyed the freedom from fear or guilt of staying in bed. Master Thomas had done this for her. She knew that a lot of masters used their slave women and Master Thomas did at first, but she knew that he loved her. He had never spoken the words to her, but the way he had treated her over the years and the sadness she had seen in his eyes when he gave her the papers to free her said more than words.

Some people would not understand how she could love the master, but she did. Sometimes she didn't understand it herself. She had seen him order slaves to be whipped for running away or for stealing, but never had he ordered a house slave to be whipped and certainly never her. It was as if he was two different men. But he was good to her and not only when he called her to lie with him. Now that she was not there would he begin to call Hattie or one of the other girls to his bed? The thought caused a feeling of revulsion that made her squirm. Best not to think about that.

Habit was hard to break, she thought, as she got out of bed a few minutes later. As much as she liked the idea that she could lay in bed all day, that had never been her life and it felt strange. She washed quickly with a basin of water and dressed before heading to the kitchen to make breakfast for her and Deborah who did not appear to be up as yet. That was not surprising since she had fallen into the habit of sleeping late when she was with Richard so she would not find it hard to stay in bed past the time the sun came up.

Putting on the kettle to boil, she let her thoughts drift to what they would do that day. She wasn't looking forward to going shopping, but she had to. She was not accustomed to being around too many people at once, or to the hustle and bustle of living in the city, but she had to get used to it. For a brief moment she longed to go back to the comfort and familiarity of The Acreage, before she remembered the mistress and how hard she made her work. How could she forget the back breaking wash days? How could she even think about going back?

She was like those people in the Bible that the children's tutor had taught them about one time. They were slaves like her, but after they were set free and things got hard, they wanted to go back to the place they had come from. They only remembered the food they had and forgot the work they had to do and the whips on their backs. Thankfully, she had never felt the sting of the whip, but Deborah had. She was glad that they were no longer under the mistress' eye.

Living in the city might not be easy, but she would do it because there was no going back. She and Deborah would work hard and make their businesses succeed and they would make a new life for themselves. Maybe Deborah would even find a free man to marry. She hoped so. As for her, she really wasn't interested in anything like that. She would welcome the master whenever he came into town and she would be satisfied with that. After all, she had what many women, both black and white, longed for: freedom to do what she wanted.

Deborah stretched and cracked open an eye. The unfamiliar room made her search her mind to figure out where she was. When it came back to her, she smiled. She was in her own room in the house that Master Thomas had given to her mother. The smile lasted only as long as it took the memory of Richard's leaving to rush in like filthy, unwanted floodwater.

She remembered how she had taken an instant dislike to him as soon as she heard the master reading the letter he had written asking to come to Barbados. He had said that he wanted to learn how they used slaves in Barbados as he was planning to invest in a plantation in Carolina and wanted to use African slaves to cultivate rice, as if they were horses or mules. When he arrived at The Acreage she was less than impressed with him. Granted, he was tall and handsome, she had grudgingly admitted to herself, but he was hateful in every other way.

Although he had a fiancée in Carolina, he had lain with Hattie, one of the house slaves, days after he arrived and several times after that. Soon he had made it plain that he wanted to lie with her. She had told him it would never happen and she had meant it. Even after he rescued her from the mistress' whip she refused him, even though she was beginning to soften towards him. Then he bought her from Master Thomas and offered her freedom in exchange for her services until he left the island. That was the price of her freedom and she had paid it.

She didn't expect him to turn out to be gentle and kind to her and she certainly never considered that she would fall in love with him and that his leaving would make her feel as if her heart had been torn out and taken with him to Carolina when he left a few days ago.

While she would prefer to curl herself into a ball and stay in bed, Deborah forced herself to get up and face the day. She swung her legs over the side of the bed and took a deep breath to fortify herself. She had survived being a slave for eighteen years. She would get over Richard and she would survive.

Deborah finally joined her mother in the kitchen a few minutes later, carefully arranging her face so that she didn't reveal the turmoil she felt inside. Her mother was probably going through her own sorrows after parting from Master Thomas. After all, they had been together for nearly twenty years. What was her two months with Richard compared to that?

"You get up at last? Richard really had you spoiled," Sarah teased her. "You don' have no trouble sleeping late now."

Deborah smiled slightly, remembering, with a pang, the morning after her first night with Richard. She had woken in his bed with the sun high in the sky to find him watching her. She had been ready to rush out to do her duties as was her custom, when he had reminded her that it was now her duty to serve him. That had the desired effect of riling her up, as he had intended.

"I hope I served you well," she had thrown back at him, only to have him retort that she did and that she was worth every pound he'd paid for her. The slap she had aimed at his face never landed as he had caught her hand and asked her if that meant the honeymoon was over.

He had been teasing her, but it brought home to her the reality of what she had agreed to. Theirs was no marriage and they were not on a honeymoon. Richard had paid the master £20 for her, with the agreement to set her free when he left. By the time his ship took him back to Carolina a few days ago, he had healed the wounds inflicted by William and he had taken her heart with him.

Sarah watched her smile fade and her face become bleak.

"Sorry. I keep reminding you about Richard," she apologized.

"You can't keep pretending that he was never here, Ma. I will live. After all, I got what I wanted – my freedom." Somehow the words rang a little hollow.

"Well, now that you are finally up, we can go and buy some goods to put in the house," Sarah changed the topic. "This will be the first time I will be buying things with my own money." She smiled in anticipation.

"There are a lot of shops here in town selling all kinds of things. Remember that Richard brought me to town a few months ago to buy some clothes."

"Oh, yes. I clean forgot that. That seems so long ago now."

"Yes. It's like it was in another life. Alright, we better go before the sun gets too hot."

They closed up the house and poked their head downstairs to tell Mamie and Jacko that they were going out but they could stay and clean up downstairs.

They headed for Cheapside, which was the main street in town. There was nothing that could not be found in Bridge Town. Stores were stocked with everything that the masters and mistresses on the plantations would need, brought in from other countries. Sarah knew some of those things because the master had often bought her gifts when he went to town, like the comb and brush he had given her for her birthday when she had turned eighteen.

Both Sarah and Deborah were excited at the thought of choosing goods and paying for them with their own money. The master had given Sarah £100 when he freed her and Richard had left Deborah £20 on the night stand the morning he went back to Carolina. She hoped the money was his way of telling her that she meant more to him than the money he had paid for her or, at the very least, that he wanted to make sure she was looked after when he left.

With money in their pockets, they entered the first shop expectantly. The shelves were stocked with all kinds of goods and the smells were both confusing and exciting as they hinted at the variety that was available for them to choose from.

"What you girls want?" The man behind the counter demanded, eyeing them. He could tell that although they were quite well dressed they were not plantation ladies. He was a solid looking man, with a red face and untidy brown hair and the clothes he wore could have done with a washing a week ago. He frowned at them and asked, "What you all doing in here without your mistress? Negroes can't buy goods, you don' know that? Get out and come back with your mistress!" With that they were shooed out of the shop.

The words of the shopkeeper stung their ears as they stumbled back into the dusty street in dismay. They walked a little way down the street in a daze before stopping next to a deserted building to collect themselves as they were shaken by his treatment of them.

"I can't believe that man talked to us like that! We are free! How dare he refuse to sell anything to us?" Deborah seethed as she recovered from her shock. "I will never buy from his shop. Come, Ma. There must be other shops that will sell to us."

Half an hour later, Sarah and Deborah dejectedly made their way to the master's solicitor, following the address the master had given them. After explaining who they were and what had happened, they followed him to several stores so that he could buy the goods they needed.

By the time they returned to the house, Deborah was fuming and Sarah was feeling discouraged.

"I cannot believe that we have money but we cannot buy our own goods! Will we have to walk with our papers to prove that we are no longer slaves?" Deborah asked in frustration.

"It seems that although we free, we not really free. The master had said he would get his solicitor to help us with ordering goods and buying from merchants, but I don' think he realized that we wouldn't be able to buy even food," Sarah said dejectedly.

"Don't worry, Ma. We will get through. It will not always be so. One of these days everybody will be able to buy and sell as long as they have money."

Even as Deborah assured her mother she began to worry about how they would sell their goods. Who would buy from them? What would make people come into their shop?

Chapter 20

A week later

Sarah rearranged the dresses on the rack for what seemed like the hundredth time. She noticed that Deborah was doing the same with her goods. She bit back a sigh as she thought that all the rearranging was not bringing anyone into the shop. Not that she had a lot to sell as yet. She had only bought a few bolts of material from the merchants in town with the help of the master's solicitor, but it was still the heavy fabrics that made them hot. She hoped that she could find the kind of material she wanted when a new shipment came in. She would make do with what she could until the goods she ordered got there.

She had sewed a few dresses and she had been able to make some undergarments with some fine lawn material she had bought, but she may as well have spared herself the sleepless nights to get them ready for today, for no one had even looked in.

She looked around at the shop, avoiding Deborah's eyes, and was pleased with how well it was laid out, even though they did not have everything in place yet. Jethro had come two days earlier in the week, with the master's permission, to build the counter that Deborah had wanted and the side door so that she could get in and out from behind it. He had even built her a rack to hang the clothes on and a few shelves where she could fold up smaller articles and store them.

The master had been truly generous to send Jethro and she had been pleased to see him at first. She kept his company as he sawed wood outside the shop, lifted it into place and hammered in nails with Jacko's help, while Mamie worked with Deborah in the small yard to make soap. She could not help but notice how his muscles strained against his thin shirt as he sawed wood and hefted it to his shoulder to bring it into the shop.

Around midday she had gone upstairs to make lunch for everybody and invited Jethro to wash and come up to eat in the kitchen. Jacko said he would eat downstairs and Deborah and Mamie asked her to keep theirs until later since they wanted to finish off making the soap one time.

Over the years, she and Jethro had become friends, but from a safe distance since he had taken the master's words all of those years ago to heart and had never tried to touch her in any way, far less kiss her as he had the day the master had discovered them. She knew that a lot of the slave girls admired him, as he was tall and well-built, but he had never married.

"This food taste real good, Sarah," he praised, finishing off everything on the plate and wiping it with a piece of bread. Sarah laughed at the gesture.

"Thank you. You can have some more if you want," she offered.

"I better not, if not I goin' be sleeping before I finish off the shop for you and Deborah and the master only give me two days to work on this. To tell the truth, I don' think he did want me to come at all, but you know he could never tell Deborah no."

"Why? He had other work for you to do?"

"No, it ain' that." Jethro laughed softly. "He know that you free now. So he can't tell you what to do. He can't stop us from kissing if we want to," he hinted.

"Jethro, that ain' why," Sarah brushed him off.

"It is the gospel truth!" he declared. "If I was him I would feel the same way. You know ever since how I feel about you, Sarah, but I never could do anything about it. Not after that morning that he catch me kissing you. But now he don' own you so he can't tell you nothing."

"Yes, but he still own you, Jethro, so don't get too bold. I am not there anymore to stop you from getting the whip across your back if he feel like. I hope that one day he would free you too."

"You think he would free me when he know that the first thing I would do is head for you?"

"Jethro…" Sarah protested.

She had just left The Acreage and the master. They had been together for more than half her life. She wasn't ready to think about anybody else. And anyway, the master… Thomas, she mentally corrected herself, would probably come to town in a week or so and she would see him again. It was not that their relationship was finished; it would just be different now.

Now she could refuse to lie with him if she wanted to. Not that she wanted to. Maybe she could have before too, but she never did. After all, he was the master and she was his slave so she did not think to refuse him and he probably would not have accepted her refusal anyway. Although that wasn't quite the truth.

The day that she had first seen Richard came back to her. It had been a wash day for her and she was holding a pile of sheets that she had just picked up from the line. Her back had been hurting from bending over the wash tubs for hours and all she could think about was lying down on her pallet that night. The master had taken Richard around the plantation that day and they had ridden into the yard where she was. The master had told her, in front of Richard, to come to his room later. All she had said was "Yes, Master Thomas", although she had cringed at the thought of going to his room that night. She had been so tired.

A smile softened her face as she remembered dragging herself to his room, beyond tired, but willing to give him what he wanted. He had taken one look at her weary face and, realizing he had seen her with a pile of sheets, asked if it had been wash day. At her nod, he had gently kissed her and told her to go back to her hut and sleep. Tears of gratitude had pricked her eyes and, even now, months later, she felt them stinging her eyes once again.

"What you thinkin' 'bout that got you smiling and gettin' ready to cry?" Jethro asked, watching her face.

"Master Thomas," she admitted.

He went quiet.

"You really got feelings for the master? After all these years? He coulda free you ever since, but he had to wait 'til the mistress nephew come here and free Deborah before he could think about freeing you. And you thinking 'bout he and smilin'?" He sucked his teeth in disgust.

Sarah immediately sobered up. Was she foolish to be thinking about the master like that? Jethro was right. He could have freed her before. Why did he not think of it? Maybe he had not wanted to let her go, she defended him to herself. She remembered how sad he had looked when he gave her the papers to free her. She didn't know what to think. Jethro was only confusing her.

"I think you better get back to work, Jethro," she said coldly. She didn't want to deal with what Jethro was saying right now.

"Yes, Mistress Sarah," he replied sarcastically, pushing back his chair.

As he walked out of the kitchen, Sarah felt a distance develop between them and she was filled with sadness.

"Ma, this is not working. I know we said that the master would send people to us, but according to Jethro he won't be coming into town for another two weeks. We can't sit down and hope that people will come in the shop. We have to give them something to come in for," Deborah announced after a while.

"Something like what? We have goods for them to buy."

"Yes, but everybody else has goods too and until we get them to come in they won't even know what we have. We can ask the solicitor to get a sign made for us. Two, in fact. One to say the names of our businesses that we can hang up and one that we can prop against the wall that will get people to come in." Deborah was starting to get excited as ideas came into her head. Sarah smiled.

"Tell me what you thinking about," Sarah encouraged her.

"Well, when Mamie and I were running out of soap we started making some smaller ones so I could offer to give away a small soap every time somebody buys a dress or something from you."

"And I could maybe give away a free ribbon when somebody buys a perfume or soaps from you," Sarah added.

"I could also boil up some herbal tea, like chamomile, and offer free cups of tea. That way once they come in I could tell them about the herbs I have and how they can use them."

"That sounds real good, Deborah. You like you born for this business thing," Sarah smiled at her.

"We all born with things we can use, Ma. It is just that sometimes we don't always get the opportunity to use them."

"Or sometimes we don't make the opportunity," Sarah said. "And what we ain' born with we can always learn."

"True. Look at Jethro. He was born to make things. Look how good he made that countertop for me and even the rack for you. It's a good thing that the master realized that he could make things and took him from the field and gave him the opportunity."

"The opportunity to do things for the plantation, not for himself. That ain' right."

"What you saying, Ma? That the master taking advantage of Jethro?"

"What else you would call it?"

Deborah looked at her mother in surprise. She had never heard her speak a word against the master. "How come you thinking like that now, Ma? I never heard you say anything against the master."

"I don't know, Deborah. Jethro said some things to me when he was here this week to make me think."

"What kind of things?"

"That the master had to wait until Richard come and free you before he could think 'bout freeing me and if he really care about me why he didn't do it before. That kind of thing. He had me confused and when he left we were not 'greeing so good. That never happened before. It left me feeling bad."

"Oh. What Jethro said is true. But it could also be that the master didn't want to let you go because he loved you and wanted you close to him. Or he may have been worried about who would look after you if he set you free."

"I hope that is the reason, although it don't really matter so much now because, whatever the reason, I free now."

"I think that Jethro is a little jealous of the master, though. So he will say those kinds of things." Deborah paused. "How you feel about Jethro?"

"I don't know, child. I don't know. Listen, you better get to the solicitor and ask him 'bout the signs before we have to shut down the shop before we start," she joked, changing the subject.

"I'm going, but you and I both know that it's not about the signs," Deborah sighed, causing Sarah to sober up. "It's about our colour and we can't change that." Sarah nodded sadly.

A few days later

Footsteps clattered over the wooden floor as a young slave girl rushed in looking stricken. Her head was uncovered and she was breathing hard as if she had been running.

"You de woman that does sell herbs?" she asked when she caught her breath.

"Yes. Can I help you?" Deborah asked with concern, coming out from behind the counter.

"My mistress send me. Her daughter been sick for days with vomiting and loose bowels. She getting worse and worse and the doctor ain' helpin'. He said that to make she drink liquids, but they just running right out." She looked on the point of tears. "My mistress ask if you have any herbs that could help her."

Deborah and Sarah exchanged glances. This was the girl they had seen fanning the woman across the street on the first day in their house. The woman who had insulted them. Indignation rose in Deborah that the woman would dare to send her slave to them, followed by the satisfaction of knowing that she had been forced to humble herself and seek them out.

She searched through the mental list of things that she had in the store that could work. "Yes. Let me put together something for her."

Hurrying behind the counter, she took down three jars and measured out some chamomile, goldenseal and ginger and combined them in a small pouch. Then she took a small jar and measured out some precious honey and gave them to the girl.

"Steep the herbs in a tea pot, sweeten it with the honey and get her to drink all of it when it cools. That should stop the sickness."

"Thank you, Miss," she gushed, taking the bag. "The mistress give me money to pay..." she started to say, digging in her pocket.

"Don't worry about that now. You can come back and pay later. Get this tea in her quickly."

"Thank you," she said again, running out of the shop.

Deborah sank down on her stool. "My first sale and it is to that sour faced woman across the road," Deborah laughed cynically.

"Look how long she waited before she sent the girl here. The child must be real sick now," Sarah commented sadly, thinking how deep the chasm was that separated people because of their colour.

"I hope the tea helps her daughter."

"I know it will. You got a gift with those herbs, Deborah."

"And you have a gift with your sewing. Once we work with those gifts and keep trying our best to give the customers more than they expect, we will do well."

"That is the truth. When she hears that you said not to worry about paying you now, but to get the herbs to her daughter right away, she will be different person. She not only going to come back and pay, but she going to tell everybody about this shop. You mark my words."

Chapter 21

Three weeks later

homas pushed his horse as hard as he dared without endangering it. The last thing he needed was to have it fall into one of the mud holes in the road caused by the rains of the last two weeks. He would have been to town earlier, but the rains had been torrential. As soon as the sun made an appearance the day before, he packed a small bag and made plans to travel to town for the weekend. Not seeing Sarah for almost a month was almost like a physical pain. After all, he had seen her nearly every day for almost two decades.

To alleviate his physical discomfort he had gone in to Hattie, but he felt disgusted afterwards, as if he had betrayed Sarah in the worst way. He had given Hattie a few shillings to alleviate his guilt. The thought of going into his wife did not even cross his mind as he still nursed a deep resentment towards her for forcing him to get rid of Sarah.

He admitted to himself, though he had never spoken the words, that he loved Sarah. At first he had desired her and wanted to possess her. Once he did, that possessive feeling only increased until he had no tolerance for any other man as much as looking at her. The only reason Jethro had escaped a whipping for kissing her that time he had come upon them was because Sarah had begged for him.

From the time she had worriedly told him that she was with child, his feelings had begun to blossom into something deeper than lust. He felt a perverse pleasure as he saw her growing big with his child and many nights he lay with her, not for the pleasure of her body, but only to hold her and feel their child moving restlessly in her womb. He had never experienced that with Elizabeth. It was not something that was done in their circles, but with Sarah it felt most natural and moving. And when he looked at the baby and saw his own eyes looking back at him, his heart was lost to both of them.

He had had many offers from visitors to the plantation over the years to buy Sarah, but he would never sell her. He had even warned Richard that both she and Deborah were off limits. Not that he had been deterred by that warning when it came to Deborah, for he had been as captivated by her as he, Thomas, had been with Sarah. He would have liked Richard to stay in Barbados and help to run the plantation, as he had come to love him like a son, but one could not always have everything.

He had written to William when Richard had left and told him to come back home. It had been two years since he had put him on a ship to England after what he had done to Deborah. That had not been the only reason, as Elizabeth had accused him, but it was the last complaint in a long list that he had gotten about William that pushed him to make that decision. He and John Bowyer's son, Henry, had developed quite a reputation in town for leaving behind unpaid debts and patronizing houses of ill repute.

Sending William to his uncle in England had further deteriorated his relationship with Elizabeth, but he was long past caring. He only hoped that William would come back a better man than when he left and that he would be more civilized after his time in England. Maybe he would finally be interested in working on the plantation rather than spending all the profits from it.

The sight of the town in the distance caused him to flick the reins on the horse to speed it up. His heart leapt in anticipation of seeing Sarah again and he laughed at himself. He was acting like a young buck, although he had reached his fiftieth birthday three years ago. He didn't feel like it, though, especially when he was with Sarah. Of course he was not as young as Jethro, he thought jealously. He had been reluctant to send Jethro to help them at Deborah's request as he knew how Jethro felt about Sarah, but he could not deny Deborah so he had put aside his mistrust and allowed him to go. He would ask Sarah about the visit.

Thomas looked around as he waited for Sarah to open the door. They had done a lot to the property in the month that they had moved in and he was proud of them. His solicitor had sent word to tell him about some of the challenges they had faced at first, but they had overcome them and persevered with their business, finding ways to get people to come into the shop.

The door opened and Sarah peeped around it. The welcoming smile that transformed her face from curious to excited warmed him right through and started a tingle of anticipation in him as he stepped through the door.

"I missed you, Sarah," he declared.

"I missed you too, Master Thomas," she said, taking his hat, coat and the bag he had brought.

Thomas smiled as he reminded her that she no longer had to call him master, but he knew that a habit was hard to change. She wanted to get him a drink and something to eat, but all he wanted was to feel her in his arms, and he could not resist pulling her to him. A noise in the hallway caused him to glance past her to see Deborah looking uncomfortable as she came upon them in an embrace. It was not something he had been free to do openly at The Acreage.

"Hello, Deborah," he greeted her, reluctantly releasing Sarah. She looked good, but a bit sad and withdrawn. But then again, Richard had only been gone for a month and it probably did not help to see him hugging her mother. He was not even sure how she felt about Richard. Did she love him? If she did, he could understand the sadness in her eyes. Sarah was not completely gone from his life and he felt heavy when he was at the plantation without her near.

Unable to help himself, he pulled Sarah to him again. How he had missed her. He wanted to drag her to her room and rediscover her, but the women were eager to show him around the house. Since he would deny these two women nothing, he put his desires aside and allowed himself to be taken from room to room and down to the shop to see the improvements that they had made.

"The house looks good. You two have done wonders," he praised them. "But I'd like to see what you've done with your room now, Sarah," he hinted. Deborah took the hint and excused herself to go and make dinner, leaving Sarah to lead Thomas to her room.

Thomas shut the door behind them with a firm click, thankful that he finally had Sarah to himself.

"You look well, Sarah."

"Thank you, Thomas." She made a slight pause before she said his name and then smiled with the realization that they were equals now and she no longer had to call him "master", as he had reminded her earlier.

"What are you smiling at?" Thomas asked indulgently, although talking was the last thing he was interested in doing.

"When I said your name just now I felt equal to you," she said quietly.

"We have always been equals in my eyes, Sarah," Thomas said seriously. "I hardly ever thought of you as a slave. Elizabeth was forever accusing me of that."

Sarah's eyes widened in surprise at the admission and she opened her mouth to reply, only to be interrupted by Thomas who put a finger over her lips.

"We can talk more later," he promised, "but right now I need you, Sarah. You don't know how much."

He bent his head and captured her lips in a possessive kiss that showed her the truth of his words. Sarah sank her hands in his hair and matched his kiss with an answering passion. She had missed him as well. All of Jethro's questions left her mind as she lost herself in Thomas' familiar touch.

Thomas' hands roamed up and down Sarah's back as he reacquainted himself with the shape and feel of her. The time they had been apart made him impatient to be joined to her, but he forced himself to slow down and savour her. They could spend all night together; something they had never done before. That thought alone was enough to make his blood rush with excitement and he had to force himself to exert great control. He had all weekend, so he could take his time. They had been together for nineteen years and he was still not tired of Sarah. He didn't think he ever would.

From that first time he had lain with her, he had wanted no other woman the same way and, in fact, he had not visited any of the other slaves since they had been together. She had been everything he had unknowingly been searching for. She understood him far better than his own wife and her arms provided comfort when he needed it.

"Tell me what you want, Mistress Sarah. I am here to serve you today," he invited.

Sarah smiled and whispered shamelessly in his ear, delighting him with the boldness that had taken him years to cultivate.

Thomas' breathing slowly came back to normal. Sarah was lying on his chest idly playing with the greying hair on it. He smiled against her hair, content that he had satisfied her as he had been satisfied. He was ready to fall asleep, but she wanted to talk, asking him deep and searching questions. How was it that he treated his slaves different to the way he had treated her and Deborah? Did he not think that if he had taken Deborah away from her and sold her she would feel the same pain as the women whose children had been sold? She had asked more questions that he could not answer, but then she had answered them for him, as if she had spent time thinking about the answer. She had said that people were all the same and whether you were a house slave or a field slave you were the same. It was only when you did not know somebody, or did not spend any time getting to know them, that you saw them as different. Years of ingrained prejudice fought with the truth of what she was saying, until he had to admit that she was probably right.

"I know I right," she had ended her case.

He wondered what brought on these thoughts and whether they had anything to do with Jethro's visit.

"Were you and Deborah happy with the work that Jethro did?"

"Of course. You know that he does good work."

I wonder what else he does 'good', Thomas thought jealously. He was being ridiculous. Sarah was free now and he had no claims on her. At least not legally. Besides, she had never been one to lie with different men, so why would she start now. He had to stop being so suspicious.

"He even made a clothes rack for me and some shelves, although he came to do the counter for Deborah."

"I instructed him to do anything that you needed him to," Thomas told her. In the shop, he added to himself.

"Thank you, Thomas."

"Although I knew that he would do anything for you, whether I told him to or not. He always had a soft spot for you," he reminded her.

"You still remembering the time that you catch him kissing me?" Sarah laughed. "That was so long ago."

"So you are saying that he does not feel that way about you anymore?" Thomas asked. Sarah said nothing, but her silence answered his question. "What about you?"

"I'm not looking to get into anything with Jethro or anybody else. You may not own me now, but I still belong to you," she assured him.

"And I belong to you too," Thomas declared.

"Not altogether, Thomas. You forgetting that you married? You belong to the mistress too, whether you like to think so or not."

Thomas had no answer for that. Wishing that things were different would not make them so. He could never be with Sarah the way he would like to be. That was just the way of the world they lived in. A great sadness overwhelmed him and he pulled Sarah closer to him. He might not be able to offer her his name, but she had his heart.

Chapter 22

The present

Sarah was surprised to find herself still sitting in the living room hours after opening the doors to let some air in, but even more surprised to feel her cheeks damp from tears as she remembered that that had been the last time she had lain with Thomas. Their relationship was different now. It had been different ever since she and Deborah had gone to the Quaker meeting in town, not long after that weekend.

At the meeting, they had learned what true freedom meant. It was not only being free from slavery but being free from all the wrong they had done in their lives, whether they had thought them wrong or not. All the thoughts running through her mind when she got home that night had given her a headache, but in the end she realized that she could not continue to lie with Thomas. It was wrong. He was married – whether he loved his wife or not – and they were not.

She had tried to talk to Thomas about her new way of life, but he did not seem to want to hear. In fact, he had been upset that they had gone to the Quaker meeting, calling them troublemakers. Although it had been very hard, she had told him that she could no longer continue to lie with him as she now knew that it was wrong and she was trying to live her life to please God. Although it had been difficult for him, and for her as well, in the end he accepted her decision and said that he still wanted to visit her and Deborah to make sure that they were alright, for which she was glad.

He had visited her a week ago and she had been happy to see him as she was lonely without Deborah in the house and she had missed him, but the visit had been a little strained. While he had accepted that, with the new life she had committed to, she could no longer lie with him, he didn't know how to react to the new changes in her. It was as if they could no longer talk to each other.

He did not understand this new joy and freedom she had outside of her relationship with him and it seemed to her as if he was jealous of the relationship that she now had with Jesus. She, on the other hand, would be forever grateful that she had made that change.

It was hard not to be with Thomas the way she used to be. Some nights her body cried out for his touch and his presence until all she could do was call on the name of the only one who could help her - Jesus.

January 21, 1697

"Richard, can you believe that we've been married for three weeks already and we've barely left the house. Shouldn't we be getting back to work?" asked Deborah, resting her chin on Richard's bare chest.

"I'm proud with what you've done with your business, Deborah, but you're becoming obsessed with it. You need to forget business while we're on our honeymoon. A honeymoon is supposed to last for a whole month, my dear. Do you not know the origin of the word 'honeymoon'?" Richard replied lazily, playing with her hair which was the only covering for her back.

"No, I never heard it, but I am sure you will tell me."

"Well, it is believed that the word originated from the practice in some European countries of newlyweds drinking mead during the first month, or moon, of marriage. Mead is a drink made with honey and is supposed to increase virility and fertility. So the first month of marriage became known as the honeymoon."

"So have you been drinking mead unknown to me?" she teased huskily, sliding up his chest until her lips hovered over his, "Because you've been very virile these last three weeks."

"You have discovered my secret!"

"You mean when the mead is gone you will have no more stamina? Oh dear! It will definitely be time to get back to work then."

"Come here, woman. I'll show you that I don't need any mead to have stamina." Richard buried his face in her neck and nibbled on a ticklish spot, making her squirm against him in delightful ways.

"Stop!" she protested, laughing as she wiggled to escape his tickling lips.

"If you continue to wiggle like that we'll never leave this bed, far less the house."

"Are you sure you're up to it?" She teased again.

"Up to it..?" he sputtered. "I'll show you."

"Well, please do," she invited.

Richard needed no further encouragement as he flipped her over and lowered his mouth to hers. He would never get tired of loving this woman.

They had barely left the house for the last three weeks, spending hours talking to each other about everything and nothing. The few times they ventured out took them only as far as the beach just outside the house Richard had rented. He loved everything about this strong-willed woman. They did not agree on everything and they even had a disagreement already, although he could hardly remember what it was about now. He had known from the time he met Deborah that he would never have a dull moment with her, and he was right.

How could he have considered marrying Ann just to be able to run her father's plantation? She had never stirred his blood like Deborah did, but he had left Barbados six months ago determined to marry her and fulfil his ambition. In the end, though, he could not get Deborah out of his mind and he had been glad when Ann broke off their engagement and freed him to return to Barbados. Never had he imagined he could be this happy.

"Do I sense that I do not have your full attention? Could it be that you are tired of me already?" challenged Deborah.

"Never! I was just thinking how glad I am that I came to Barbados and met you. I can't imagine ever getting tired of you."

She rewarded him with a kiss.

"Well, stop talking and show me," she demanded huskily.

Richard laughed delightedly. Deborah was everything he wanted in a woman, both in bed and out. How blessed he was.

One week later

"Master Richard, a letter has come for you," the housekeeper informed him, handing over the letter. He and Deborah had just sat down to breakfast, the last one before they started back to work after their honeymoon. He broke the seal and scanned the contents, knowing from the handwriting that it was from his mother. He read it out loud.

January 10, 1697

> *My Dear Richard*
>
> *I hope this letter finds you in good health. Since you neglected to write us after your return to Barbados we have had to rely on the report from Bostick who told us about the storm that you were caught in on the way to the island and assured us of your safety, for which we were very glad.*
>
> *After Ann broke off your engagement, you confessed that you had fallen in love with the daughter of a plantation owner, but you offered no further confidences. Your father and I therefore feel that it would*

> be beneficial to pay a long overdue visit to your aunt
> and uncle at The Acreage and make it our business
> to meet our future daughter-in-law. We trust, of
> course, that it is your plan to marry this girl, as-
> suming you have not done so already without the
> courtesy of inviting us to the wedding.
> We will set sail soon and should arrive in Barbados
> in the last week of the month or early the following
> month. We look forward to seeing you.
>
> Your mother
> Mary Fairfax

"'We trust, of course, that it is your plan to marry this girl, assuming you have not done so already without the courtesy of inviting us to the wedding'," Richard repeated mockingly. "That is my mother for you."

"Your parents are coming to Barbados?" Deborah moaned. "Do they know about me?"

"A little. I told them that you were the daughter of a plantation owner," admitted Richard. "I felt that the less said at that time, the better."

"The daughter of a plantation owner?" Deborah laughed derisively. "So they do not know that the plantation owner is Thomas Edwards or that my mother was his slave."

"Uh…no. I really did not want to provide too much information at the time and I was anxious to get back to you as soon as I could. And do not forget that I was unsure of what I would find when I got here. I did not know if you would even want to see me again," he reasoned.

"Oh yes, I had forgotten. But what will they say? I do not think I'm ready to meet your parents. And I know that Elizabeth Edwards will have nothing good to tell them about me."

"Don't worry, my uncle will sing your praises. Anyway, I do not care what they say; they do not control my life. I am married to you and I love you. They do not have to approve of our marriage." Richard knew that his mother, in particular, would very likely be difficult. Not only was Deborah coloured, but his mother tended to be controlling and Deborah could not be controlled. He smiled at the thought of how his mother would react to his wife.

"It would still be good to have their blessing," Deborah fretted. "Blessings are very important, you know."

"We have God's blessing, and that is all that matters. Let us not worry about things before we have to address them," advised Richard. "Today is our last day, so let us not waste it with concerns about my parents. Are you sure you want to go back to working in the shop now that we are married? You do not have to, you know. I am more than able to support both of us."

"I know, but I have worked hard to get my business up and running, and I now have regular customers so I want to continue with it. As it is, I have left my mother to look after my side of things, with help from Mamie, of course. So it is time that I went back to work."

"All right, my dear. I know that it means a lot to you. But when we have children, I hope you will cut back on your hours."

"Children?" Deborah had not really thought about having children. She had started back using the herbs that she used to take when she was with Richard to prevent herself from becoming pregnant. In all of their talks they had not discussed having children. They would still be considered coloured, but they would be free. What would life in Barbados mean for them? She was definitely not ready to bring children into the world right now. They had not had to deal with other people so far, but soon they would have to leave the comfort of their house and face the prejudiced people on the island. Could she subject her children to that?

"Hello, Ma. I'm back," Deborah greeted her mother with a huge hug.

"Deborah, I missed you. But the month did you good. You look real happy. Richard like he treating you good."

"Yes, he is, Ma. I'm very blessed to have a husband like him."

"I am happy to hear that, Deborah. Who would have thought that you would end up married to him?" She shook her head in disbelief.

"Certainly not me," said Deborah. "So how is my business doing?"

"Good, but not as good as if you were here to run it your-self, because you know more about what you sell than me and Mamie. A lot of people been asking for you so I told them that you were on a little holiday."

"Ma, this is Barbados. They will all know by now that I married Richard. I don't think it is the people who live in town that will give us as much trouble. It is the ones from the planta-tions. And now his mother and father are coming to Barbados soon."

"They know about you?"

Deborah shook her head. "Not much. In fact, all they know is that I am the daughter of a plantation owner," she said smiling.

"Oh loss. I hope they don't cause no trouble between you and Richard."

"Richard is his own man, Ma. He said that he doesn't care what they think."

"You got a good man there."

"Yes, and it's time for you to get one," teased Deborah.

"I don't need no man in my life right now. I am very happy as I am."

"Have you seen Jethro recently?" Deborah asked slyly.

"He stopped by two weeks ago when the master sent him to town to buy some wood. Why?"

"Just wondering. He had always liked you, Ma."

"So what he can do about that? I am free, but he still belong to the master."

"If the master was to free him, what would happen?"

"I don' know, girl. I like Jethro, but I don' know if I like him that way. Anyway, I don' know if the master would ever free him."

"You never know," said Deborah. "Now I better take stock of what I have in here and what I need. Time to get my mind back on my business."

Sarah wished she found it as easy to get her mind back on her business. She was a little torn by the feelings she was starting to have for Jethro, in spite of what she had told Deborah. He understood about her new life and he encouraged her to live it. In fact, he was the one who had tried to talk to the slaves at The Acreage about a Quaker meeting he had been to years before, and to explain things to them, but they had not understood. So now they could discuss the Bible together and she found herself enjoying talking to him more than she had with Thomas when he came last week. Was she beginning to have greater feelings for Jethro than she had for Thomas?

Chapter 23

Thomas read the note from Richard that accompanied the letter that Mary Fairfax had addressed to him and Elizabeth. The note warned him that his parents were planning to come for a visit and would be there in a few days. He also told him that he had not shared much about Deborah with them, apart from the fact that she was the daughter of a plantation owner, so he was bracing himself for the meeting.

Thomas smiled wryly. Well, Deborah was certainly that, but he was sure they would be horrified to discover that he was the plantation owner and that she and her mother had been his slaves less than a year ago. Thinking about it now gave him a feeling of discomfort in his stomach. His daughter had been his slave. Surely there was something wrong with that. Nevertheless, that was the case and he was prepared to face their judgement, but he did not want Deborah to be slighted by them.

Elizabeth and the girls were scheduled to go to England in order to secure husbands for them as there was a deficit of marriageable men on the island. But now that would have to be delayed if they were to entertain her brother and his wife.

He had recently secured a passage to Jamaica for William, where he had arranged for him to work on the plantation of a friend of his. If he proved himself, he would consider investing in one himself and leave William there to manage it. Land was still very plentiful and relatively cheap in Jamaica and he knew that the country would soon take over from Barbados as the largest producer of sugar for England. He hoped that Jamaica would change William from the man he had become. He had hoped so of England as well, but he had hoped in vain, for as soon as he returned he had tried to attack Deborah again. He was only glad that Richard had not killed him, although he would have deserved it. He had failed in being a good father to William.

He knocked on Elizabeth's door and let himself in at her invitation. Since Sarah had talked to him about how her life had changed and that she regretted how Elizabeth must have felt about their relationship, he had begun to see things through new eyes as well and he admitted to himself that he had grossly disrespected Elizabeth. He had not gone so far as to ask for her forgiveness, but he now treated her with more courtesy and respect and he found that she had responded to that. So much so that he had even gone in to her one night to lie with her and she had not turned him away.

"Elizabeth, I have good news," he announced.

"I could certainly use some good news," she answered. He acknowledged that she had been through several shocks recently, with Richard marrying Deborah and then William being sent off to Jamaica mere weeks after he had returned from England. It could not be helped.

"Mary and James wrote to say that they are coming to Barbados to stay with us for a month or two."

"Well, that's certainly good news. I have not had the pleasure of seeing my dear brother for years. It will be lovely to see them both. I suppose they are coming out in hopes of seeing Richard get married. Too bad he has already done the deed."

"Now, Elizabeth, try not to prejudice them against Deborah. She and Richard are very happy together and that is the important thing, is it not?"

"Humph," Elizabeth replied, promising nothing.

Thomas shook his head in despair before continuing, "That will mean that your trip to England will have to be put off for a while."

"The girls will be disappointed, but I can't say I was looking forward to the voyage. I hate sailing."

"Perhaps we can send them on ahead after they meet their uncle and aunt, as long as we can find a suitable chaperone to accompany them."

"Kathryn Smith is returning to England soon, as her school has not done as well as she had hoped. Maybe she would be willing to chaperone them. Do you think they will be all right?"

"Of course they will, dear. They can travel on my ship and the captain will make sure they are well taken care of. They can stay with my uncle and their cousins until you get there."

"When will Mary and James be arriving?"

"I believe the letter said either this week or next."

"What? We have to prepare for them and make them feel at home."

"Don't worry, dear. I have every confidence that you will make them feel very welcome when they come, as you did with Richard."

"Yes, well he certainly made himself right at home with our slaves as well," she couldn't help adding.

Thomas was about to protest when he stopped himself. After all, it was he who had told Richard that he was free to make use of any of the house slaves for his needs, except, of course, Sarah and Deborah. Well, Richard had certainly not heeded him in that regard and now he would have to face the judgement of his parents and, without a doubt, the planters on the island, if he intended to stay in Barbados.

Richard watched as his mother was helped from the tiny boat onto the dock, followed by his father. It had been less than three months since he'd seen them so he was surprised by the pleasure he felt on seeing their familiar faces. No doubt by the end of the day he would wish his mother to be back in Carolina if she was true to form.

"Mother, Father," he greeted them and signalled for the driver of the carriage he had rented to come and collect their luggage. "Welcome to Barbados. I hope you will have a most enjoyable stay."

"Oh, Richard, I missed you," replied his mother, hugging him. His father shook his hand and slapped him on the back.

"Good to see you, Son."

"I will take you to the house I'm renting. You will spend the night with me and then travel to Uncle Thomas and Aunt Elizabeth tomorrow."

"And when do we get to meet this mysterious woman who has caused you to abandon family and country and move to Barbados?"

"Now mother, don't start. You will meet Deborah at our house shortly. She should be home from her work by now."

"Work? She works?" His mother sounded horrified at the thought.

"Work is not part of the curse, Mother. God gave man work before the fall."

She ignored him and continued, "And did you say she would be at your house? Tell me you are not living in sin, Richard. It was bad enough that you had that French trollop in Carolina even though you were engaged to dear, sweet Ann. So I hope you are not carrying on your shameful practices here in Barbados."

"Not at all, Mother. We are married."

"Married? You got married without us being here? Richard, how could you?" she accused. He looked to his father, who had not got a word in yet, for help.

"Don't fuss, Mary. He's a grown man. You had Charlotte's wedding not that long ago, and when we go back to Carolina we will have Charles and Ann's. By the way, your brother sends his regards, Son."

"Yes," his mother piped up again. "Thankfully he and Ann are very happy together. I must say they are much better suited that you and she ever were."

221

"I am glad that we agree on something, Mother."

"Let us go. I am dying to meet my new daughter-in-law."

"You probably will die when you meet her," Richard murmured under his breath.

"What was that, dear?"

"Nothing, Mother. Let me help you into the carriage."

He spent the next half hour giving his parents the guided tour as they travelled to his rented house which was situated between Carlisle Bay and Maxwell Bay, right on the sea. He brought them up to date on what was happening in the island, all the while silently praying that Deborah and his mother would not kill each other when they met, as they were both strong women. His mother always tried to control his life, unsuccessfully, so he hoped that she would not try to control Deborah's too, as Deborah was not a woman to be controlled, even when she was a slave. He silently prayed for divine intervention.

The carriage drew to a halt outside the modest two storey house and Richard got out to help his mother down.

"Nothing beats the smell of the ocean," his father said, taking a deep breath of the salty air.

"It smells like raw fish to me," complained his mother. Richard rolled his eyes.

The door was thrown open and Deborah came out to meet them. He left his parents' side to go to hers and take her hand. She looked beautiful with her hair loose over her shoulders the way he liked it and she was wearing a dress he had never seen before. Her mother must have made it for her. His blood stirred just from looking at her.

"Father, Mother, meet Deborah, my wife," he announced proudly.

"Richard, she's coloured!" his mother shrieked and fainted dead away.

"Oh dear," said his father as he moved too slowly to break her fall. "My goodness, Richard. This is a surprise! Although I can see why you were ready to give up everything and come back to Barbados." His father seemed as shocked as his mother even as he assessed Deborah with his gaze, appreciating her beauty with a man's eyes. "You say you're married?"

"Yes, sir," Richard assured his father.

"Well, I guess there is nothing to be done then."

"No," Richard said emphatically.

"You know, of course, you will be unable to come back to Carolina with her."

"I am aware of that, Father. I have no desire to return to Carolina."

"We should take your mother in," his father suggested, changing the subject.

Deborah's mouth tightened at his lack of acknowledgement of her, as if she was not a person because she was coloured.

Richard knew it would take his parents a while to come around, if they ever did. After all, prejudices that were ingrained did not change overnight. He should know. He had been the same way when he came to Barbados.

"Father," Richard prompted before he moved.

"Deborah," was all his father said. She nodded in response.

"I'll get Mother," Richard said, stooping to lift her up in his arms. It had not taken long for the pleasure of seeing his parents to wear off. If they could not be civil to Deborah, they would not be welcome in his house, far less his life. He could not wait for them to travel to The Acreage tomorrow and he was sure that they would have no desire to tarry either. Meanwhile, they still had to get through dinner when his mother came to. He braced himself.

"So tell me, Deborah, how you managed to snare, I mean, meet, Richard."

They had sat down to dinner prepared by the housekeeper. Deborah had obviously instructed her to prepare a lavish meal as there were more dishes on the table than he was accustomed to having. There was fresh fish, but also roasted pork and chicken, as well as a host of starches and vegetables making up the meal. Richard was proud of the table that Deborah had laid in her effort to impress his parents. He loved her all the more for it, for he knew that she was well aware of the reception she would get from them, yet she had done her best to honour them with the sumptuous meal.

"He stayed at my father's plantation when he came to Barbados. That is where we met." Deborah held her peace although she could not help but seethe inwardly at his mother's insult.

"Your father's plantation?" his mother repeated, confusion wrinkling her brow. "I did not realize that you had stayed with anyone apart from Thomas, Richard."

"I did not, Mother." He let that sink in and knowing that his mother was not slow of wit, he waited for the eruption.

"So you mean… Thomas is her father?" Shock contorted her face. "She is the illegitimate child of Thomas and some free coloured woman?"

"Her mother was not free until a few months ago and neither was Deborah. I bought her from Uncle Thomas and –"

"You bought her?" His mother interrupted, incredulously.

"Yes and then I set her free before I came back to Carolina and Uncle Thomas set her mother free."

"You married a slave?"

"Mother, she was not a slave when we married."

"Such a marriage is against the law!" she protested.

"Not in Barbados, Mother."

"Richard, have you gone mad?" his mother began.

"Excuse me," Deborah interrupted. Richard wondered that she had managed to hold her tongue for so long. "Please do not discuss me as if I am not here, Mrs. Fairfax. Yes, I was a slave and yes, Richard bought me and set me free. So does that make me less of a person than you? I think not! In fact, I think you are rather –"

"Okay, dear," Richard intervened before it deteriorated further. "Let us say grace and eat our meal before it gets cold. Father, thank you for this food that you have provided. Give us the grace to be more like Christ and to love one another as we love ourselves. Help us to remember that a brother or sister offended is more unyielding than a fortified city and that people will know that we are your disciples by our love. Amen."

He opened his eyes and smiled at his mother, challenging her to go against the word of God. He was rewarded by a slightly strained smile in return. That would be enough for now. This battle had been won, but he knew there would be a whole war to be fought.

Chapter 24

"Mary, James! It's so wonderful to see you after all these years," Elizabeth hugged her brother tightly and then her sister-in-law. Tears made their faces blur before her.

"I can't tell you how happy I am to be here, Elizabeth," Mary agreed. "It was even worth braving the trip from Carolina. I am so ashamed that we own ships and we have not been to Barbados in years, but I do so hate to sail."

"I am exactly the same way. Well, at least you are here now," Elizabeth allowed magnanimously.

"Thank you for your hospitality," James added.

"Don't mention it. You are family. It is good to have you here."

"I would thank you for taking in Richard last year, but now I've lost him to Barbados," James accused half-jokingly.

"Yes, well about that..." Thomas began.

"Say no more. I know it was not your fault," James assured him. "We have seen Deborah so I can well understand." He shared a look with Thomas.

"I can't believe that Richard actually married that woman," Mary began, before noticing that Elizabeth was looking uncomfortable with the turn of the conversation. Belatedly, she realized that she was introducing a topic that would not be at all in good taste, considering the circumstances of Deborah's birth.

"Where are the girls?" she asked instead. "I'm dying to meet them."

"They will be down shortly. They're very keen to meet you as well. Come and sit so that we can chat. We have years to catch up on. How was Charlotte's wedding?"

The ladies settled themselves in rocking chairs on the patio while Thomas offered to show James the mill.

By the time the men re-joined them, Hattie, the house slave that Richard had availed himself of when he had first come to Barbados, came out bearing drinks. She eyed Richard's parents surreptitiously to see who he got his looks from, and shamelessly eavesdropped on their conversation so that she could report back to the other slaves.

Hurrying back to the kitchen with her news, she took great delight in telling the other slaves about the visitors.

"You should see Master Richard parents. He get most of he looks from he mother, but the height from he father."

"What they talkin' 'bout?" asked Cassie, one of the other slaves.

"Who is Master Richard?" interrupted one of the new girls that Elizabeth had bought to replace Deborah and Sarah. She was rather plain to look at, heralding the end of an era of The Acreage having the best looking slave women on the island.

"He is the mistress' nephew. You don' remember we talking about how he come from Carolina and buy Deborah from the master and then set she free when he left?"

"Oh, yes. And then he come back and marry she. I would like something so to happen to me," she said wistfully.

"Well, you ain' look nothin' like Deborah, girl, so that ain' goin' happen," Hattie stated uncaringly.

"Hattie, you ain' got to say that so," Cassie chided. "And you can' talk neither, because when Master Richard see Deborah you didn' last too long in he bed."

Hattie sucked her teeth at that.

"We did always know that Deborah would be different. She did never act like a slave," Cassie continued, smiling.

"Well, from the time Sarah bring she into this world, Ada did say that Deborah would do something that none of we would do. She get she freedom and she marry and now living good. I glad for she," Sally added. "I wonder how Master Richard's parents tek to the two of them gettin' married."

When the girls came down there was a great deal of hugging and exclaiming by Mary. They wore two lovely morning dresses which were elegantly fashioned but looked cool and well adapted for the weather in the island.

"Your dresses are lovely," complimented Mary Fairfax. "And they look wonderfully cool. Where did you get them?"

"Father bought them for us from town," Mary volunteered.

"Thomas, you'll have to take me to that merchant so that I can get a dress or two while I'm here. My dresses will be uncomfortably hot in this weather."

"Certainly, Mary," Thomas agreed, looking somewhat ill at ease. Elizabeth said nothing as she could guess who had made the dresses. Even though Sarah was no longer at The Acreage, reminders of her are still very much present, she thought resentfully.

"We should have a party to introduce you to our friends," she announced, changing the subject.

"It would have been nice to celebrate Richard's marriage as well, if he had not married that coloured woman," Mary Fairfax declared.

An awkward silence followed her words, and she belatedly remembered that Thomas was Deborah's father and that he had likely bred her mother while she worked for Elizabeth.

"I'm sorry…" she began, colouring uncharacteristically.

"Well, as much as we would like to deny it, we cannot pretend that Richard has not married Deborah. But it is unlikely that they will be accepted by society, at least not the plantation society," Elizabeth bravely answered.

"I wonder if Richard thought that through when he decided to marry," his mother said.

"I'm sure that would not have been enough to deter him," Thomas spoke up for the first time. He was very uncomfortable with the conversation, but he felt the need to defend Richard as he understood the power of attraction to make men do things they might not normally do.

"Marriages of their kind are not permissible in our country," Mary pointed out.

"It is not against the law here, but I must confess that they are rare," Thomas informed her. "Nevertheless, they are married and I intend to invite them to the party and acknowledge their marriage," Thomas declared. His tone invited no further comment from anyone.

In spite of his assertion, Thomas was not overly optimistic that Deborah would be accepted by the plantation owners. Thankfully, they only represented a small percentage of the white population in the island, the rest being indentured servants and merchants. The few free Negroes and mulattos in the island might also be open to friendship with them, so she and Richard would not be short of people to socialize with.

"It is rather ironic that the last time we had a party, Deborah was serving the same people that you now seek to introduce her to as an equal," Elizabeth couldn't resist adding.

"Well, she is certainly a great beauty and very well spoken," James said, speaking up for the first time. "I am sure she will be no embarrassment to Richard."

Thomas nodded at him approvingly. At least Richard and Deborah had his and James' support. While their wives did not approve, they really had little say in the matter.

Richard handed the note that Thomas had written to Deborah and watched for her reaction. It had accompanied an invitation to him and Deborah to attend a party at The Acreage in two weeks to celebrate his parents' arrival in the island and to introduce them to the friends of the Edwards. He knew what that meant; the same people that he had met months ago when he had first come to the island.

He had observed that when Deborah had served them the men had examined her as if she were a choice piece of meat that they could not wait to partake of. If he was perfectly honest with himself, he had done the same thing. What a low creature he had been then.

He had cornered Deborah in the hallway and ordered her to come to his room after the party. He couldn't help but smile as he remembered the lie she had told him to avoid his advances. She had said she was indisposed and the vast quantity of alcohol he had consumed had slowed his wits so that it took him a while to grasp her meaning and brought a curse to his lips when he finally understood that she would be unable to come to his room. What she had been was unwilling, not unable, but she had managed to outwit him in that instance.

Deborah read the note and handed it back to him.

"Shall we go?" Richard asked.

She knew that it was not as simple a question as it appeared. He was asking if she was prepared to stand at his side and face not only his aunt but also the highest echelon of society in the island. People who would no doubt snub her because she had been a slave and, although she was almost as white as them, would consider her beneath their notice because she had her mother's blood in her.

Richard saw her chin rise a notch. The chin that was so similar to Thomas' and he knew before she spoke what her answer would be. He felt proud of his wife who would not back down from a fight or run from difficulties.

"I'll need a new dress," she said, giving her answer. "And I know just the place to get one made especially for the occasion."

"The one you wore at the last party caused quite a sensation," he reminded her, pulling her into his arms.

"Yes and earned me a whipping. Did I ever thank you for saving me?"

"You did, but you can thank me again. Better yet, you can show me how very thankful you are," he suggested huskily, picking her up in his arms and heading to their room.

Two weeks later

There was a hush as Richard and Deborah entered the living room of The Acreage. It was the same room where Deborah had served him and many of these same people months ago. He saw her chin come up and, although no one looking at her would know it, he felt her tension in the tightness of her hold on his arm.

Tonight she looked more beautiful than ever. Her hair was done in an elaborate style, piled high on her head with long tendrils dancing in front of her delicate ears. Sarah had produced an emerald green dress that matched her eyes and favoured the colour of her hair. Although it was satin, she had lined it with a light lawn material so that it was not stifling in the heat as some of the dresses that the other ladies were sweltering in.

The emerald pendant that Richard had recently gifted her with was nestled just above her bosom, while the matching earrings dangled from her lobes. To Richard, she was the most beautiful woman there and he was enchanted by her. Looking around at the men in attendance who were openly devouring her with their eyes, he was not the only one. It looked as if it would prove to be a long night.

"Richard, Deborah, welcome." Thomas greeted Deborah with a kiss and shook Richard's hand. Elizabeth kissed Richard's cheek and nodded coolly at Deborah who responded in kind. Richard sighed quietly with relief. At least his aunt had not openly snubbed her.

"Thanks, Uncle Thomas and Aunt Elizabeth, for your kind invitation. Mother, Father," he continued on, greeting his parents. His father greeted them warmly while his mother took her cue from Elizabeth and offered a similar nod to Deborah.

"Let me reacquaint you with some of the people you met last time, Richard," Thomas offered. Richard knew that Thomas was accompanying them in order to smooth the way and he was grateful for Deborah's sake.

"John, Henry, Benjamin. You remember Richard Fairfax, my wife's nephew from Carolina. We've made a Barbadian out of him and he has returned to live here. Richard, you remember the Bowyers, my neighbours. And this is Benjamin Middleton."

Richard shook hands with the men and added, "Allow me to introduce you to my wife Deborah."

"You cannot be serious, man. I would have congratulated you on succeeding where we failed, but this is unheard of," John Bowyer protested.

He drew reference to the party where Deborah had served them and they had asked Thomas if he was ready to sell her. Richard felt sickened as he recalled telling them that he had already expressed his interest in buying her to his uncle but could not persuade him. As if Deborah had been a new horse to acquire.

"Nobody marries their mistress," Bowyer admonished. "Far less parades them in society as if they are one of us."

Richard drew his arm into a fist and had to forcibly quell the urge to plant it in John Bowyer's red face.

"Your desire was to own Deborah and have her for a mistress. I do not own her. She is my wife. In fact, I would have to confess that, if anything, she owns me," he admitted, looking at her lovingly and causing the men to laugh knowingly.

"No one should own another," Deborah asserted, silencing the men. A movement at one of the doors to the hallway caught her eye, distracting her, and she was surprised at the pleasure she felt on seeing Hattie and Cassie entering bearing trays. Not that she and Hattie had ever been friends, but Cassie had always been good to her, especially after the episode with William.

"Please excuse me." She released Richard's arm to cross the room to greet them, knowing that the other guests would no doubt look down on her for acknowledging them. She didn't care what the guests thought or she would never have come to the party. Anyway she would much rather be among friends than be in the presence of those disgusting men.

Deborah could feel the stares of the guests on her and she held her head high. The women's were of disdain, while the men's were of lust. As she passed a group of women, she heard one of them say to her companions: "Can you imagine that Elizabeth actually invited that girl here? Why, she served us at the last party. Does she think that marrying Elizabeth's nephew makes her equal to us now? For heaven's sake, she was a slave. What could Elizabeth be thinking?"

"Well, you know Elizabeth would never do such a thing. It would have to be Thomas who would insist upon her being here. He seems to have become a slave lover and then she is his spitting image. I need not say more." There were nods of agreement.

"Imagine that good looking boy Richard throwing away his life to marry that coloured girl. That would never have happened if he had been from here. Maybe that is permitted in Carolina where he comes from," another one said.

"It certainly is not! So I cannot imagine why he thought he could do it here!"

"I understand that there is no law against it here..." started a quiet lady, who was a visitor to the island.

"You can't say that you are condoning this despicable joining, Lottie," protested Margaret Bowyer. "There doesn't need to be a law. Everyone knows that they have their coloured mistresses, but marriage is not dreamt of."

"Hello, Cassie. Hello, Hattie," Deborah greeted them, doing her best to ignore the malicious women that she could not help overhear as she passed through the room.

"Hello, Deborah. I mean Mistress Deborah," Hattie corrected herself. Deborah made a face at her.

"You look real sweet, Deborah," Cassie complimented her.

"Thank you. How is everybody?"

"Good. The mistress buy two new slaves since you and Sarah left. How Sarah?"

"She is good."

"Your business doing good?" Cassie asked.

"Yes. It was hard at first, but it is a lot better now."

"Good."

There was an awkward silence that Deborah did not know how to fill. She did not have anything in common with these women anymore. Neither did she have anything in common with her father's guests. She was no longer a slave, she was free, but she belonged to neither group. She suddenly felt very alone and out of place. She mumbled her excuses to Cassie and Hattie and turned to find the only one to whom she felt she belonged – Richard.

She returned to Richard's side and clung to his arm as if it were a lifeline. Richard looked down at her in concern. He would have liked to ask her what was concerning her, but it would have to wait until later. He placed his hand over hers and squeezed it comfortingly. They would not endure this gathering much longer.

"So, Uncle Thomas, you have once again separated me from my best friend," complained Henry Bowyer. "Poor William has been shipped off to Jamaica," he informed Benjamin Middleton, while looking accusingly at Deborah.

"Jamaica? What will he be doing there?" Middleton asked Thomas.

"A friend of mine owns a plantation that he will be managing," Thomas informed him.

"May God be with him," Middleton said sympathetically. "Jamaica will either make him or break him."

"Let us hope it makes him," Thomas said fervently.

Chapter 25

William stood on the deck of the *Sea Princess* watching Jamaica grow larger in his sight. The ship sailed past the harbour that he was told was Port Royal and headed into the Kingston Harbour. One of the crew told him that Port Royal had once been one of the busiest and riches ports in the colonies, but it had been destroyed by an earthquake and a tidal wave five years earlier. It was estimated that three thousand people had been killed and over twenty thousand injured. Two thirds of the city had sunk into the sea and it had not been successfully rebuilt as yet, so Kingston Harbour was being used as the main harbour.

The sailor had chuckled as he told him that Port Royal had been known as "The Sodom of the New World", and had been a haven for pirates and inhabited by the worse sorts. Apparently, before its destruction, it was believed to have about one hundred taverns. Needless to say, drunkenness and debauchery abounded in the city. William smiled to himself thinking that he would have been right at home there. Pity it had been almost destroyed. Apparently some had said that it had been the judgement of God. He smiled cynically at that as he doubted that God troubled himself with the affairs of men any longer.

As they sailed into Kingston Harbour, he could see why it was said to be one of the largest natural harbours in the world. There were almost as many ships in its protected bay as one could see in Carlisle Bay on a good day. As their ship dropped anchor and butted against a wharf, William left his position near the rails to get his belongings and make ready to go to shore.

Once he climbed down the ladder and onto the wharf, he had to take a few minutes to steady himself and adjust his feet to the feel of solid ground beneath them. He had done more than his fair share of long voyages and he hoped that this was the last for some time. Hopefully he and Jamaica would get on well together.

He had gotten a full history lesson on his voyage and it seemed as if the sailors took delight in telling him all the worst things about Jamaica. Unlike Barbados, which had never been successfully invaded, he'd been told that the Spanish had been the first Europeans to occupy the island but were ousted by the British in 1655 although it had taken another fifteen years before they officially conceded defeat. The British had had to ward off constant threats of attack ever since, the last one being from a French squadron just the year before. The last thing he needed was to be caught up in the war of another country.

From what he had heard, the plantations had enough problems dealing with the maroons, descendants of African slaves who had been freed from slavery by the Spanish as they fled from the English. They lived in the hills and constantly came down to raid the plantations. They were said to be so fierce and wily that not even the military could thwart them. He hoped that they were not close to the plantation he was heading to.

Did his father know all this when he decided to banish him to Jamaica? Not only did it seem to have more than its fair share of violence, but he had been warned that disease was rife in the country and many of the population died every year. So, if he wasn't killed by maroons or other aggressive slaves, he had a good chance of not making it to his next birthday by catching some deadly disease.

How he longed for Barbados and the tranquillity of the island. They had had their share of slave rebellions and diseases, but nothing like what was rife in Jamaica, at least not recently. And once again, he'd been forced to leave his country. Did he not learn from the last time? What demon was it that had driven him to attack Deborah a second time? Although he hardly considered the first time an attack. He had simply been taking what belonged to him. After all, she was his father's slave and that meant that he could use her at will, or he would have been able to if his father did not favour her.

His hand drifted to the scar on his cheek that was healing but still pained him occasionally. It could have been worse, he supposed. His cousin could have cut his throat. He was fortunate to have escaped so easily. He would have to watch his throat in Jamaica, as he had a particular fondness for it.

He planned to stay two weeks in Kingston before he travelled to Westmoreland to the plantation he was to manage. From the map the Captain had shown him, Westmoreland was at the most western tip of the island and was as far as anything could be from Kingston. Jamaica being more than twenty times the size of Barbados, he could not imagine how long it would take him to get there and what perils awaited him on his travels.

Kingston was certainly no Bridge Town. In fact it was still very underdeveloped and rather swampy. Perhaps he would pay what was left of Port Royal a visit. It would be interesting to see the famous port and perhaps patronize a few of the remaining establishments there and partake of the debauchery that he'd been told about.

William cracked an eye open and tried to remember where he was. His head was paining him terribly. Carefully turning it, he saw curly hair strew across the pillow beside him. The fog partially lifted from his brain. He had had another night on the town as he'd done for the past week or more. He was due to leave for Westmoreland in a few days and might not have the opportunity to indulge in the pleasures of sin for a while. He remembered drinking vast quantities of rum at a tavern before being propositioned by a beautiful mulatto girl whom he had brought back to his room at the boarding house. Yes, that was where he was.

As he turned his head again a wave of nausea assailed him and a series of shivers shook his body. He had been drunk many times, but he had never felt like this. The chills particularly disturbed him and he tugged the sheet up to cover his naked body. He couldn't seem to get warm.

His tugging at the sheet woke his companion who rubbed her eyes and rolled off the bed to dress. Looking back at him shivering under the sheet, she said, "You don't look so good. You sick?"

"I don't know. I thought it was the rum I drank last night, but I am cold and my head is hurting."

"You may have malaria. A lot of newcomers to the island get it. It is from the mosquitoes in the swamp."

"M-malaria?" he stammered, shivering. "Does it kill you?"

"Sometimes. But some people survive. I can find a doctor for you, although there is not much they can do."

She dressed quickly, helped herself to some money from his purse for services rendered, and let herself out. He hoped that she would send a doctor as she had promised, if there was one to be found in this God-forsaken town. Did he come to Jamaica to meet his death? Would he die alone in Kingston, with no one the wiser about his death? Sweat now broke out over his body, causing him to throw off the sheet.

He must have drifted off to sleep because when he woke up the sheet was covering him again and a man with unkempt grey hair was peering over him.

"Who are you?" he croaked.

"I'm the nearest thing in this town to a doctor. What ails you?"

"My head hurts like the devil, I feel like vomiting and I'm going from chills to sweating."

"Sounds like you have malaria, young man. Are you new to Kingston?"

"Yes. I arrived about ten days ago."

"Oh dear. That is bad luck. And what are you doing in this wonderful country?"

"I'm here to manage a sugar plantation in Westmoreland."

"Hopefully this is not the more serious form of the disease and you will recover to manage your plantation. I walked with some cinchona bark which will help with the fever. I will speak to the proprietor to see if he can find someone to help you. I take it you have money to pay?"

"Yes. And please ask someone to send me some water."

"I will have the bark made into tea so that you can drink it and I will return tomorrow. The symptoms will only last six to ten hours, but will recur in two or three days until it passes, provided it does not get worse."

"I trust it does not," he murmured weakly. "Thank you, doctor."

The doctor left, leaving William alone in his misery. He had never felt so sick in his life. This was his father's fault. If he had not sent him here he would never have caught this horrific disease. Once again Deborah had been the cause of him being sent from his home. He cursed the day she was born, for from that time his mother had not been the same. Only when he got older did he discover why. His father was such a hypocrite! He had no doubt lain with Deborah's mother because he owned her and could use her as he wished, yet he would condemn him for doing the same with Deborah.

His head began to hurt worse than ever and all thoughts fled from his mind as he quickly reached for the chamber pot that the doctor had left within his reach to empty the meagre contents of his stomach. Lying back weakly, he closed his eyes and moaned in pain, praying for an end to his suffering.

William sat up and swung his legs over the side of the bed. He had had two more bouts with the malaria, but nothing for the last three days. He was weak, but finally beginning to feel better than he had in days and now he longed for a bath. He hoped the maid that the owner had sent to him would come in soon so that he could get her to arrange it.

Standing up slowly, he steadied himself by holding onto the bed and then cautiously let go and made his way over to his trunk. Digging into it, he found some writing material and sat down at a small desk near the window to write a letter to his father to let him know of his illness. Hopefully he would agree to allow him to return to Barbados. Apart from the pleasures of the last week or so, he had no love for Jamaica and it was not where he wanted to spend the next few years of his life. Assuming, of course, that some disease or maroon did not kill him first.

Donna Every

February 14, 1697

Kingston, Jamaica

Dear Father

I am only now getting the opportunity to write to you as I have been woefully sick with a disease called malaria. I started to sicken about ten days after I got to Jamaica and, although the sickness only lasts for about ten hours at a time, it is the most horrible feeling. It causes severe headaches, vomiting and fever, which gives way to chills. I would not wish it on my worst enemy.

I have been told that disease is rampant in the country and if I don't succumb to one of these diseases, there are maroons which raid the plantations who could easily take my life. I am sure that you could not have known this when you sent me here. If you are of a heart to reconsider my banishment to this God-forsaken country, I would appeal to you to speak to Richard on my behalf and see if he would be in agreement with my return to Barbados. I give my word that they would have no further trouble from me.

As soon as I am stronger I will set out for Westmoreland and hope to receive a letter from you while I am there with good news that I can quit this country soon.

Your son
William

William let the ink dry before he folded the letter and put it to give to the maid when she came in. He wondered if his father would pay him any heed or if he had finally washed his hands of him. Until he heard from him, he would have to set out for Westmoreland as planned and begin his new life. He wondered how he would survive the trip, far less how he would survive in this hard land.

Chapter 26

Richard put the finishing touches on the manifest for the shipment he was sending to Carolina. The ship was filled with sugar, molasses and rum from Barbados and would come back with lumber, grain, flour and, now, rice. It still galled him every time he saw increasing quantities of rice coming from Carolina. He knew that it would eventually take over from tobacco, but he had been unable to convince his father to invest in rice. He'd even been prepared to marry Ann to achieve his ambition, but that was now in the past. He would not change his life now, even if he and Deborah had challenges.

After they had come home from the party at The Acreage, they had spent some time talking about it. Deborah had shared how she felt that she no longer fit into plantation life. She did not know what to say to the slaves anymore and the ladies of the plantation wanted nothing to do with her. Thankfully, she had a few Quaker friends whom she and Sarah had met when they first moved into town and she had developed casual friendships with some of the merchants' wives. However, she

248

was concerned for her mother whom she feared was lonely but kept it to herself.

A knock at the door disturbed his thoughts and he looked up, pleased to see Thomas coming into the office.

"Uncle Thomas, this is a nice surprise," he said, rising to shake his uncle's hand. "What brings you to this part of town today?"

"We've just put the girls on a boat to England. There was a lot of weeping and wailing and gnashing of teeth, but they have gone. Your father and mother accompanied Elizabeth back home to recover from the ordeal."

"I had forgotten that they were to go to England soon. Please have a seat. So, when will Aunt Elizabeth be joining them?"

"When your parents leave she will follow them. Fortunately, the girls are being chaperoned by a school teacher who has given up on Barbados and is returning to England."

Richard nodded.

"I am hoping they find good husbands and settle there. Eligible young men are scarce in Barbados."

"What about you? Won't you be lonely when Aunt Elizabeth goes?"

"As you know, my dear boy, it is not as though your aunt and I spent hours in each other's company, although our relationship has improved somewhat. And, of course, I'll still come into town and see Sarah, although our relationship has become a bit strained, I'm sad to say."

"I'm sorry to hear that," Richard sympathized. "But she has changed her life and cannot go on as before."

"I know. I know," Thomas acknowledged resignedly.

Richard weighed his words carefully before saying, "Deborah is concerned that she is lonely and in need of companionship."

Thomas stiffened slightly as if he knew where the conversation was leading.

"Oh?" he said cautiously.

"She hoped that perhaps you would consider freeing Jethro so that they could marry."

"Free Jethro? Why would I do that? He's my best carpenter and my right hand man."

While that was true, Thomas knew that was not the real reason. He was jealous of his own slave, or what he could have with Sarah if he freed him. Not for the first time, he regretted that their skins were of different colours. Why was it that the colour of someone's skin could create such a great divide?

"Besides, what would he do? He cannot work for you because an Act was passed only two years ago to ban Negroes from ship and dock work."

"I did not know that and obviously Deborah did not either, because that is what she was thinking. But there is a lot of work for skilled people, black or white. He would not lack for work."

"Those were poor excuses, I know. The truth of it is that I am the lowest of men. If I cannot have Sarah then I want no one to have her and certainly not Jethro. I don't know if you know this, but many years ago, before Deborah was even born,

Jethro saved Sarah's life. A runaway slave who learned of my attachment to her had planned to kill her to avenge himself because I had him whipped. Before he killed himself, he told Sarah that he had planned to kill me too."

"I did not know that."

"I owe her life to Jethro and possibly even mine. He has always liked Sarah, maybe even loved her. But I, too, love her. I do not know if I can bear to stand by and see him have what I cannot. It is a hard thing that Deborah is asking."

Richard was surprised to hear Thomas voice his feelings for Sarah. He looked pained as he spoke the words, causing Richard to remember how he had felt when he imagined Deborah with someone else, even though he had chosen to return to Carolina.

"I know what you mean. I felt the same way about Deborah even though I had no right to, as I was returning to Carolina to marry," Richard grimaced slightly. "I am just glad that I came to my senses in time."

"Ah, my boy, count yourself blessed that you had a choice you could make. I wish such a choice was available to me."

"If it was, would you make it? Would you give up everything to be with Sarah?"

Thomas thought for a moment and then he said with great gravity, "That is a question I cannot answer unless I am presented with the opportunity to act on my words. And I do not foresee how that can ever happen."

He stood up, looking older than Richard had ever seen him.

"I will pay Sarah a visit before I return to the plantation. I have a lot to think about."

Thomas noticed with alarm that the doors to Sarah's shop were closed. He quickly tied his horse to a post and mounted the side steps to knock at the door. He waited impatiently for the door to open.

"Hello, Thomas. What are you doing here at this time of the day?"

"Sarah. I was worried when I saw the shop closed. Is everything all right?"

"Yes. Come in." She held the door open for him. "I just came up for lunch and to have a little rest. Deborah went to buy goods and took Mamie and Jacko."

"Good. I'm glad to have you to myself for a while," Thomas smiled. He drank in the sight of Sarah with her hair plaited and down her back. Even in her work dress she looked lovely to him. And she seemed delighted to see him.

"Are you hungry? I was just about to eat something." Thomas realized that he was hungry, but seeing Sarah filled him up.

"I was hungry, but now I've seen you I feel full."

"Thomas, what you mean?"

"I miss you, Sarah." He pulled her into his arms knowing that he was going beyond the boundaries that Sarah had asked him to observe, but he could not help it. He was surprised that Sarah did not resist.

"I put the girls on a boat to England today. It seems that I am losing people all around me. Richard, you and now the girls."

"Oh, I forgot that Deborah told me they were going. How are you doing?"

"I am okay. It is for their good. Hopefully they will find good husbands in England." Sarah nodded understandingly, but he saw a fleeting sadness cross her face. "What about you, Sarah? Do you want to get married?" He searched her face.

She pulled away and started to take out plates to put on the table. Thomas was sorry that he had asked the question.

"I don't really think about that," she lied.

"How are you doing now that Deborah is not here?"

"I'm alright, Thomas. I have my work and a few friends from Bible study."

Thomas stayed her movements by taking her wrist and pulling her back to him.

"Are you really alright, Sarah?" he asked, with his lips hovering close to hers. "Do you not lay in bed at night aching for me as I ache for you?" His breath, which was now coming faster, mingled with hers.

"Thomas..." she protested weakly.

"Tell me that you don't, Sarah."

"I-" She could not lie. That was all Thomas needed to hear before he devoured Sarah's mouth like a man starved of food and then coming upon a feast. Sarah felt a stab of conviction that she was doing wrong, but she ignored it as her flesh gloried in the feelings that Thomas was arousing in her. Her hands restlessly moved over his back and she revelled in the strength she felt there. Thomas' hands began to make their own discoveries, making Sarah tremble with need. He did not need to ask any more questions as Sarah's response gave him all the answers he needed. He picked her up and strode quickly to her room.

Not giving her the chance to think, he continued to explore her mouth, only pausing to nibble on the sensitive place where her neck joined her shoulder. When she pulled his mouth back to hers and pushed his jacket from his shoulders and encouraged him to take off his shirt, he knew that she was past protesting. He hurriedly unbuttoned her dress and shed it and the chemise she wore. The sight of her brown skin against his and the feel of her softness crushed against his hardness was almost his undoing. Thankfully, Sarah was as ready for him as he was for her and they fell into her bed in a tumble of limbs, past caring about the right or wrong of it. Minutes later their mingled cries signalled the culmination of their frantic joining.

Although almost silent, the sound of Sarah's tears reached Thomas' ears, even as she tried to hide them by turning her face into the pillow. He rolled over and held her as she silently shed tears born of guilt and shame.

"I'm sorry, Sarah. It was my fault. I should never have kissed you."

"I am like that woman in the Bible who was caught in adultery. I would have been stoned for what I have done," she cried.

"No, Sarah. The blame is mine. Please don't cry." Thomas felt as if his heart was being rung out. This was even worse than when Sarah had cried tears the first time he had lain with her. He knew the source of her tears and he knew that he had caused her to fall from grace.

"Even for that woman Jesus had compassion," he assured her.

"Yes, but he told her to go and sin no more. I knew I was doing wrong and I still did it. How can I ask for forgiveness when I deliberately sinned against God?"

"King David took another man's wife, got her with child and had the man killed to cover his sin. Yet, when he repented God forgave him. I am sorry, Sarah," he said again. "I take this sin upon myself." As he accepted it, a feeling of revulsion and shame came upon him, almost crushing him under its weight. If that was how Sarah felt, he knew he could never bear to make her feel that way again. A great pain occupied the place where his heart was; so great that he felt as if he would die from it.

"No, Thomas," Sarah said in a stronger voice. "Jesus already took the sin upon himself so that we don't have to."

He was amazed that as Sarah's simple words sunk into him and he believed them, the weight lifted and the vice around his heart eased. An overpowering love for her filled his heart and he knew what he had to do.

Jethro knew that the master had come back from town and now he wanted to see him. He could not help the dread that accompanied him as he headed for the master's office. Did he find out that he had been to see Sarah the last time he had been sent to town? Was he going to warn him about spending time with Sarah, or worse? Jethro fretted while he waited for the master to answer his knock. Had he heard the first knock? He had not said to come in. He debated whether to knock again, but he couldn't stand there all day. Lifting his hand, he knocked more loudly on the door.

"Come in." The master sounded irritated at the interruption.

"Sorry, Master Thomas, but Cassie told me you wanted me."

"Yes, Jethro. Come in and close the door." Jethro obeyed and stood waiting expectantly.

"Jethro, do you still have feelings for Sarah?" The master came straight to the point. How was he to answer that? He searched the master's face briefly as if to discover what was hidden there. He lowered his eyes before answering.

"Sarah is a good woman, Master Thomas," he prevaricated.

"Yes, she is. But I didn't ask you that. I asked if you still have feelings for her. Would you marry her if you could?"

"I don' see how that could ever happen," he answered, avoiding the question again.

"If there was a way, would you marry her?" Thomas persisted. Jethro looked back up at the master and the earnestness that he saw on his face gave him the courage to say quietly, "Yes, Master Thomas. I would marry her."

Thomas closed his eyes at the stab of pain that went through him. When he opened them again, he was composed.

"All right, Jethro. That's all I wanted to know. I am going to give you your freedom so that you can marry Sarah if she will have you. I know that you will be good to her."

Jethro could not believe he had heard right. He wondered if the master was testing him to see how he really felt about Sarah. He looked at him again questioningly and the master nodded.

"I will get my solicitor to draw up the manumission papers and once they are signed, you are free to go."

"Master Thomas, I-I don' know what to say. I can't believe you would do that for me."

"I can't truthfully say it is for you, Jethro. It is for Sarah. But I also owe you for saving her life all those years ago, so this is your reward. A life for a life."

"Thank you, Master Thomas. Thank you. Thank you." Tears were forming in Jethro's eyes as he backed out of the office. Thomas felt tears prick his as well and he dropped his hands in his head as he heard the door close. He steeled himself against the pain in his heart as he prepared himself to truly set Sarah free.

Two weeks later

Thomas looked up at the sound of a rider approaching him. It was John Bowyer. He wondered what he was doing at his plantation at that time of the day. He did not have long to wait to find out.

"Thomas, what is this I am hearing?" He got straight to the point. "I understand that you are freeing that carpenter fellow of yours. First the girl and her mother and now this boy? What is this? You becoming a slave lover or something? You turned into a Quaker?" he scoffed.

"This has nothing to do with you, John."

"You think not? You didn't think that it would cause unrest among my slaves and at the other plantations when they keep hearing that slaves at The Acreage are being set free?"

"I didn't give that any thought," Thomas admitted. "I'm surprised that they would know what is going on at my plantation." He really did not care what was happening at the Bowyers' plantation. He could barely get through each day as he thought about Jethro and Sarah together.

"They find ways to talk among themselves, so think about it carefully before you free anymore, for the sake of the rest of us planters. I never thought I would see this day," he shook his head in disgust.

"Bowyer, if that is all you have come to say, consider it said. Good day to you." Thomas turned his own horse and rode away, leaving John Bowyer with his mouth open. He may have just damaged a good friendship, but he really did not care. He was sick at heart and the last thing he needed was someone adding to the burdens he was already carrying. They were his slaves and he could do what he wanted with them. He had freed Jethro for Sarah and that was surely a good thing, so why did he feel so bad?

Chapter 27

One month later

"T'ings really changing 'bout here," declared Cassie. "I ain' sure if they for the better or the worse," Sally added.

"Well, Jethro getting he freedom is a good t'ing. I glad for he. He tell me that Master Richard goin' pay he to help build things for he and he promise to help he get other work. He even lettin' he live downstairs their house until he catch heself."

"And the mistress goin' to England today and carrying Peggy with she. I wish it did me she was carryin'. I wonder if the master goin' start to sell some of we, 'cause he ain' goin' need all of we when they ain' got nobody in the house but he," Hattie added. "The last to come should go first," she said pointedly, looking at the other new girl who had come at the same time as Peggy.

"I feel sorry for he, because when the mistress gone, nobody ain' goin' be here with he. He goin' be lonely enough," the new girl said, ignoring Hattie. "He is the best master I ever had."

259

"Why you think he let go Jethro, Cassie? To marry Sarah?" This was from Sally.

"I don' know what was in the master head. But if he free Jethro to marry Sarah, who say that Sarah would take up with Jethro just because he free? She did like him, but I don't know if she did like him that kind of way to marry him," Cassie said.

"When you lonely you does do all kind of things," said Hattie knowingly.

"Wha' you know 'bout it?" Sally laughed. "You best go and see if the mistress ready," she advised.

Elizabeth descended the stairs and looked about her as if imprinting the memory of the house on her mind. She would be gone six months and she knew that she would miss her home and, of course, Thomas. She almost did not want to go because he was a different man. He now seemed to have some sort of peace that she had never seen in him before and he had become very solicitous towards her. Mary even remarked upon it before they left.

The girls were all lined up at the bottom of the stairs to say their goodbyes. She knew that she had not always been the best mistress, but then she had not been the worse either. She had never had any of them whipped, except, of course, the one time that she had ordered Jethro to whip Deborah, but that had been the final straw of a lifetime of frustration with Deborah. And jealousy, she now admitted to herself. She realized that she would miss them, but she was taking one of the new girls whom she had come to like.

She would be going to England to stay with Thomas' family, not even the mistress of her own house. Still, she would be glad to see the girls, for she missed them terribly. The last letter she had gotten from them had been full of excitement about the parties they were attending and the young men they were meeting. She smiled to herself, happy for them. She would do everything in her power to make sure that they married for love and not for position. She had learned the hard way the emptiness of an arranged marriage. Still, she loved Thomas even if she never really had his love. Perhaps when she was gone his heart would grow fonder.

"Are you ready to go, Elizabeth?" Thomas asked, coming into the foyer.

"Yes, I suppose I am. Girls, look after Master Thomas well. I will see you in six months, God willing."

"Goodbye, Mistress." The house slaves bade the mistress goodbye and unexpected tears pricked their eyes as she went through the door. Elizabeth paused to run a hand along the back of her favourite rocking chair, recalling the many occasions she had sat in it entertaining friends or rocking the children as babies or reading a book. She would miss sitting here and looking out at the beautiful flowers or over at the mill.

The carriage came around from the yard and stopped in the driveway. Elizabeth walked out to it and Thomas helped her up before climbing in next to her. As they drove away from The Acreage, she wondered what poor Thomas would do in the house all alone. In the past she knew that he would have visited Sarah, but from what she could gather he no longer seemed to do so and he had hinted that Jethro may be courting her now that he was free.

She had been shocked that Thomas was setting Jethro free, but he did not explain it to her so she could only assume that somehow he was doing it for Sarah. That was when she knew without a doubt that the love he had for Sarah was greater even than the love he had for himself.

Thomas stood by the wharf watching as the ship sailed away. Elizabeth and her maid, Peggy, had stood at the rails waving. Peggy had been excited at the thought of the adventure of going to England, something she never in her dreams would have imagined. Elizabeth, on the other hand, had looked deeply saddened at the parting. He, too, had been surprised to feel a heaviness at her leaving.

Love for her had begun to blossom in the last month. Not a romantic kind of love or the kind of love that came close to what he felt for Sarah, but an unconditional love that was born of forgiving her for causing him to set Sarah free. He knew that he had been wrong to try to hold on to Sarah for selfish reasons, so he, in fact, should have thanked Elizabeth for forcing him to come to that place. He lifted up a brief prayer for her safety on the trip and turned away to mount his horse. He had sent the carriage back to The Acreage, but he had no desire to go back to the empty house; he would have dinner and spend the night with Richard and Deborah after he finished his business in town.

He wondered if he would run into Jethro who was living downstairs of their house until he was able to afford to find somewhere to live. At least he was not living with Sarah. He had not been to see Sarah since the last time they had lain together and he ached to do so, but he forced himself to stay away. He had no desire to tempt her, or himself, again. Something was happening in his heart as well, ever since that day, and he knew that he could no longer live as he had lived before.

His business took him several hours, as he arranged with his solicitor for additional money to be sent to an account in England to keep Elizabeth and the girls and then dealt with some other matters that needed his attention.

He was happy to dismount and give the reins of his horse to a boy to look after before he knocked at the door of Richard and Deborah's house. Richard opened it with a smile on his face.

"Uncle Thomas, come in. Good to see you."

"Thank you, Richard."

"How did Aunt Elizabeth get off?"

"Good. It was a good day for sailing and she was well settled in her cabin with the new maid she is taking with her."

"Good. I am glad to hear that, but now I am concerned about you all alone at The Acreage."

"I will be fine, son." His heavy tone belied his words and Richard's heart went out to him.

"Well, you know that you are most welcome here any time," Richard offered generously.

"I am in total agreement," Deborah said, coming into the room. She looked beautiful with her hair loose and wearing a brightly coloured dress.

"Deborah, you look beautiful," Thomas praised his daughter. "Have I told you how proud I am to be your father?"

Tears immediately flooded Deborah's eyes at her father's words. For the first time in her life he openly acknowledged that he was her father and that he was proud of her.

Thomas opened his arms and Deborah fell into them, sobbing loudly as emotions she had held in over the years overflowed and healing that had started with Richard became complete. Richard felt a lump in his own throat and had to clear it lest he start crying as well, although he knew there was no shame in a man's tears.

"I love you, Deborah. Never doubt that. I am so happy that you have found love with Richard. It is a rare gift. Treasure it."

"I love you too...Father," she returned, smiling through her tears. "I'm just sorry that you and my mother-"

"Let us not speak of it, Deborah. It can never be, although it pains me to say so. I pray that she will find happiness with Jethro at least. Have they been seeing each other?" He could not help asking.

"Uh...a few times," Deborah answered. "I believe he has gone to see her this evening," she added quietly, avoiding the pain on his face.

"Good, good," he said with false cheer. "Glad it's progressing well. So, are you going to feed me this evening?" he teased Deborah. She smiled as she took his arm, leading him to the dining room. Richard followed them, happy that Deborah had finally been acknowledged by Thomas but sad that her father could not enjoy the happiness that they had.

"Sarah, that food was real good. You can cook nearly as good as you can sew," Jethro teased her, making her smile.

"Thank you, Jethro, although you would say anything so that I would invite you back another time," she accused.

"You find me out," he laughed.

"I never see you laughing so much, Jethro. You had some drinks before you came here?" Sarah teased him.

"I didn' have much to laugh 'bout before, but since the master free me, I feel so happy I want to laugh all the time." Sarah nodded understandingly. Jethro had only been freed a few weeks so she knew that the newness of it had not worn off yet. In fact, sometimes she still found herself not able to believe that she was truly free after being owned for over thirty years.

She was very thankful to Thomas for setting her free while he was still alive, because his solicitor had told her and Deborah that it was not something that happened often. Most slaves who were set free were granted their freedom in their master's will when he died and sometimes the family disputed the will so that they could keep the slave. She would not have wanted to be owned by William. There was something evil about that boy. She could not believe he was the same boy that she looked after when he was small.

"I know what you mean," she said at last, leading the way into the sitting room. "So you got any work outside of what Richard giving you?"

"Yes. Only yesterday a shopkeeper ask me to build a counter like what I build for Deborah."

"Good. Always get some of the money up front so that people don' try to cheat you. Some of them people like to try and cheat us. Like they think we don't have any sense."

"I know that you is a big business woman, Sarah, but I ain' no fool neither."

"Sorry, Jethro. I know you ain' no fool."

"I must be, though, because you free and I free and I ain' ask you to marry me yet although I been coming 'round here since I move to town. I ain' even try to kiss you or nothing', but I want to real bad, Sarah," he admitted, moving closer to her. Sarah said nothing so Jethro took that as consent and put one arm around her shoulder and turned her face towards his with his other hand.

His lips caressed hers and he cautiously parted her lips and explored her mouth. He restrained himself from releasing his desire for her so that he did not cause her to pull back. He could not believe that he was free to kiss Sarah without fear of the master or anyone stopping him, save Sarah herself and she was not doing so. Joy made his heart sing.

Sarah put her hand around Jethro's neck as he deepened his kiss. It was pleasant to feel desired especially since she could feel him holding back. She allowed him to kiss her and kissed him back before gently pulling away. She could feel him breathing hard while her breathing remained calm. Kissing him was pleasant, but it did not move her to great passion.

"Sarah, you know that I did love you for a real long time. In fact, that day that Master Thomas catch me kissing you, I tell you that I would want to marry you if we was free. Well, I never thought I would see the day, but we free now. You would marry me, Sarah?" Jethro held his breath as he waited for her answer.

Sarah looked at Jethro's face and saw the vulnerability there and the love that he had for her. He could have married long before, for many of the girls wanted to marry him, but he had waited for her. He had been a good friend to her and she loved him as a friend. If they married she would no longer be lonely. They could have a good life together and she was still young enough to have more children. She opened her mouth to answer him.

"Jethro, you have been good to me all these years and I would marry you, but I need to pray about it first. You know that I don't do anything without praying about it now."

He nodded. "Alright, Sarah. Pray and let me know. I goin' pray too, that you say yes."

She laughed.

As Sarah led him to the door, she could not help but admire his height and strong build and sadness filled her that he did not stir her as Thomas did. It would have made everything so much easier. Maybe she wanted too much. After all, she never expected to be free in this life, far less have a good looking, hardworking man like Jethro want to marry her. She could do a lot worse.

Chapter 28

*S*arah spent a restless night. Her thoughts kept her awake long after the town had gone to sleep. It was only in the deep of the night that she could almost imagine that she was still in the country. She had become accustomed to the noises of town now, though, and she liked being able to get everything that she needed without having to drive for hours in a cart or carriage. Her business was doing well and she had a few friends in town. Her daughter was happy and free and so was she. Her life was good. It was more than she could ask for. And Jethro had asked her to marry him.

She had prayed many hours about how to answer him and yet she had not found the peace that she was seeking. Why not? He was a good man. He said he loved her and she loved him too, as a good friend. Maybe her love for him would grow into something more. Or she did not have to marry. She could continue her life as it was, work in her business and maybe begin to help teach other women to sew.

A pang of loneliness hit her as the silence of the house pressed down on her. She wanted someone to share her life and to share her success with. She wanted someone to talk to when she closed up the shop and came upstairs. Someone to sit with her while she worked late at night to finish a dress for a customer. She wanted someone to caress her body and hold her in the night. Was that someone to be Jethro?

She got dressed the next day and ate automatically, not really noticing what she put into her mouth. For once, she was not eager to go into her shop and take pleasure in serving her customers. She suddenly longed for the spot at The Acreage where she could look out and see the ocean and let the beauty of it bring her the peace she sought. She had not done so for years, not since George had jumped off the cliff. That had become Deborah's favourite spot.

Deborah was already in the shop when she got there.

"Good morning, Deborah," Sarah tried to sound bright and cheerful.

"Good morning, Mother." Deborah examined her mother's tired face. "Jethro spent the night?"

"You know better than that, Deborah. I didn't sleep too well."

"Why was that?"

"I had a lot to think about. How was your evening?" Sarah changed the subject.

"It was wonderful. My father had dinner with us and stayed the night."

"Your father?" Sarah had never heard Deborah refer to Thomas as her father.

"Yes. He was in town yesterday to see Elizabeth off to England."

"She has gone? How is Thomas?"

"He is alright, but he looks a little sad and lonely."

Sarah wondered if it was because his wife had left or if it was for another reason. There was no point to her thoughts. She felt for him because she knew what it was to be lonely.

"Anyway, he came to the house for dinner and he told me that he was proud that I am his daughter and then he held me in his arms for the first time and hugged me. He said he loved me," she ended in a tear-soaked whisper.

"Oh, Deborah, I'm so happy to hear that." Tears pooled in Sarah's eyes and she moved to hug Deborah.

"He seems to have changed, Ma. I mean, he was always good to me, but he never called me his daughter before or said that he loved me. Maybe God is changing his heart."

"I hope so. That would be real good."

"So what about you, Ma? What had you awake last night?" Deborah refused to be put off.

Her mother was silent for a minute before she sighed and said quietly, "Jethro told me that he wants to marry me last night."

"You don't look excited about it. You don't want to marry Jethro?"

"I don't know. I love him like a friend, but he don't make my heart beat fast…"

"Not like Thomas," Deborah finished. Sarah smiled sadly.

"No, not like Thomas. But he's a good man. I could do a lot worse."

"Yes, but you don't want to settle for that. I can understand why you couldn't sleep. You prayed about it?"

"Of course, but it seems that the Lord keeping the answer to himself for right now. All I can say is that it make sense in my head to marry Jethro, but my head and my heart not agreeing."

"Take your time, Ma. You don't have to rush and answer him. Maybe you should spend some more time with him and see how things turn out."

"You're right, Deborah. That make me feel better already. Since when you become the mother and I the daughter, with you giving me advice?" she teased.

"It's just that I am wise beyond my years," Deborah answered, smiling.

Elizabeth emptied the contents of her stomach into the bowl that her maid held for her. How could she have forgotten the sickness she suffered when she sailed to Barbados from England? Granted, it had been many years ago. At least she had had Thomas to comfort her then. She knew that it would settle down after a few days, but already she felt weak from the constant vomiting. Peggy, on the other hand, had no such problem. Sickness was no respecter of persons.

It had been three days since she left Barbados and all she wanted to do was turn around and return to the island. The prospect of being on the ocean for six to eight weeks was not appealing. She fervently hoped that the winds held and they made good time to England because she knew that sometimes a trip could take as long as thirteen weeks. It was enough to make her shudder in dismay.

She felt terrible in the confines of the cabin, so, with Peggy's help, she cleaned up and managed to go up to the deck. Peggy helped her to find a spot to sit and she was glad to find that she felt somewhat better with the refreshing wind blowing in her face.

The captain saw her and made his way towards her to inquire after her wellbeing. "Mrs. Edwards, how are you faring today?"

"The fresh air has made me feel marginally better, Captain. Thank you for asking."

"In a few days it will pass and it will be plain sailing after that. Excuse my little joke."

Elizabeth smiled faintly at his attempted humour and asked, "How many passengers are on board?"

"I'm carrying twelve souls on board. A few of them are suffering as you are, but most are in fine form. I'm hoping that the winds hold and that we make England in good time."

"So do I," she agreed fervently.

"How long will you be there, if you don't mind my asking?"

"Not at all. I plan to be there for three months. My daughters are there already."

"So Mr. Edwards will be all alone?"

Elizabeth stiffened slightly at his familiarity. "He has many friends and acquaintances. He will hardly be alone." She wondered if he would seek out Sarah now that she was not there. He had not spent the night in town for a very long time. Maybe he was no longer seeing her, especially now that he had freed Jethro. Maybe he would join them in England for a while, if he could leave his precious plantation.

A particularly big wave caused the ship to lurch and her stomach to heave again, forcing her to flee to her room with Peggy at her heels.

Elizabeth felt well enough after a week to venture into the dining room where she met with the rest of the passengers. The meals were not as elaborate or tasty as what she was accustomed to at The Acreage, but there was a limit to what the ship's cook could do without fresh meat and vegetables. She was just grateful that she could keep food in her stomach, so she did not complain.

There was a family who had come to Barbados to spend time with their relatives; two young ladies and their mother, that she was acquainted with, who were journeying to England much for the same reason they had sent their daughters; a couple from a smallish plantation that she had heard of who were moving back to England and two young fellows who had come out to the West Indies for adventure. There were about twelve of them in all.

The captain joined them most evenings, but she did not warm to him. She did not like his familiarity, not to mention that when he sat with them, that made their number thirteen, which was surely no good thing. But at least he was a veritable treasure when it came to sharing information about current events in England and what they could look forward to when they reached.

Thankfully, the next few weeks were bearable and she helped to pass the time writing in her journal and doing embroidery. She sometimes sat with the lady and her two daughters talking about people they knew in Barbados and speculating on what England had in store for them. She had started a letter to Thomas as soon as she recovered from her sea sickness and most days she would add a little to it to let him know how she was passing her time. She planned to ask the captain to deliver it to him when he returned to Barbados.

On berthing in England, she found the cool weather of May a welcomed change after years of living in the tropical climate of Barbados and the clothes that she had brought with her, that had kept her hot on the island, were now suitable. It had been wonderful to reunite with the girls who looked healthy and happy and had blossomed and matured in England. Once she had settled down at Thomas' uncle and aunt's house, she sat down to write him a letter to let him know that she had arrived safely

May 30, 1697

> *My Dear Thomas*
> *I hope that you are keeping well. After seven gruelling weeks at sea I arrived safely in England and was never so glad to feel solid ground beneath my feet. I was extremely happy to be reunited with*

the girls who have grown in both beauty (it seems to me) as well as in confidence.

Your uncle and aunt have been very kind and I have settled in well. The only drawback is a minor cold that I seem to have picked up from somewhere and an annoying cough. Hopefully they will pass soon.

I miss you already and cannot imagine how I will get through the next three months. I must confess that I am not looking forward to the voyage back to Barbados. Perhaps I should remain in England and you can come back here to live instead. Not that I can imagine you giving up The Acreage for anything.

Please give my regards to Margaret Bowyer when you see her next time and any of our friends. Hope all is well at the plantation and that the girls are taking care of you.

Your loving wife
Elizabeth

Days after writing the letter, Elizabeth's cough grew worse and she developed a fever. Her chest pained her when she coughed and her breathing became difficult. The physician was called and pronounced that she had pneumonia. He bled her and left instructions on what to give her to help the cough.

Unfortunately, she grew weaker and weaker until she was barely able to breathe. Finally, one beautiful day in June, a day too beautiful for anyone to die, Elizabeth drew her last painful breath and departed from the earth.

Chapter 29

Thomas read the letter in his hand again in disbelief. He had received a letter penned by Elizabeth only a week past and now his uncle was writing this to him? It did not seem possible.

June 15, 1697

> *My Dearest Nephew*
>
> *It is with great sadness and regret that I write to inform you that your dear wife Elizabeth passed away today. She contracted a cold shortly after she arrived and a persistent cough. When she finally allowed me to call the physician, he diagnosed her with pneumonia and treated her as best he could, but she did not respond to the treatment and quickly grew worse.*
>
> *We are consoling your dear daughters as best we can, but they are naturally distraught over the loss of their mother. We know that you would want to be here for them, although by the time you arrive we*

would have buried your dear Elizabeth. However, you will be able to visit her grave, which will be in the family plot, to pay your respects and say your goodbyes.

My sincere condolences to you.

Your uncle
Jonathan Foxworth

Thomas stared at the letter in stunned disbelief. Elizabeth had written only of a minor cold and cough. How could it have turned into pneumonia so quickly and taken her life? His heart grew heavy with grief. He wondered how his daughters were faring and for the first time in his life, he longed to hold them in his arms and comfort them as he had held Deborah a few months ago.

His mind started planning all he would have to do to prepare to go to England. He would leave Bentley in charge of the plantation, but he would ask Richard to have an eye to things once in a while. He would have to write and inform William of his mother's death. That would be no easy thing, for in spite of all William's faults, he loved his mother and they were close.

He went to the door of his office and called to the new house boy he had bought to take over some of Jethro's duties.

"Len, pack a trunk for me and send Cassie to me. I have to set sail to England immediately. Pack for several months."

As the words left his mouth, it was as if he suddenly realized what he said and what it meant. Elizabeth was dead. He had known her for more than half his life and, though his love for her was not great, he keenly felt her loss and regret that he had never loved her as she had desired.

"Yes, Master Thomas?" Cassie interrupted his thoughts.

"Cassie, the mistress has died in England," he announced baldly. Cassie gasped and put a hand to her chest.

"Oh, Master Thomas, I sorry to hear that."

"Thank you, Cassie. I have to sail to England to be with the girls. I've sent Len to pack for me and I will head to town tomorrow and try to catch a boat to England. I will be gone for several months as the voyage takes as much as two months and I will probably stay for a month with the girls. Look after the house. Bentley will be in charge."

"Yes, Master Thomas."

"All right, you can go."

She quietly closed the door behind her, leaving Thomas with his thoughts and his regrets. He remembered Elizabeth in the past coming to sit in his office on rare occasions to talk and a few years before, when things had come to a head over William, she had thrown open the very door he now looked at and demanded to know why he was sending William to England. Regret pierced his heart as he remembered how harsh he had been with her. After all, William's behaviour had not only been the result of her spoiling him, but also because he had not been a good father.

He tried to shake himself out of the melancholy mood, but the heaviness remained with him. Regrets would not change anything. What was done was done. All he could do was make sure that he didn't end his life with more regrets. Life was just too short and uncertain.

The next day dawned dark and dreary, as if even the island was mourning the news of Elizabeth's passing. Thomas had barely slept the night before, working long hours in his office to put things in place for his long absence and then tossing and turning as thoughts of Elizabeth and their life together flitted through his mind.

Although he had promised himself he would not waste time on regrets, he could not help but chastise himself for not loving her more, although love was not something that one could command. The great disrespect he had shown her tugged at his now renewed conscience. There was nothing he could do about that, but he took comfort in the fact that he had been kinder to her in recent times and their marriage had been better than at any time in the past. He hoped that she had been happier before she left for England. At least she did not appear to have suffered too long, which was a great blessing.

He looked out of the carriage as Len drove him to town, grateful that it was still overcast but not yet raining. How he loved this country that had become his. When Elizabeth was leaving, did she ever imagine she would not see it again? Would he? So many things could happen. No one was assured of a long life and death was unavoidable, so the choices that one made were very important. Of that he was convinced.

He was both glad and sorry when they came into town for it meant that while the journey from The Acreage was over, he would soon have to be on a ship for six or eight weeks, doing nothing of consequence. What would he do to keep his sanity on the trip? He had instructed Len to take him first to book a passage to England, for his own ship had left not more than a week ago. Then he needed to see his solicitor to conduct some business and he would go and stay with Richard and Deborah until he left for England, hopefully within a day or two.

And he needed to see Sarah to let her know. He had stayed away from her, giving her the chance to see Jethro without him interfering. It was hard to let her go, but he asked after her every time he saw Richard and Deborah. He had to admit that he was selfishly glad to hear that she and Jethro had not married as yet as Deborah told him that Sarah had asked for time to get to know him better.

A thought shocked him into stillness. He had been so focused on Elizabeth's death and all that he had to do that it had not occurred to him. He was now a widower. What did that mean for him and Sarah? What could it mean? Or was it too late?

The first place Thomas went after he paid for his passage to England and met with his solicitor was Deborah and Sarah's shop. As the carriage approached it, his heart leapt in anticipation of seeing Sarah again, for he had not seen her in several months. He was quickly consumed by guilt that he could feel that way with Elizabeth scarcely in her grave.

Len drew the cart to a halt outside the door and he entered the shop, hoping that it would be deserted save for Deborah and Sarah. Luck was not with him, for they were both dealing with customers and others were milling about waiting to be served. He was proud of them for running their businesses successfully, but at that moment he wished he could usher all their customers through the door.

Sarah caught sight of him first and her eyes widened in surprise. She gave him a slight smile and turned her attention back to her customer. That gave him the opportunity to study her intently. She was beautiful with her hair tamed into a single plait, but a few stubborn tendrils escaped and hung loose by her cheeks. She did not look a day over thirty, but he knew that she was close to forty. He had known and loved her for nearly twenty years. He could say that their relationship had almost come of age.

He paced impatiently, waiting for the shop to clear. Sarah sensed his mood and was very efficient in wrapping up the transactions with her customers. Before the last one had even turned away properly he was at her side.

"Sarah, can you come upstairs for a few minutes. I need to talk to you." The urgency on his face communicated to her that something was very wrong.

She nodded and called to Deborah that she was going upstairs for a few minutes. Deborah looked up and met her father's gaze. She worried about what was wrong. As soon as she got rid of her customers she would go up and find out.

"Thomas, what has happened?" Sarah asked as soon as they left the shop.

"I'll talk when we get inside," he answered.

Sarah could hardly get the key in the lock properly as her hand had started to shake. She hoped that nothing had happened to Richard, for it would devastate Deborah. As soon as they were inside she asked Thomas again, "What happened? Did something happen to Richard?" she asked fearfully.

"No, not Richard." Sarah sagged with relief. "Elizabeth had died in England."

Sarah sucked in a shocked breath. "Oh, Thomas, I am so sorry. What happened?"

"She caught a cold and a bad cough which turned into pneumonia. It seemed to have happened very quickly."

Sarah pulled him to her for a comforting embrace, saying how sorry she was for him and for the children. He enjoyed the comfort of being in her arms. Somehow it lessened the pain of the grief that he was carrying.

Pulling back after a few minutes, he told her, "I am sailing to England tomorrow to see after the girls and to pay my respects to Elizabeth. I will be gone for about five months."

Sarah nodded in understanding.

"Sarah…" Thomas began, only to be interrupted by the door being thrown open.

"What has happened?" Deborah demanded.

"It's Elizabeth. She has died in England," Thomas told her.

"Oh! I'm so sorry, Father." Although Deborah and Elizabeth had never seen eye to eye she was genuinely sorry for his loss.

"I've been fortunate to get a passage on a ship leaving for England tomorrow. I hope to pass the night at your house."

"Of course. We would be pleased to have you. You can have your driver take you there now if you have finished your business in town. We need to move closer to town, but we do so love being near the beach."

"Thank you, Deborah. I will stop by and see Richard before I go to your house."

"Fine. I will see you when I get home," she said, turning to leave.

Thomas took Sarah's hands in his. "I won't see you for five months or more Sarah, God willing that I return safely."

"I will be praying for you, Thomas."

"Thank you, Sarah. I can certainly do with your prayers." He hesitated, not knowing how to continue or what it was he really wanted to say.

In his heart he wanted to ask Sarah if she would wait for him, but wait for what? What could he offer her? Was she now considering a life with Jethro? It would certainly be easier for her. Could they ever have a future together? He knew that she would settle for nothing less than marriage and, truth be told, he would not disrespect her with anything else. But how could they ever have a marriage in Barbados?

He remembered Richard's question to him not too long ago: Would he be willing to give up everything for Sarah? He had said he could not answer that question until the opportunity to make that decision presented itself. Now the opportunity was before him. Was he willing to give up everything for

Sarah? Did she still love him? The thoughts that raced through his mind silenced his tongue, as he had many questions and no answers to give.

"I won't say 'goodbye', but I will say 'until I see you again'. I love you, Sarah." He hugged her briefly and left quickly as if overcome with emotion.

Sarah stood where he left her.

"Go with God," she said softly, even though he had already left. Would she ever see him again?

"Sarah, I hear that Mistress Elizabeth dead in England." Jethro announced when he came by the next evening.

"Yes. Thomas stopped by to tell me yesterday when he came into town."

"I real sorry to hear that. She wasn't a bad mistress. Only the time that she tell me to whip Deborah." He shook his head reminiscently. "She did real vex that day. I didn' know what to do. Then she say 'If that girl is not stripped and tied to the post in ten minutes, you will get the flogging instead'," he mimicked her voice, making Sarah smile. "To tell the truth I did never so glad to see Master Richard riding in the yard like the devil was behin' he. He was so vex that when he grab the whip out of my hand, I thought he woulda turn 'pon me."

"That seems like so long ago, but it was only last year. So much happened since then."

"True. How the master takin' it?"

"He grieving, but he holding up good. You didn't see him at the house last night?"

"I hear his voice but I keep to myself." There was silence as both of them became lost in their thoughts. Then Jethro said, "This make me think how easy things is happen. You here today and gone tomorrow."

"I was thinking that too," Sarah agreed.

"So maybe we should get married now 'cause we ain' got tomorrow put down. You think any more about marrying me?"

Sarah was quiet for such a long time that Jethro wondered if she had heard him. Although her face remained emotionless, inside her was in turmoil. She should just go ahead and tell Jethro yes. And yet something held her back. Was it some hope that she and Thomas could be together somehow? She could not imagine how it would happen or even if he wanted it to. He had said nothing when he came to say goodbye, although she had felt he was about to say something when Deborah had come in.

"Jethro, you been real patient with me and good to me, but to tell the truth I still can't say yes yet. I just don't know what to do."

"What you mean, Sarah? You think that now the mistress dead, Master Thomas goin' marry you? You goin' become the mistress at The Acreage and rule over Cassie and Sally and the rest?" He laughed mirthlessly. "You dreamin', woman. Master Richard marry Deborah, but she look nearly white and, besides, he ain' own no plantation so he ain' got to mix with them people from the rest of plantations. But Master Thomas big up in this island. You really think he goin' marry you when he know that the rest of them planters would laugh at he and want to know if he gone mad?" He sounded angry now.

"I never said anything about marrying Thomas," Sarah protested, with her own voice rising.

"But you thinkin' it," accused Jethro.

"You don' know nothing about what I thinking, Jethro. Look, you better leave. I don't want to talk about this no more."

"Whenever you ain' want to hear what I got to say, you does tell me to leave. Well, I leavin'." He stood up and looked at Sarah's bent head. "When you come to you' senses lemme know. But I ain' plan to wait for you forever. They got a lot of other women who would marry me quick so."

Sarah raised her eyes to his. She knew that he was right and that she should really make a decision rather than keep him waiting. It was not fair to him. She opened her mouth to answer him, but Jethro held up his hands.

"Don' say nothing now. You tek your time and think hard about what you want to do and then let me know. I givin' you another month to mek up you' mind."

He let himself out and the sound of the door closing caused a dam to burst in Sarah. She sobbed for the injustice of a life of slavery she had endured and she cried because, even now she was free, the same prejudice that created that life made sure that she could never have what she truly wanted.

Chapter 30

November 30, 1697

homas stood on the deck of the ship and watched as his beloved Barbados came into view. No one could have kept him below deck. Carlisle Bay was as full of boats as it ever was and, as he cast his eyes up the hills, he could see plantation houses hidden among the trees. He had missed Barbados more than he had thought he would.

How he had survived the voyages, he did not know. Days and weeks of endless sea and terrible food, of sleeping in a cabin a quarter of the size of his room at The Acreage and very little to do except write in his journal. At least the voyages gave him ample time to make plans of how he could improve the yield of his canes and to consider what diversifications he could make so that he was not only dependent on sugar and rum. While they were not doing badly, he knew that the island would soon be challenged by Jamaica which would, no doubt, take over as the main producer of sugar in the colonies. The sheer size of it alone would guarantee this and the soil was virgin, unlike that of Barbados'.

On reaching England, he had found that the girls had come to a place of acceptance of their mother's death so it had not been as hard to deal with as he had thought it would be. Nevertheless, as soon as they saw him it was as if their grief resurfaced and he was glad that he was there to comfort them and remind them about the good times they had with their mother in a way that his uncle and his wife had been unable to.

By the end of the month, he asked them if they wanted to return to Barbados with him, but they preferred to stay in England with his uncle, although he did not think that state of affairs would last very long as there were quite a few young men who had expressed interest in courting them. He had met the two of them who seemed to be most popular with the girls and he was pleased with the way they treated his daughters. At least he was assured that they would not have husbands as unloving as he had been to Elizabeth.

He had gone out to her grave the day after he arrived and had a long talk with her. He knew, of course, that she was not in the grave, but it still helped him to say aloud the thoughts that had been plaguing him on the voyage and to ask her to forgive him for not loving her the way she had wanted to be loved. When he left the grave he felt as if a burden had lifted from him and as if he could now go forward with his life.

He still did not know what that meant. When he had said his goodbyes and boarded the ship, he found himself with weeks ahead of him and nothing to do but think. So he wrote every day in a journal he had bought for the trip and he read many books. He had always liked to read, but the busyness of plantation life had robbed him of his reading time. That was something that he promised himself he would start to do again when he got back to Barbados.

Elizabeth's death had caused him to examine his life and he was committed to making some changes. He now realized that while the plantation was important and he wanted it to be successful, it was not as important as his family and the people around him. Never again would he spend more time working on it than he would with his family. Not that he had a family to be with, as the girls were in England and William was in Jamaica.

Maybe he would bring William back from Jamaica if Richard and Deborah were in agreement. After all, from the letter he had received after his sickness, he seemed as if he was now willing to leave Deborah in peace if he came back. He hoped so. He wanted another chance to get to know his son better. Maybe in a few months he would let him come back or he would pay a visit to Jamaica.

He also wanted another chance with Sarah. There was not a day when she did not cross his mind. He tortured himself wondering if she had married Jethro. It was ironic how he had set Jethro free to be with Sarah, only to find himself free. But how could they ever be together? Assuming that she and Jethro had not married in his absence. He had desperately wanted to ask her to wait for him, but he had no right. He only hoped that the love they shared would have prevented her from settling for affection with Jethro. Unless, of course, that affection had blossomed into love.

What do I really want? He asked himself. He wanted Sarah and the only way he could have her was to marry her. For a plantation owner to marry one of his slaves, even if she was free, was unheard of. They would not be welcomed at any of the plantations on the island. And, anyway, how would she feel being mistress at The Acreage? He could not see it and she would not want him to own slaves anyway. He wouldn't be surprised if she had freed Mamie and Jacko by now.

The boat gave a lurch as the anchor dropped in Carlisle Bay and soon he was on Barbadian soil once again. He thanked God that he had made the trip to England and back safely. But what awaited him in Barbados?

Thomas was undecided as to whom he should visit first. He longed to see Sarah, but he did not want to go to her shop only to find out that she had married Jethro. Instead he headed to Richard's office. He knew that Richard was not one to write letters, so he had not expected to receive any, which meant that he had no news of what was happening in Barbados and, more importantly, with Sarah.

He knocked at the door of Richard's office and opened it at Richard's invitation to come in.

"Good day, Richard," he greeted, closing the door behind him. Richard's head flew up and he bounded around the desk to embrace his uncle.

"Uncle Thomas, it is so good to see you. How are you? When did you arrive?"

"It's good to see you too, son. I am much better than when I left and I came straight from the boat here. It is so good to be back on Barbadian soil. I don't think I want to go anywhere in a hurry."

"I know what you mean. Deborah will be overjoyed to see you."

"And I her." Thomas paused, wanting to ask the next question as much as he dreaded hearing the answer. "How is Sarah? Has she - ?"

"No, she has not married as yet," Richard interrupted, knowing his thoughts. He remembered when he returned to Barbados not knowing how Deborah felt about him and how uncertain he was.

Thomas released a breath that he did not know he was holding. "Thank you, Richard. You read my thoughts. I have thought of nothing else every day that I have been away."

"So, what are you going to do?"

"I don't know. Your aunt's death has taught me that life is too short not to grab happiness when we can. I just have not figured out how best to go about this. I love Sarah and I'm hoping she still loves me, but I don't know what to do about it."

"Don't worry, Uncle Thomas. Let God's will be done."

"But what is his will? Certainly not to help me, for I do not deserve his help. I deserve his judgement."

"None of us deserves the gift he has given us. That is why it's called grace; undeserved mercy."

"Thanks for that reminder, Richard. I believe that I will go and find a boarding house to stay at, have a bath and a good meal and then go and see Sarah. Hopefully by then I will have a better idea of what to do and what to say to her."

"I'll be praying for you," Richard said as he opened the door.

"Thank you, son."

The stairs to Sarah's door seemed longer than they had before. Thomas' heart began to race in anticipation of seeing Sarah again. He smiled to himself as he wondered if that would ever change. He knocked on the door and waited several minutes without an answer. He knocked again and Sarah quickly opened the door. Her mouth dropped open in surprise and her eyes filled with tears.

"Hello, Sarah." His simple words belied the emotions that roiled around inside of him at the sight of Sarah with her hair loose and damp, looking as if she had quickly pulled on a dress. She must have been bathing when he knocked.

"Thomas! Come in, come in." She ushered him in and closed the door.

Thomas stood awkwardly, not knowing what to do. He wanted more than ever to pull her into his arms and crush her to him, but he was not sure of her feelings. Would she welcome an embrace from him?

"Come, let's sit down," she said and turned to lead him to the sitting room.

"I missed you, Sarah," he said quietly to her retreating back."

Sarah turned around and fled into his arms.

"Oh, Thomas, I missed you so much. Not a day went by that I didn't think about you," she confessed.

"Me too, Sarah." He held her to him tightly. "Marry me, Sarah."

Sarah pulled back and searched Thomas' face. "Thomas, you gone mad! That could never happen. We would have to leave the island. Where would we live? Who would welcome us?"

"I don't know. I have not thought it through. All I know is that Elizabeth's death has shown me that we only have this one life and it is short. We need to live it to the fullest and not let anyone tell us how we have to live."

"That sounds good, Thomas, but we both know it is not as easy as that."

"Sarah, I have changed a lot. When I first saw you at the Holdips I wanted to own you. I didn't care that Jonathan's wife needed you to keep her company after her daughter died. I just saw something I wanted and I took it. For my whole life I have thought only of myself. I took your innocence because I wanted you. I gave you no choice. But when I freed Jethro so that he could marry you and look after you, for the first time in my life I did not act in selfishness. Your happiness meant more to me than mine. And now we are both free, I feel as if I've been given a second chance to be a better man and to make up to you all the years that you suffered."

"I didn't suffer too much, Thomas. You were always good to me. You were a good man before and you're even better now. That tells me that how we start does not have to be how we end. Whether somebody is a slave or a master, the way they start out doesn't have to be the way they end up. It is up to them to decide how they will turn out."

"You are a wise woman, Sarah."

"Too wise to even begin to dream about marrying you."

"Do you love me, Sarah?" Thomas pressed her. She paused before answering.

"Too much to let you sacrifice your life to marry me."

"That is my choice, Sarah, not yours," Thomas insisted, beginning to feel as if Sarah was slipping away from him.

"Yes, but it will affect me too. Later on, when your friends stop inviting you at them and people start to shun you, you will be sorry that you married me."

"That is not going to happen, Sarah."

"You can't say that, Thomas. Who could ever say what going to happen in the future? So I think the best thing might be for us to carry on as we were before; as just friends. I have my shop and it is doing well and I have this house that you gave me. Thank you for that. When you were in England I decided not marry Jethro either, because I love him like a friend, not a husband. Who say that I have to marry anybody?"

"You don't have to marry anybody, but I hope you will marry me. Promise me you will think about it, Sarah. Even if it means we have to leave Barbados and live somewhere else.

I would rather be with you somewhere else in the world than without you in Barbados."

"Thomas, I don't know if there is anywhere in the world for us, but I will think about what you said."

Thomas stood up and pulled Sarah into his arms. He held her close for a long time, so still that they could feel their hearts beating against each other as one. For some reason he was reluctant to let her go, feeling that if he did, he would never again have the opportunity to hold her like this.

Epilogue

*S*arah looked around her living room at the five girls who were sitting and concentrating on their tasks. They ranged in colour from white to black. In addition to the fine clothing she produced for her shop, she had been hired, through Thomas' connections, to produce clothing for slaves on the plantations. It gave her great pleasure to find some girls in town who were the children of free servants, freedmen and slaves and teach them the skill of sewing.

On their laps were pieces of material that was far from the quality she used in her shop, but they were working on the clothing for slaves, her new source of revenue. She paid them for their labour and the money helped them and their families to survive in the harsh conditions of the island. She knew well that if you had no land and no skill, life was unbearably hard in Barbados and she was grateful that God had given her the skill to sew and, she had discovered, to teach.

She could already see which of her students would continue to make the slave clothing and be happy to do so and which ones would go on to sew fine clothes for her shop or for their own customers in the future and it gave her great pleasure to know that she had helped them in that way.

A slight smile lingered on her face as she looked proudly at her girls. A sense of peace and joy filled her, dispelling the small pang of regret as she thought about Thomas and what they could not have. She worried about him sometimes for he seemed lonely. She wondered if he would remain in Barbados, for it appeared as if he had lost his love for the plantation and, sometimes, even for the island.

For the most part, though, she was content and she silently thanked God for all her blessings. She was free, Deborah and Richard were happy, she had friends, her business was thriving and she was helping to change the lives of these girls. What more could she ask for? She had more than most of the people on the island, slave and free. She did not regret her past; she had loved and been loved. She did not even regret that she had been a slave, for out of that she had Deborah. Now, her whole life was ahead of her, God's plan for her was unfolding and her end would be far different than her beginning. She smiled. She may have started her life as a slave in the country, but now she was free in the city.

The End

Author's Note

I hope you enjoyed *Free in the City* and that you were not too disappointed that Sarah chose not to marry, but to enjoy her freedom and help to equip poor girls in the city. After many of my readers of *The Price of Freedom* heard that I was planning a prequel/sequel, they said they hoped Sarah would marry Thomas. However, in order to keep the book as historically accurate as possible, I could not, in good conscience, force a marriage between them.

I must confess, though, that I, too, wanted them to be together, as they genuinely loved each other, and I wrote an ending with them marrying and staying in Barbados. However, I was not at peace with it. From my research I knew that although there was no law in Barbados against interracial marriages, the dictates of the society were so strong that it was almost unheard of. There was only one recorded case that I could find, which was between a black man, Peter Perkins and a white woman, Jane Long, in 1685. It was that marriage that I made reference to in *The Price of Freedom* when Thomas told Richard there was no law stopping him from marrying Deborah. In spite of that knowledge, I went back to the

301

library and the museum to do further research to see if I had overlooked any other such marriages, but I found no evidence and, in fact, I found some convincing commentary as to why it would not be likely.

I could have married her to Jethro, but I did not think it would be fair to Jethro since she did not really love him in a romantic way and I also did not want Sarah to settle for marriage as if she could not survive on her own.

So I have left her unmarried at the end of this book. Meanwhile, I have already started tossing around some ideas for William's book in my mind, and, even though he'll be in Jamaica, some of these characters will make a reappearance, so who knows what may happen with Sarah in his book when I bring an end to the series.

If you enjoyed this book please write a brief review on Amazon to share with other readers.

Sincerely
Donna
E-mail: donna@donnaevery.com

Donna Every Novels

The Merger Mogul
Daniel Tennant, aka The Merger Mogul, is one of
Manhattan's top merger consultants. His past has made him
vow never to be poor again and so he lives by the philosophy:
"Women are great but a profitable company and a healthy
stock portfolio are better and definitely harder to come by."

The High Road
In this exciting sequel to The Merger Mogul, Daniel Tennant,
formerly known as The Merger Mogul, has landed the project
of a lifetime – to help transform the nation of Barbados.
However, he doesn't bargain for the opposition he will
receive, or the lengths to which the conspirators will go to
discredit him in an attempt to bring an end to the project.

The Price of Freedom
He owned her and was prepared to give her freedom, but
was she prepared to pay the price? An exciting, page turning
historical novel set in Barbados and Carolina in 1696.

What Now?

Rock star Nick Badley has no bucket list; he's living it. He's been there and done that, yet a part of him is still unfulfilled and he's beginning to ask himself the question: What now?